THE GYM SHOW

A novel

Kelly Springer

The Gym Show

The Gym Show

kellyspringer126.wordpress.com

The Gym Show

Dedication

For JRA and SBA — you inspired me.

The Gym Show

Author's Note

Once I decided to leave teaching and do something—anything—else, I figured it was time for me to write a novel. Lord knows I've read enough novels to get the gist of what goes into writing one (or so I thought).

Writers are always told, "Write about what you know." So I did. I wrote about a small town, its quirks, its idiosyncrasies, and its colorful characters. Oh, and there's plenty of gossip.

In doing so, I had to be careful to not only protect my family's privacy, but the privacy of the town that I will always call home. I believe I have. My family has many secrets, and my town has many more. However, you won't read about any of *those* secrets in this story.

The Gym Show is a work of fiction. Any traces of yourself or shadows of events you may have been a part of during *your* time in our hometown are purely coincidental.

--Kelly Springer, March 2014

The Gym Show

The Gym Show

The Gym Show

PROLOGUE

November 5, 2011, Indianapolis, Indiana

The gymnast approached the unevens looking serious and contemplative. She was petite except for her massive shoulders, which appeared to be developing a sizable dowager's hump. The rest of her body was out of proportion with her shoulders—she had no hips, no breasts, and possessed rather short, mighty legs, every muscle bulging and defined. Her hair was slicked back, pinned, and beribboned. Her leotard looked as if she had sprayed it on with electric blue and white sparkled paint. She paused, dipped her head as if in prayer, then tilted her chin toward the judges and flashed a brilliant silver orthodontically enhanced smile as if she had planned it this way all along. With a quick flick of her wrist, she signaled her readiness then mounted the apparatus with a simple glide kip. Now it was all business. The rest of her routine was anything but simple, characterized by releases, reverses, twists, and Giants. Her hands would fly from the bar, and in a blind move, grasp the bar again in the opposite direction. It was almost too difficult to follow exactly what she was doing and how she was able to

13

execute each move, but she certainly made her tricks look seamless and easy. She punctuated the end of her routine with a double twist and landed nearly flawlessly, only leaning slightly to the right upon landing first on one foot then the other.

"Elfie, that bobble will cost her at least one tenth of a point."

"Ah, that's true, Bart. And I *did not think* that her difficulty level was *of the same caliber* as we've seen in the past."

"Let's wait for the judges' scores..."

"Nine-five! Nine-three! NINE-OH! Oh, my, Bart, that's *going to be devastating*...wait...nine-six...I *do believe* she's dropped to fourth place behind teammate, Alyssa Sanderson. *Not a good day for Chelsea Manning...*"

All right, Elfie, you get *your* fat ass up there and try to do what she just did.

Julie hit the 'last' button on the remote and went back to *The Barefoot Contessa.* Ina was whipping up cheddar and dill scones, chicken salad, and a carrot salad with golden raisins. She sighed. The last thing she needed to be doing was watching another cooking show. Feeling like a manatee, she was perched in a ratty-looking Lay-Z-Boy, the arms of which were caked with grease — the result of too many grimy hands clutching its sides to fling it back into the recline mode. She had the chair tilted back, but

14

only back as far as it took the footrest to appear. Julie sat nearly immobile, her left knee couched in an inflatable device with icy water running through its vinyl veins. The device was attached to a tube that was attached to a cooler, which was, at least earlier in the afternoon, filled with ice water. She wasn't so sure now, and this, combined with the need to use the bathroom, would soon necessitate a shift. However, she was too afraid to move too much to check the ice. The knee had, earlier in the day, been scoped, its shredded meniscus removed, rendering the knee's owner temporarily inert.

Julie didn't even have a good story to go along with the knee injury that had resulted in the removal of the cartilage that had afforded her, for years, the ability to perform all manner of athletic tricks. No, this injury was the result of a jump. Up. As in, "My daughter had sunk a three pointer at the very last second of a basketball game—not even a championship game, just a regular game—and they won. And I jumped—up."

Already bored with Ina, Julie tenderly and awkwardly reached down to grab the edge of the FedEx box that contained a stack of books her sister Jenny had recently sent her. These weren't just any books, though. The box was filled with yearbooks from Julie's high school, not her own documentation of her time at Mercyville High School, but memory-filled archives encapsulating the years when her father had been the high school's principal, and her mother had been the girls' physical education teacher. The yearbooks, the contents of which had been poured over, memorized, and analyzed by both Jenny and Julie when they were children, had always been shelved in her family's living room until her dad had sold the house in 1987, and the contents of her childhood home were cast about her small hometown in an estate sale. During the sale, Jenny had surreptitiously set the yearbooks aside, even though she knew that many folks from the area would have paid a substantial price for the entire collection of Mercyville memories.

Julie had recently asked Jenny to send her the yearbooks. A few years ago, she had come up with the idea that she wanted to, somehow, between working full time and mothering her three children, document the years that her parents had spent working together at Mercyville High School. She was especially interested in capturing the years when her mother's signature creation—the Gym Show—had established itself as the school year's most exciting, eclectic, and intriguing event. Those yearbooks (placed, maddeningly, just out of her reach from the Lay-Z-Boy) contained decades of memories that she was sure would somehow inspire her to write some kind of synopsis about the Gym Show. She could just about get her left hand on the edge of the box, and if

16

she shifted — however, when she shifted, a sharp stab of pain ran through her knee and she gave up.

This entire knee episode had turned into a colossal pain in the ass.

Two weeks after the untimely jump that had caused the injury and many, many painkillers later, Julie had conceded to have the knee scoped. It was a simple outpatient procedure, and it went fine; that is, until her doctor arrived in the post-surgery suite to issue his instructions for her post-surgery behavior. As an aside, he had informed her that he had *just* looked at the MRI pre-surgery and the tear that he had only previously suspected was present was, indeed, much worse than he had initially thought given the trifling injury that led her to him in the first place.

"I had to take it all out. There just wasn't any meniscus left at all; it was in shreds. Are you sure that you just jumped up that one time?"

"Well, yeah. I mean, I've been running about 30 miles a week for the past three years, and it hasn't given me any problem at all before then." Julie waited for his eyebrows to indicate a surprised and somewhat impressed countenance.

"Do you ever run on concrete?"

"Well, yeah...in the wintertime, I run at my school. You know, run the halls — it's carpeted, but I'm pretty sure

17

it's concrete underneath. It's a pretty big school. One level. It's a middle school." As if he cared! Julie was a teacher in a large suburban middle school. Running in the halls after school had dismissed was about the only perk she could enjoy at work after spending an entire day with 180 hormone-ravaged, ill-mannered eighth graders.

"You know that concrete is, like, the absolute worst surface you could be running on. That's wrought havoc on your joints. Any other sports? Were you an athlete growing up?" For a genius with an MD after his name, he certainly sucked at sentence structure.

"No. I wasn't an athlete. I was just a gymnast."

As soon as the words were out, Julie regretted having spoken them. She had been saying, "No, I was just a gymnast" for most of her adult life, and certainly when asked by friends why her three children were such good athletes. Gymnastics in the new millennium was highly athletic, artistic, competitive, and elite. Just ask Chelsea Manning. Julie, however, had never participated in gymnastics competitively, unless one factored in her YMCA experience as an eighteen-year old tumbling phenom. The 1970s was still a nascent era in the gymnastics milieu, especially in her small, obscure hometown in western Pennsylvania.

"You're, what," Dr. Knee consulted her chart, "forty-seven? How long did you say you have been running?"

18

Julie cast her eyes toward her swollen left knee, and absently rubbed her thigh above the bandaged site. "Well...since my fortieth birthday. You see, I had lost a little bit of weight, and I started running, and I really, really liked it. I figured since I hadn't been a runner when I was young—you know, because I was just a gymnast— then I wouldn't be compromising my joints. You know."

"Well, you're done running. It's simply out of the question. You have no more cartilage left in that knee. Why don't you try swimming?"

She could feel the hot tears well up in her eyes. Julie genuinely loved to run. She didn't run fast, and she knew that she probably looked stupid doing it, but it was something physical that was giving her some satisfaction—a release from the tension, the stress, and the spiritual draining that teaching sucked out of her soul, one long kid-filled day at a time. Running provided Julie with a time to think. Teaching school all day and having three kids was hard enough; when she was running, she had time to sort out her day, plan her week, dream a little, and know that when she was done, she could reward herself with a glass of wine—sometimes the whole bottle—and a hot bubble bath.

These were the thoughts that had occupied her mind as she watched the World Gymnastic Championship, probably over now, and a second episode of *The Barefoot*

Contessa. Ina was making dinner for her sweetheart, Jeffrey who apparently loves her unconditionally, as long as she cooks him his favorite foods, all rich in fat, sugar, and calories. She wondered if Ina had ever been a runner. It was doubtful that she had ever been a gymnast.

With an audible sigh, Julie flipped back to ESPN, but the gymnastic spectacle was over, juxtaposed by what appeared to be a news conference. Like an old friend, the Penn State logo was visible at the bottom of the screen, catching Julie's attention immediately, but the words "Penn State Ex-Coach, AD Among Others Charged in Child Sex Case" replaced whatever warm feelings she may have had at any reference to her alma mater. A lifelong Penn State fan and 1985 graduate of the Main campus, Julie listened in gradually increasing stages of disbelief then abject horror as the sports pundit revealed details alleging that the team's former defensive coordinator had just been indicted on forty counts of sex crimes against young boys. This was unbelievable, incomprehensible.

Repulsed beyond reason, Julie felt as if she had to throw up. She sat stock still, eyes targeted at the television and strained to hear more as the story continued to name the school's athletic director and another university official as complicit in the cover up of the ex-coach's crimes, but stopped short of accusing head coach Joe Paterno of any wrongdoing. Julie let out her pent-up breath, somewhat mollified. To her, Joe Paterno represented all that was pure and good about college sports, and she, along with every other kid who grew up in Pennsylvania, idolized the venerable football coach. After all, it was Penn State football that had drawn Julie toward the State College campus just as students at Alabama or Notre Dame flocked to those universities because of their storied football programs.

She flipped through the remaining channels looking for other coverage, some other story that would, she hoped, downplay the severity of Penn State's involvement in this nightmarish crime, but every other news outlet reported the same events with the same details that essentially named the University as a co-conspirator in this man's crimes. Not surprisingly, but with a sadness and an ache in her heart that she could not explain or assuage, in the coming days Julie would find that her beloved Joe Paterno, a man who represented all that was good, wholesome, and down-to-earth in the world of collegiate sports, would be viciously vilified. It was not only the media who cast him out as an abettor of abuse, but the public in general maligned his name and his reputation and associated him with the scandal in the worst possible way—and that scandal would be the end of his career and, indeed, his life.

Julie turned off the TV and stared at nothing,
21

forgetting about the trivialities of her torn up knee, absorbing the news with a sickening dread that this announcement was the end of her fascination with Penn State. What did Joe Paterno know and when did he know it? What would this scandal do to all of those, like her, who had worshipped Penn State, its history, its sterling reputation in the world of collegiate sports? In these coming days, her friends and even her own husband would politely suggest that her concern was altogether misguided—that her real sorrow should be directed to those young boys who had been ruined by this man. While that was true, the reality of what had happened to them, especially as more sordid details were revealed through the press, was simply too evil to comprehend, and as a way to defer that evil from creeping into her consciousness, Julie focused instead on the collateral damage.

All of this reflection about her beloved Penn State and her childhood growing up in Pennsylvania invariably made her think about her parents. She missed them both, but she especially missed her father. What would he have thought about all of this? In Joe Paterno's shoes, what would he have done?

Julie's involvement in gymnastics had put her in touch, literally, with any number of coaches—male and female. Any of these adults at the various camps and clinics she attended could have taken advantage of their respective positions — they could have committed the same revolting acts as this ex-coach had committed — a man whose name would soon become synonymous with all that was evil and sickening in the universe. Julie wasn't naïve enough to think that this man's crimes were committed in a vacuum; as a teacher, child abuse was a reality she faced quite often, and, unfortunately, teacher-student liaisons were becoming more and more prevalent but no less abhorrent. But at what point had this kind of appalling behavior become so commonplace? Or, was it just that the public's insatiable hunger for salaciousness made for better TV ratings? Try as she might, she couldn't imagine anything like this happening in her childhood.

Gymnastics had dominated her youth to the extent that it defined her. Whenever Julie's name came up in any conversation, people would preface it with "That gymnast." Her love for gymnastics began as a child and continued throughout her high school years. Though her debut on the gym floor had little to do with gymnastics and everything to do with being the daughter of two of the town's most interesting people, Julie never forgot that spring in 1970 when gymnastics became the most essential part of her being. It was her first real Gym Show.

Her father would never forget that spring, either, though Julie was never to know the reason why. Nor would she ever know just how much her own father had in common with her beloved hero Joe Paterno.

Julie reached down again, more determined than before to pull the box of yearbooks close enough so she could find the 1970 edition of "The Walleye," this time more to return to her childhood than to revisit memories of the Gym Show — and to return to an era when her world was an innocent place where men didn't hurt little boys.

1969

The Gym Show

I

November 1969, Mercyville, Pennsylvania

He waited eagerly among the dusty folds of the draperies, Blade did, wanting to watch to see if his "Old Sport" as he called him — as he called all of his boys — would follow through with this next acquisition. A camera affixed upon a tripod sat next to Blade, who was fast becoming conscious of the sound of his increasingly powerful breathing.

In the context of their games, the man never used his real name, only "Blade," which was the name he used, and "Old Sport," which was the name that he had given to the each of the other boys.

He could feel that this "Old Sport" was nervous, yet Blade sensed in him an energy that the boy usually lacked during their prior couplings. That momentum, Old Sport, is called Desire.

The boy, for his part, was at first reluctant to approach his next mark, but upon the pretext of digging for information about a girl, he gained an uncommon confidence. The boy really didn't know this kid that well;

27

he knew that the kid's older brother had been a friend of Blade's before he had graduated, but other than that, there was nothing remarkable about the skinny, dark-haired boy. But now that the boy was here, the boy excitement began to increase and knowing that Blade was hidden within the curtains waiting and watching made this eventual tryst all the more thrilling.

II

From her vantage point in the backseat of her parents' 1966 Ford Falcon station wagon, Julie wasn't able to see exactly how far they still had to go before they made it to Erie. It was dark, rainy, and cold, and wedged between her older brother and sister, she sat uncomfortably in the humpy middle of the backseat.

Julie's parents, Carol and Jim Adamson, talked quietly in the front of the steamy vehicle and woe to the child sitting in the back who dared cause a commotion, no matter what the circumstances. Julie's dad, much older than his pretty wife, was, this particular evening, without the anesthetizing effects of his nightly fifth of Seagram's 7, and made it known, once again, that he hated driving, hated driving in bad weather even more, and could never abide children who whined, complained, giggled, or even whispered to each other while he was "concentrating on the road." His foul mood was coupled with the reminder that the rolled up newspaper wedged between the dashboard and the windshield would be liberally applied for any breach of backseat etiquette. With Carol's oft-repeated mantra of "Please! Your father has had a very stressful day at school, so do not do *anything* to upset

29

him," none of the three risked a clout across the snot box
with the ersatz truncheon; however, it was highly unlikely
that Julie's brother Jimmy, the oldest and more responsible
and grown up of the three, would ever endure their
father's wrath. Carol always made sure of that.

November in Mercyville, a place tucked in the
western-most portion of Lake County in the northwest
corner of Pennsylvania, was notorious for freezing rain,
snow, and all manner of inclement weather, all of which
Julie was used to as a seasoned five-year old. But what
had her stomach in knots and her head hurting was not
the awful weather, the hot, moist, and moldy-smelling air
coming from the car's heater, nor the fact that she was, as
always, sitting on the hump. It was not the fear of getting
smacked with the newspaper, nor was it the fact that she
was beginning to feel as if she had to pee, and she knew
that it would be another twenty minutes before they
reached their destination. No, it was much more than that.

She was going to be on television, and she was scared
to death.

Miss Olentick was her kindergarten teacher, but she
had recently taken some time off to get married (though
Julie couldn't for the life of her imagine who would want
to marry someone that fat who seemed to get fatter each
day), so her substitute teacher was Miss Marpy. Miss
Marpy was somewhat older than Miss Olentick, but was

far, far prettier. Her dresses were shorter, her legs slimmer, her hair was piled high atop her head in swirls and swirls of blond confection, and her smile was simply dazzling. In addition to that, her large blue eyes were accentuated with a shade of aquamarine that reminded Julie of their tour last summer of Marine Land — her blue eye shadow was the perfect match for the aqua blue tanks filled with frolicking dolphins. Miss Marpy, unlike her predecessor, never raised her voice, and was forever calling each of her young charges "Sweet Pea," "Honey," "Little Darling," or Julie's favorite, "Bunny Boo-Boo" — and whether it was out of love for the little ones or her inability to memorize thirty-five or so names, it was a far cry from Miss Olentick's grumpy demeanor. Oh, she was so glad that Miss Olentick had gone off to get married and left Miss Marpy in her place. She was positively in love with the beautiful Miss Marpy.

Chaos nearly ensued when, shortly after she arrived to take Miss Olentick's place, the dazzling Miss Marpy had taken the opportunity one morning after the Pledge of Allegiance and the class' daily homage to the calendar to ask if any of her new students would be interested in being on *television*. Miss Marpy explained to the class that not only was she a substitute teacher; she was also the star of a television show called *Peggy's People*. She breathily informed the class that her special television show featured a clown, a cowboy who did magic tricks, and various children who served each episode as the guests of the show. She further explained to her now visibly excited charges that the cable-access television program was taped on Monday evenings at a small television studio in Erie, and whoever was chosen to be on the show would have to come with his or her parents at seven o'clock the following Monday evening.

Not surprisingly, thirty-five hands immediately shot into the air, presenting Miss Marpy with a rather uncomfortable conundrum, since all thirty-five kindergarteners could not possibly be guests on *Peggy's People*.

It so happened that on that particular day, Julie was sitting in the very front of the row of children all sitting Indian style on the tile floor during calendar time, so when she shot up her right arm and shouted, "Me, me! Ooh, pick me! Me! I want to be on your special television show!" Miss Marpy, through proximity if nothing else, happily obliged her, telling the other disappointed children that there would be plenty more opportunities for them to be on her show. Julie was thrilled. She took the letter Miss Marpy had given her (but couldn't read herself) to give to her mother, and sat back down in her spot in the front row, smiling and hugging herself for the rest of the day.

The Gym Show

Her mother had never shared with Julie whatever was in the letter, so all the information that Miss Marpy had provided in class the day she was chosen was all that Julie knew. Julie herself had never even heard of the show and did not know anyone who had been a guest on *Peggy's People*, but she knew that she was still excited that Miss Marpy had picked *her* to be on television. Her favorite show with cowboys was *Bonanza*, and all during the day of her big television adventure, she had imagined that the show might be like an episode with Little Joe, Hoss, Pa, and, well, a clown. The trouble was that she did not know what the people at the TV studio were expecting of her once she arrived at the studio. Was she supposed to have learned lines like a real actor? What about costumes? She knew that the people on *Bonanza* did not dress like that in real life, but how was she supposed to know if her plaid jumper, red turtleneck, white knee socks, and Buster Browns were appropriate for the show? What if she arrived at the studio and everyone else who was to star on that evening's episode of *Peggy's People* were already in their costumes and already knew their lines? She would feel stupid, she would feel dumb, and they probably would tell her to go home and never come back.

Once this thought crossed her mind, she began to cry. Of all of her classmates, Miss Marpy had chosen Julie Adamson to be on her special television show. Not smart

33

and good at everything Shelly U. Not Debbie R. with her very curly hair and big blue eyes — Debbie, who knew all the words to "Harper Valley PTA" and sang it loudly, with gusto, at recess every day. No, it was Julie that Miss Marpy had chosen, although now Julie was regretting ever having raised her arm in the air to shout, "Ooh, pick me!"

Julie's parents were unaware that their youngest child was sitting on the hump in the backseat crying, but her brother and sister on either side heard her sniffling, and took this opportunity to do what they did best and usually without Jim or Carol ever catching them in the act. Her older sister Jenny, and Jimmy, the oldest and most responsible of the three, turned to her and began to taunt.

"What's a matter, *sissy*?" Jimmy whispered hotly in her ear. "You better not cry or they're not going to let you be on TV. Your boogers will show."

"I don't know why they picked you anyway," hissed Jenny. "You aren't that pretty and with all that snot running out of your nose, they're probably going to tell you to go home."

"I think she has to pee," continued Jimmy.

"Aw, does pooy Jooey have to pee?" Jenny asked. "If I press here," she proceeded to flatten the fingers of her right hand on Julie's lower belly, "does that make you have to pee more?"

"Stop it. Mum! Jenny's poking me in the belly!"

"Jenny, don't. Julie, why are you crying? You keep that up, missy, and I'll give you something to cry about!" Carol turned to glare at Julie sitting awkwardly in the back seat. Julie's mother looked tired, and she was most decidedly annoyed at having to drag all three of them and Julie's father out on a school night, especially in the middle of November, and especially on a Monday, knowing full well that the rest of the week was going to be as busy as this day was. Carol and Jim Adamson had a knack for anticipatory exhaustion.

Julie's parents were Mercyville's version of a first family, though, looking back, anyone who rose to any kind of position or had any manner of public life in the small town that was Mercyville was placed on somewhat of a pedestal. James Adamson, 'Mr. A.' to his students, was the principal of Mercyville Junior-Senior High School, enrollment 500. Carol Adamson (Mrs. A.) was the girls' gym teacher at Mercyville, but woe to the person who had the audacity to *call* her a gym teacher—she taught *health* and *physical education*. Jim, as a married principal, had hired the newly graduated Caroline Tanner right out of Slippery Rock State Teachers College, and within the space of a few weeks had begun a clandestine and rather scorching love affair with the pretty, petite blond. Carol, for her part, had broken off her engagement with her college sweetheart and waited patiently for Jim to divorce

35

his current wife, all the while maintaining a cool detachment in public to her new and much older man. In all fairness to both Jim and Carol, Jim's first marriage had been teetering on the brink of disaster for some time, either for reasons not known to Carol or known but not acknowledged, and the day after his divorce was granted, Jim and Carol drove to Virginia and married.

By the standards in most small American towns in the late 1950s, this was a scandal unlike any other—after all, most people were blindsided by the news that Mr. A, had married the new gym teacher, but fortunately Jim was popular with the townsfolk, and it didn't hurt him that, at the time, his father James Sr. was a school board member. Besides, no one had really cared too much for the first Mrs. Adamson—a woman who maintained a dispassionate aloofness from her husband's affairs at the school, and a woman whose very existence would remain a secret from her ex-husband's three school-aged children for at least two more years. Thus, the people in the small town of Mercyville soon grew used to the new Mrs. Adamson. Her acceptance into the community was as easy as Carol's acceptance into any group—her sweet features, small but curvy form, and her ebullient personality made her a generally likable person. Much like a grown-up Gidget, those around her couldn't help but fall under her spell— all smiles and bright green eyes, quick laughter, and perky sense of style. Unlike the first Mrs. Adamson, the elusive Constance, who had remained throughout her marriage bored with Mercyville and its small town garden clubs, church circles, and summer parades, Carol loved life in Mercyville, and she was truly a breath of fresh air in a small community that was sorely in need of the bit of excitement that Carol provided.

The May-December relationship between Jim and Carol surprised few of Carol's close friends and absolutely none of her family. Though Carol grew up in a female-dominated world full of strong-willed women whose dependence upon men was clearly not needed, some in their small circle of friends (and most of Carol's and Jim's immediate families) felt that perhaps Carol was searching for the archetypal father figure. The difference in their ages notwithstanding, Carol was a dynamo, an extrovert, and liked to be on the "go" all the time, whereas Jim was content to be the first one home in the evening, and in the spring and summer, found peace and serenity perched high on his father's ancient International Harvester tractor, plowing or tilling fields on their ten acres of property, fields that would never be planted in anything but soybeans just so they could be plowed under the next spring. And always, Jim was accompanied by his beverage of choice, a fifth of whiskey still secreted in its paper sack from the State Store.

Carol's involvement in the lives of her students took the form of cheerleading advisor, volleyball coach, and sponsor of a variety of girls' clubs and organizations at the high school. The depth of her involvement in school was only limited by time—her position as Jim's wife gave her carte blanche to organize, assemble, create, and produce anything she felt would put her and the school in the town's spotlight.

However, her most lasting and memorable contribution to the community and school of the small town of Mercyville was the school's annual Gym Show.

At the time of the Gym Show's inception, the world of women's gymnastics had yet to introduce the likes of Cathy Rigby, Olga Korbut, or Ludmilla Tourischeva; thus, gymnastics' popularity, especially among the residents of the small farming and mill community of Mercyville, was non-existent. However, once Carol Adamson became Mercyville's female *physical education* teacher, she set about to change all of that. At Mercyville High School, and at most small schools at that time, girls did not participate in sports—there was no girls' basketball team, no girls' softball or field hockey teams. Carol set out to remedy this, and so she had orchestrated the revolutionary idea of teaching her female students the beautiful, graceful, and *womanly* art of gymnastics. Her style of gymnastics was less about technique, athleticism, or competition, but had more of a theatrical, more of a circus or pageant feel. It was, in fact, a *show*.

When enough girls had acquired enough awe-inspiring gymnastic skills to wow a crowd, Carol knew it was time. Her first Gym Show in 1963 was such a success that the following week, she and her gymnasts replicated the "Show" two more times to standing room only crowds. That gave Carol the idea to take her "Show" on the road the following year and travel to other small high schools in other small communities, further widening the audience that couldn't get enough of Mercyville's girl gymnasts.

Now approaching its seventh year, the Gym Show remained the school's crowning event, growing in scope and popularity. In 1965, the Gym Show expanded with the addition of the May Queen crowning. Every January following the Christmas holidays, preparations began, practices ensued, and the boys from the shop class happily built for Carol a voluminous stage constructed on one end of the school's gym that would seat the Gym Show's May Queen and her Court. They built the stage with two by fours, plywood, chicken wire, and tissues. Each year, Carol chose a different color scheme, but white was the predominant color, suggesting the purity and innocence of the girls on the Gym Show's May Queen Court. The Show was performed the first or second weekend in May, first

39

on Friday night (when the May Queen would be crowned), then again on Saturday night when the May Queen and her court would either reign over the Show, or, in many cases, peel on a leotard and perform with the other gymnasts.

Everyone, it seemed, had a hand in the production of the Gym Show. In addition to the "shop boys," there were other technical aspects to consider. Someone had to be in charge of music, and this entailed the operation of a large record player with its bulky beige speakers attached to either end. The music was an important component, not only of the girls' floor exercises, but of the entire Show itself. Between "acts," music played while two or three girls would perform a dance in the center of the gym — more so Carol could involve as many students as possible and not so much as a distraction from the movement of mats, apparatus, equipment, and props. Those "managers" who moved this stuff between acts were as important to the show as the girls who could execute twelve back handsprings in a row. Who else would there be to shove equipment, mats, and even people out of the way when those same girls would flip all the way out to the lobby?

Without a doubt, though, the highlight of the Gym Show was the annual crowning of the May Queen. For a school without a football team, the May Queen was

40

The Gym Show

Mercyville's answer to a homecoming queen; however, her reign was much more important and held much more significance. She was the ambassador of the school and of the community at large, the shining example of wholesomeness, and always, always, virginal and pure of mind and soul. Her court included the queen herself, her stalwart escort (a boy of equal transparency), usually an athlete in good standing and always, always the most popular among his peers. In addition, there sat four other young ladies whose fellow student body members had voted them onto the court, but those same students had not honored them to reign as queen over the Gym Show. All of the young ladies, though, were models of beauty, goodness, and propriety; the boys handsome, dignified and honorable. When the Gym Show crowned its first May Queen in 1963, girls wore hoop skirts shaped like frothy white bells, and yearbook pictures of the queen and her court took prominence in the middle of each annual, that space reserved for the most important event of the school year. At home, Julie would pour over these yearbook photographs, longing for the time when she and her special little man would preside, to the collective "Awe's" of the crowd, as the flower girl and the crown bearer.

Unlike the crowning of the May Queen, the selection of each year's flower girl and crown bearer was a fait

41

accompli.   Shortly after the Christmas break, Carol
Adamson would change out of her physical education
teacher attire, and over a girdle and stockings, she would
don a wool skirt and tasteful blouse, slip her size five feet
into a pair of stylish pumps, and click her little self across
the street to the elementary school. Upon her arrival, she
entered the kindergarten wing and visited each of the two
classrooms, looking for the prettiest little girl and the most
handsome boy.   These two lucky little children would
have the honor and privilege (and two complimentary
Gym Show tickets) of serving as that year's flower girl and
crown bearer for the May Queen Crowning. The children
were always kindergarteners, except for the year that
Jenny was in kindergarten and Jimmy was in first grade.
Carol simply couldn't help herself; she *had* to have her first
two children front and center of the May Queen court. It
was difficult for her to wait until Jimmy was a first grader,
but worth it all to see Jenny in her yellow and white
flower-girl dress, her blonde bob capped off with a yellow
ribbon and Jimmy, so grown-up looking and handsome in
his bow-tie and suit strutting down the floor with his little
man-like styled hair slicked back from his forehead.

This year's Gym Show, 1970, was Julie's year, and
although her mother had not mentioned it yet, Julie knew
for sure that there would be no other little girl in the
kindergarten at Mercyville Elementary who would be

42

walking step-together, step-together across the gym floor to take her place of honor beside the 1970 May Queen. She just didn't know who her escort would be. That would be something her mother would decide. Julie had her favorites, but she knew better than to mention these boys to her mother. After all, it was Carol's show.

And Julie's show was about to begin. They had finally arrived at the tiny cinder block studio of Erie's cable access television station, Channel 10, a channel that was as unfamiliar to Julie as *Peggy's People* was. The Adamsons had one television set, and, because they lived in "the country," only one channel was available most of the time. Often, though, on rainy or stormy days, they could rotate their aerial antennae and pick up a station or two out of Cleveland, but that was hardly enough to become familiar with the shows that some of the kids talked about in school—*Gillligan's Island* and that new show *The Brady Bunch*. Since the Adamsons had never had the opportunity to view the programming from Channel 10 out of Erie, no one in their household had ever seen *Peggy's People*, and no one had thought to discuss if they would ever get to view the episode with Julie as the star.

Once inside, the wet and somewhat chilly Adamsons were ushered into a small, dark studio featuring a stage with cutout decorations—a hitching post, a mock-up of a building with 'Saloon' written on its shingle, and next to it,

43

a makeshift jail. Even a child could tell that these weren't real buildings, especially since, adjacent to the cardboard decorations there sat what appeared to be a small set of aluminum bleachers. There were other families standing around with their children – probably the other stars of the show, Julie guessed. But before she could get back to the task of worrying about her role in tonight's drama, there were more pressing matters to attend to. Julie tugged on her mother's coat, "Mum, I have to go to the bathroom."

Her mother looked down at her with a touch of disgust, wrinkled her nose, and said, "This place is dirty. You can wait until we're done here and you can go at Ricci's." Ricci's was the restaurant where the Adamsons liked to frequent when they came "...all the way into Erie." It was a nice, quiet, Italian eatery, and Julie liked going there because she always ordered the ravioli and a Shirley Temple. Thinking about the Shirley Temple made the urge to pee that much more intense, but Julie knew better than to cross her mother. Carol was obviously very tired and somewhat taken aback by the overall shabby look of the inside of the studio, as evidenced by the pinched look on her face. Julie could tell that her mother was beginning to run out of patience with the events of the evening, even though they had not really started. What would have been an exciting adventure for most families was turning out to be an ordeal for the Adamsons.

Julie looked closer at the other people gathered. The other children were not from her kindergarten class, but looked to be of varying grade levels, ages, and sizes. She also noticed, with relief, that none of the other children were wearing costumes, and no one carried props or had on make-up; they simply wandered around with their parents looking just as confused and out of place as Julie felt.

It wasn't long before a tired looking middle aged man appeared, all dressed down in a rumpled short sleeved shirt and greasy striped tie, his pants hitched way down under his belly, the straining waistband curled under his protruding gut. "Listen up, folks. I'm Fred, the production manager. Thanks for coming out tonight. I know the weather stinks and all, but we're real glad here at Channel 10 that yinz could make it. I need all a yinz kids ta follow me over ta the seats. Now." Julie noticed a gap in his shirt where the buttons were just about to pop. His pasty skin was visible, black, curly hairs escaping the trappings of his yellowed and somewhat pilled shirt. Fred started herding the children toward the bleachers. Julie made her way along with the others, when Fred, at once, did something that surprised all of them. He had stopped suddenly, spun on his heel, and walked toward Jenny who was standing next to Carol, looking bored. With a look of beatification, Fred's stretched out his arms as if he was

45

going to embrace Jenny, as if he alone was making the awesome discovery of this enchanting and beguiling young girl. He had walked right past Julie, and as he did, the sweet brine of his underarms wafted past her wrinkled nose. He silently beckoned Jenny, ever so gently and tenderly, to sit on the very first bleacher. Jenny looked at first surprised, looked up at her mom and dad, and, getting the 'okay' signal from them, shrugged her shoulders and giggled. She took her front row seat and looked smugly left and right at her fellow bleacher partners, obviously enjoying the attention. At that point, Julie suddenly felt even more awkward and self-conscious than she did sitting in the car. And she still had to pee.

Finally, out of the corner of her eye, she spotted the beautiful and majestic Miss Marpy — "Peggy" — dressed in a stylish plaid belted dress that accentuated her long legs. Tonight, her blonde hair cascaded over her shoulders with a little flip at the ends, and her makeup was more exaggerated than it was when she was Miss Marpy in the kindergarten room and not the enchanting Peggy of *Peggy's People*. Like Fred, she, too, was smoking a cigarette, but for some reason, her sophisticated mannerisms, her long, slender fingers with the cigarette blithely resting between them seemed much more elegant than the crumpled mess sticking out of the side of Fred's mouth. She was talking fast with another man who was dressed in a plaid sports jacket, the kind that her own conservative father called "fruity." Julie didn't know what "fruity" meant, but she was sure that her dad would never wear a purple tie like the man's either.

Fred had told Julie to sit on the third bleacher behind a boy whose glasses were affixed to his head with a black elastic band. His dirty blond hair was oily, and white flecks dotted the part that she could imagine his mother had sliced down the side of his head in preparation for his big television debut. He must have felt Julie staring at the back of his head because he turned around and smiled at her baring a mouthful of blackened and graying teeth, some missing here and there. She didn't smile back, not necessarily because of the bad teeth, but because she was trying to remember where she had seen him before. He was dressed even more formally than the other children who were dressed in their "school clothes" — slacks, nice shirts for the boys; dresses or skirts for the girls. This boy was actually wearing a jacket and tie coupled with an altogether too short pair of trousers, white socks, and old fashioned black shoes that appeared to be two to three sizes too big for him. The boy continued smiling with his gap-toothed self until Julie, in a rare show of meanness, stuck out her tongue at him.

As if she didn't stand out enough on her own, with her green eyes and long, shining blond hair, Jenny was wearing what her mother referred to as "play clothes"; the clothes that the Adamson children were to change into after school. Her ensemble included pink corduroy pants and an Oakland Raiders football jersey — Daryl Lamonica, Jenny's favorite quarterback. Leave it to Jenny to buck tradition and choose a west coast team to follow instead of the Steelers or the Browns.

Julie clearly remembered Miss Marpy telling her to wear her school clothes, but somehow Jenny's breach of the dress code had bothered neither Fred nor Miss Marpy. And she knew for sure that it wasn't Miss Marpy's idea of inviting Jenny, in her boy clothes, to join the group of children on the bleachers; however, Miss Marpy didn't seem to care or even notice Fred's addition to the clan.

At once, a bright light turned on and suddenly and without preamble, the show began. No directions, no costumes, and no idea of any kind what she was supposed to do. This was, indeed, alarming, especially because Julie was still holding out for a restroom — she really had to pee! A voice from somewhere in the depths of the studio's darkness introduced the beautiful Miss Marpy as "Peggy," and she and the cowboy, who had materialized while Julie was scrutinizing Four-Eyes' hair part, began a chatty dialogue about cattle rustling, Indians, and magic tricks. It wasn't long before the cowboy brought out a rope, fashioned it into a lasso of sorts, and asked for two

48

volunteers. Not surprisingly, before any of the other youngsters had a chance, Jenny's hand shot up.

"Well fur starters, how 'bout this purdy little gal ratcheer in the front row? How 'bout it, Peggy? Think she'd be up for a lasso-in'?"

"Why Cowboy Bill, I think she might! What is your name, Sweet Pea?" Miss Marpy's sugary voice oozed with sweetness.

Jenny popped up out of her aluminum bleacher seat and bounced toward Miss Marpy. Affecting the same twang-y faux western accent as Cowboy Bill, Jenny stated, first staring at both Miss Marpy and the cowboy, then shooting a glance toward the only camera in the studio, "My name's Joe and U'm eight. That there's my sister back there, and I bet she'd want to be picked, too!" She gestured with her thumb, "Her name's *Joo-lie*."

All eyes, including the lucky kids in the first three rows, turned on Julie. She stared, frozen, waiting for Miss Marpy to continue.

"Why, yes! That *is* Julie! Come here, Julie, and stand beside your sister Joe!"

Julie felt her face become very hot, and for a moment, she couldn't move a muscle. She had no idea what she was about to be asked to do; she knew she was courting trouble if she was to stand right beside Jenny, especially this new Jenny-Joe who was, Julie was sure, at that very

49

moment plotting an elaborate prank that would certainly humiliate Julie in some way. It was this, combined with her continued need to release her bladder, which froze her to her spot. It wasn't until some girl sitting beside her poked her hard in her side with her finger that she shook out of her numbness and slowly stood up on the aluminum bleacher.

"Come on down, Julie! Cowboy Bill has something to show you!"

Julie stared, first at Miss Marpy, then at Cowboy Bill, whose eyes were widening with every passing second, willing Julie to get a move on and get her little cowgirl ass down beside her sister. Julie then looked warily at Jenny, who began to flare her nostrils in and out, in and out — Jenny's surefire tactic to get Julie to either begin crying or start giggling non-stop. Julie quickly averted her eyes and concentrated on the arduous task of parting the seated children in front of her and placing each of her Buster Browned feet carefully upon the bleacher seat in front of her, mindful not to wobble or tip. Finally, she took her place beside Jenny.

"Well you two sure don't look much alike, do ya'?" Bill exclaimed, running his eyes up and down Julie's sturdy frame, taking note of her mousy brown hair and her turtleneck and jumper. "Are ya' sure you two are sisters?"

"Oh, yeah, we're sisters," Jenny said with a new confidence—some might call it a swagger—heretofore never seen by any of the Adamsons, "but Julie's real dad was the milkman."

Though Julie never quite knew what this pronouncement meant each time Jenny had said this about her, she was pretty sure that Jenny herself had no idea of the implications of the statement. Apparently, given Julie's darker hair contrasting with the rest of the Adamson's shiny blond-ness, someone, possibly an inebriated relative at a family gathering, had made a joke that Julie was the milkman's progeny. Jenny overheard this and used it relentlessly to tease Julie; however, never within earshot of her mother. As soon as the words left her mouth, Julie could hear a sharp intake of breath offstage—no doubt Carol's—but what was about to happen eclipsed all of that.

Though visibly amused, Cowboy Bill returned to his rather surprisingly professional duty as co-star of the show and continued with the setup of his trick. He turned to Jenny and said, "Well, now, little gal...how 'bout you hold this here end of the rope. I'm gonna' show ya a trick I learned when I was a-livin' in the wild, Wild West. I'm gonna' take the other end of this rope and tie it around yer little sister here."

Cowboy Bill proceeded to loop the heavy rope around
51

Julie's middle, ending with a slipknot that allowed Jenny to either loosen or tighten the rope, depending upon Cowboy Bill's next set of directions. Julie, with terror in her eyes and her need to pee nearly bringing her to tears, watched as Jenny flared her nostrils once again, smirked, and pulled on the rope with as much strength as one would expect from a girl wearing a Daryl Lamonica jersey.

In impressive and spectacular fashion, rivaling any college fraternity boy after a night of heavy and continual beer drinking, Julie issued forth a stream of urine that, under different circumstances, might have won her a prize for both velocity and volume. It not only filled both of her shoes, but it splattered so far afield that both Miss Marpy, the now horrified "Peggy," and Cowboy Bill jumped out of the stream's way.

Not a drop landed anywhere near Jenny.

What happened next was as surreal to Julie as the entire television debut experience had been. A flurry of activity ensued, gasps from the other parents were clearly audible, swear words were uttered, muttered, and spoken by the adults in charge, and Julie's mother grabbed her under her arms and swung her out of the puddle and off of the makeshift stage. Julie remained too stunned to cry, too embarrassed to even open her eyes, and before she knew it, someone had thrown her winter coat over her shoulders, and once again, she was sitting on the hump in the backseat of the car flanked by her brother and sister. No one said a word.

The only who spoke on the twenty minute drive home was Jim, grumbling a lament about how his dinner at Ricci's — his one chance this week to go out to eat — was completely ruined and all because of a stupid television show. Julie, meanwhile, sat silent in a cold, wet puddle of her own urine, an old blanket from the back of the station wagon between her bottom and the vinyl seat of the car. Fighting the urge to cry again, she wondered just how in the world she would ever again face her lovely and beautiful Miss Marpy.

The Gym Show

III

Stanley Czerniawski was late for the bus again. It wasn't his fault; this time, his mother had delayed his trip down the long driveway by insisting that he wear the hideous rubber galoshes with the toggle fasteners over his too-tight school shoes — shoes that Stanley had been hoping to ruin once and for all by running through the mud puddles left by last night's rain. He hated those damn shoes.

As he plodded toward the bus, whose driver was honking incessantly even though she could see him coming, he dreaded the day ahead. Clutching his lunch pail and a yellow plastic tote that his mother used during the summer to carry her onions in from the garden but was now put into service as a book bag, he couldn't help but think that Mrs. Chapin, his bus driver, deliberately made a point of failing to wait the requisite thirty seconds after stopping the bus at the end of his driveway and flipping on her flashing red lights to make sure that Stanley got on the bus each day. In fact, he was certain that Mrs. Chapin hated him, hated his awkward entrance onto the bus each morning, hated his woman-like plastic book bag with the summer's onion skins still nestled at the

55

bottom, hated the smell of the stinky cheese he carried in his lunch pail every day, and hated everything that Stanley Czerniawski represented. It was no skin off her nose if he didn't make it to school on time—or ever. To make matters worse, Mrs. Chapin's son Billy served as the bus' sergeant-at-arms, a loud-mouthed bully who made sure every bus rider bowed to his whims and his insufferable teasing.

Stanley was the only child of Polish immigrants—his parents had both arrived in the U.S. shortly after the Second World War, having survived an invading Nazi juggernaut and the occupation of their country only to begin witnessing the devastation of their beloved homeland by the conquering Soviets. When they arrived, they had already been married for several years, and the ensuing years were dedicated to finding a way of life in a country that was more inclined to welcome back their own returning war heroes with the best jobs and opportunities, not waste the post-war excesses on two seemingly undereducated immigrants who spoke broken and heavily accented English.

In fact, though, both Aggie and Lube Czerniawski were bright and hardworking, brought up in decent homes and, though lacking any kind of formal education, both families worked hard to make sure that their children could read and write, and both Aggie and Lube could speak a little bit of English—at least enough English to eventually gain them passage out of Poland. Both families were fiercely and devoutly Catholic and amid the sorrow-filled tears of a painful goodbye, Aggie and Lube promised their families that they indeed intended to continue their devotion to the Church as new Americans.

Once Aggie and Lube arrived in America, they moved in with a distant cousin in a small mining town south of Pittsburgh. Lube worked in the coalmines while Aggie set about making a home for them in the small, cramped company-owned house they shared with the cousin. They desperately wanted a family, but it didn't appear as if the American contingent of the Czerniawski family would be added to (not to mention the awkwardness of sharing a bed with Cousin Jakub). Lube, never robust as a child and young man, was even less healthy as an adult creeping toward middle age—eight hours working underground in a damp and dusty environment began to age him exponentially—so Aggie set about to find somewhere else for the two of them to make a life. Through her involvement in the church (Lube preferred to take literally the commandment regarding rest on the Sabbath), she discovered an opportunity to live on a farm located near a small town in the northwest corner of Pennsylvania that was run by an elderly Pole who had just lost his wife and wished to hire a young couple to take over the running of the place; in turn, they would be provided with a small mobile home on the farm's property, and together they would run the farm and take care of its elderly proprietor until his death. This was what Aggie had been looking for, though, for his part, Lube was somewhat skeptical about the prospect. Had they not left Poland to find a better opportunity than to care for an aged farmer and work his land? What about having something of their own? They had left their families' subsistent farms back in Poland to find that axiomatic American dream, and Lube felt as if all of their struggles and sacrifices would be for naught and they would wind up back where they had begun.

Aggie was persistent, though, and in 1956, they left the coalmines of southern Pennsylvania and moved their few belongings north to Mercyville, a town known, among other things, as being the exact mid-point between Chicago, 500 miles to the west, and New York, 500 miles to the east. Few of Mercyville's residents thought to challenge the sign that hung above Betty's Bait Shop, a faded black arrow pointing west and a matching arrow pointing east, and actually measure whether Chicago was indeed 500 miles to the west or if New York was 500 miles to the east. Few of Mercyville's residents would ever travel that far, anyway.

Aggie and Lube found Mercyville to their liking. It

was clean, it was fresh, and the couple became used to the idea of spending the rest of their lives nestled on this small farm between two lakes—one picturesque and plentiful with all manner of wildlife, the other, a playground for Pittsburgh's upper middle classes. A peaceful area of lush, green, and abundant fir trees was exactly what they had in mind when they had left Poland.

The old farmer was kind to the young couple and left them alone (for the first time in much of their married life), preferring to spend most of his days in town drinking beer at the Knights of Columbus out by the Shenango Reservoir boat launch. Though older than both Aggie's and Lube's parents, Mr. Danof did not appear to be leaving this earth any time soon and did not require all that much care for himself, leaving Aggie with little more to do than tend to the meager menagerie residing in the barn and clean both Mr. Danof's house and their own small trailer.

A swiftly moving creek ran through the middle of Danof's property and became, over the years, a popular campsite for a small band of gypsies that roamed western Lake County at the end of each summer; they were, presumably, leftover carnival folks from the Lake County Fair. The travelers must have found the area near the creek a tightly enclosed hiding place where they could set up camp with their caravans, trailers, and rusty pick-up trucks while the women and children in the group dispersed into town and grifted their way up and down Main Street in Mercyville.

The gypsies were generally harmless, but, like raccoons or possums that nest in attics or haylofts, they were a nuisance. No one in the Mercyville area ever locked their doors, and the gypsies would raid families' refrigerators, freezers, and root cellars, and would occasionally walk right inside of folks' houses and help themselves to any little trinket or tchotchke that happened to take their fancy. Danof detested these intruders, and one of Lube's jobs each summer was to flush out the area by the creek on his property where the gypsies usually made camp. Lube, a loaded shotgun in hand, would nervously patrol the area, hoping he would never have to fire the damn thing — he was a poor shot at best — and the idea of hurting another human being, after all he had seen during the war, was repellent to him. He had known bands of gypsies back in Poland, Bohemians whose nomadic ways during the war often made them the target of Nazis who simply shot them on sight. Lube felt as if the gypsies of the world had suffered enough, and, as long as they weren't stealing from Danof, they should be able to stay put, but Danof was his landlord. Lube and Aggie, much like gypsies themselves when they had first arrived at Danof's, had a good thing going living on his property in their warm little trailer, and so Lube did as he was told.

Lube proved himself a poor hunter, because if there were gypsies camped down by the creek, they were gone by the time Lube arrived.

Apparently the country air released something in the couple because in the late fall of 1961, Aggie found she was expecting a child — and soon. In their early forties, the two never imagined that a child was in their future and though they were excited, they were a bit wary of what to do with a child in their little home on the farmer's property.

Stanley was born during a snowstorm in January of 1962. The couple doted on him, but because they had relatively no exposure to children — not even the children who attended the Catholic church in town — the couple, through either ignorance or fear, isolated Stanley from other children who would have made his introduction into the public school system much smoother.

The idea of sending Stanley to school terrified Aggie. She knew nothing about the concept of kindergarten, so when all of Stanley's peers had turned five and were sent to learn the alphabet and their numbers, Stanley remained in the trailer with Aggie and Lube speaking mostly Polish with a only little bit of English thrown in now and then. Once Stanley turned six, Aggie was forced to send her baby boy to first grade where his lack of the basics made for one excruciatingly long year, for both Stanley and his teacher. To no one's surprise, Stanley, in elementary school vernacular, flunked first grade.

Undeterred by any shame in having to repeat the first grade, this was the year that Aggie prayed that her Stanley might begin to make some new friends and gain a bit of confidence with regard to his schoolwork. So it was a pleasant surprise that he was chosen by his school to appear in a television show. Aggie had poured over the letter sent home by the school, painstakingly trying to figure out what all was involved on her part in preparing Stanley for this most important event.

Last night, Aggie and Lube had made the rare trip into Erie in the family's Ford pickup truck with Stanley tucked safely between them, wearing his best shirt, a tie, jacket, pants that were too short, and a pair of shoes borrowed from a neighbor who lived about a mile down the road from them. Though Aggie was now earning a little bit of spending money by cleaning some houses in the area, the couple was careful with their meager savings, choosing to stash as much money under their sagging mattress for emergencies only; thus, it had made sense to borrow shoes for this occasion. Aggie was planning to save enough money to outfit Stanley in a new blue suit and new black shoes just in time for his First Holy Communion next spring. Following the taping of *Peggy's People*, Stanley's parents had made sure that he knew how proud they were

62

of their son, and had later remarked to each other that had it not been for the unfortunate incident with the nervous little girl wetting her pants right in the middle of the show, and right in front of God and everyone, the night would have been perfect.

Stanley, for his part, had been excited about his appearance on the television show, girl peeing her pants notwithstanding, but this excitement was eclipsed by the letter that remained in his plastic satchel—the letter explaining to Aggie and Lube that Mrs. Haines, Stanley's teacher, felt that it would be in Stanley's best interest to start all over again in school, this time in kindergarten. Apparently, the idea of repeating the first grade simply wasn't enough for Stanley's teacher, the highly- strung and notoriously impatient Dorothy Haines—she used whatever political capital she possessed at Mercyville Elementary to lobby for Stanley's demotion to kindergarten. Besides, with the unlikely return of Joyce Olentick and her obviously pregnant pre-wedding self, it would be an easily accomplished move, and it would serve that Barbara Marpy right, getting all of these children so worked up about a stupid television show.

Stanley, for all of his apparent academic deficiencies, had an intuitive sense that Mrs. Haines was simply trying to get rid of him and the sweet-natured Mrs. Marpy would be too polite to refuse her. These were the thoughts that

63

weighed heavily on young Stanley's mind as he took a seat on the school bus next to a shy girl with blond pigtails and a river of snot running out of her nose. Stanley was supposed to have given to his mother the letter Mrs. Haines had pinned to his plaid buttoned-down shirt when he returned home from school yesterday and before the Czernaiowski's big trip into the television station in Erie, but he simply did not have the heart to disappoint Aggie when she was apparently so excited about his being on television. So while he rode the bus home, he carefully removed the note, folded it, and placed it in the bottom of the onion satchel.

Stanley knew that come Sunday morning after the eleven o'clock mass that Aggie would somehow make sure that all of the parishioners at Immaculate Heart of Mary would know that her son, her baby boy, had been especially chosen to represent his school on television. The irony was almost painful to Stanley. The Czernaiowski's did not own a television set.

Once the bus arrived at the school, and the bus duty teachers herded the cold and wet children into their classrooms, Mrs. Haines cornered Stanley and asked if he had given his mother the letter.

"Yes. I did."

"And did your mother agree with me that it would be best if you were to go to kindergarten this year?

The Gym Show

Remember, Stanley, you're the only one in this first grade class who hasn't been to kindergarten."

"Yes. She said 'all right.'"

That apparently was good enough for Mrs. Haines. She marched Stanley over to his desk and asked him to remove his books and workbooks, his crayons, his safety scissors, and the fat thick pencil that was badly in need of sharpening. Almost as if she was afraid of catching cooties, she gingerly gathered up the contents of Stanley's desk, wrinkling her nose with one distinctly raised eyebrow.

"Miss Marpy is going to be your teacher—for now," she snapped at Stanley, obviously anxious to be rid of him and his seemingly contaminated accoutrements. "She will give you all of the supplies you need in your new classroom." Mrs. Haines unceremoniously deposited the contents of Stanley's desk on a small table near the door and Stanley doggedly followed her down the hall and into the kindergarten wing. No one had said anything to Stanley on his way out the door, which was both good and bad—good because he didn't have to face any teasing from his classmates, and bad, because no one, apparently, was going to even care that he was gone.

Miss Marpy greeted Stanley at the door with a knowing smile toward Mrs. Haines and ushered Stanley into the kindergarten room.

65

The Gym Show

She sat him right next to Julie Adamson.

IV

Jim Adamson sat across from the heavy-set girl, eyeing her with a mixture of pity and disdain as she stood awkwardly in front of his desk sniffling and trembling. The home economics teacher Mrs. Pennycroft had sent Betty Handy, who clearly had been crying prior to her audience with Mr. A., to the principal's office near the end of third period. Of all the kids in this school that that old biddy Pennycroft could have sent to him, Betty was the last he ever expected see. This should be good.

"And why again did Mrs. Pennycroft send you down to me, Betty? Here—here's a Kleenex—now, blow your nose."

Betty hiccupped, blew her nose loudly, and began, "She said I was eating crumbs. I wasn't, Mr. A., I swear. You can ask Sandy Clemmons; she was my partner."

"Betty, what were you baking today?" Jim asked patiently.

Betty drew in a snot-ravaged breath and whispered, "Apple Brown Betty, Mr. A., and there *were* crumbs, but I didn't eat any of them. Sandy did, but I didn't, but Mrs. Pennycroft blamed me anyway a...a...and said that I had to come down here and get a...a p...p...paddling!" With that, Betty broke into a fresh round of sobs. Jim handed

67

her the entire box of tissues, suppressing the violent urge to walk upstairs and strangle Doris Pennycroft.

Instead, Jim sighed and tried to lighten the mood a bit. Poor Betty, it was bad enough that she was such a big potato of a girl, but to make matters worse, the kid's heartbreaking blubbering was   almost painful. In an effort to assuage her sobs, he crooned, "'Betty was baking Apple Brown Betty. She tried to eat crumbs, but Sandy ate them already.'" Hoping to see her smile just a little through all of those tears, Jim continued.

"Okay, Betty, here's what we're going to do. You go to the girls' room, wash your face, go back to class, and tell Mrs. Pennycroft that instead of paddling you that I gave you a good, stern talking to then tell her that I said to bring down me a dish of that Apple Brown Betty. Does that sound like a good plan?"

Betty sniffed again loudly, and this time she *was* smiling, "Yes, Sir, Mr. A. You're the nicest man in the world. And I'm so sorry I used up all your Kleenex. Thank you! Thank you! I'll be right back with your dish!"

Christ almighty, that Doris Pennycroft needed to retire *yesterday*, Jim thought to himself. Irritated, he leaned back in his chair and fished the last cigarette out of the pack of Kents lying on his desk, lit it, and let the inhaled nicotine calm his ire. Mrs. Pennycroft was really only one of a handful of teachers on Jim's staff at Mercyville High

School with whom he loathed working; he figured he should count himself lucky in that regard. Her incessant whining and bitching about the most insignificant and unimportant minutiae of her tenure as the home economics teacher, though, spoke volumes about her need to retire. That, and the fact that she was probably the oldest teacher on his staff.

Whereas Jim prided himself on the relationship he had with his staff, he valued even more the relationship he had with the student body at Mercyville. He was firm, fair, set clear boundaries, was consistent, and, whenever possible, he found the humor in every situation. He liked joking around with the kids, telling them that they should feel fortunate that he was messing with them—it was a sure sign he liked them. In turn, they "messed" with Jim. For years, the Adamsons never had a mailbox for more than a few weeks. The running prank at Mercyville High School was to blow up Mr. A.'s mailbox with M-80s. As soon as Jim would replace the mailbox and again became accustomed to stopping at it every evening to get the family's mail, he'd find the next morning bits and pieces of it scattered all over the road like shrapnel. He and Carol had finally resigned themselves to gathering their mail at the post office. Instead of getting angry, he joked about it, knowing that these assaults upon his mailbox weren't personal, and if that was the worst that ever happened to

69

him as a high school principal, well, he was doing a pretty decent job.

Jim treated his staff fairly, too. As much as possible, he tried to make all of the teachers at Mercyville feel as if their positions were equal—he regarded the demands upon the physics teacher and those of the physical education teacher, for instance, with the same importance (as well they should since his own wife was the girls' P.E. teacher), but when petty little crap like this was tossed at him, he couldn't help but think that the entire school would be better off without Doris Pennycroft's bullshit. And today, this was the last thing he needed.

Yesterday after school, Jim had gone in search of Charlie, the school's custodian. He had initially used the PA system to page the older man, but Charlie was hard of hearing, and if he was using the buffer or running water somewhere, it was likely he wouldn't have heard Jim calling for him. So reluctantly, Jim heaved his 300-pound frame out from behind his desk and started walking through all of the places in the building where Charlie might be. At least the walking was supposed to be good for him—after two heart attacks, his doctor had warned him that he not only needed to lose about a hundred pounds, he should also consider giving up the smokes. Dr. DeKreif did not, however, suggest he stop drinking so much since Jim managed to hide that particular vice from just about everyone. Good thing he can't see my liver, Jim thought.

The school's gym served multiple purposes at Mercyville. When the school was built in 1952, the trend in school architecture was to combine the gymnasium with an auditorium. Mercyville's gym featured a full sized stage on one of the long ends. That Monday was one of those rare November afternoons when the boys' basketball team had not yet started practicing, so the gym was uncharacteristically unoccupied, the lights were off, and the heavy black velvet curtains framing the stage were closed. That in itself was unusual, so Jim made his way up the steps stage right and back behind the drawn curtains. Once on the back of the stage looking front, there hung several sets of lighter-weight gray curtains that were situated behind the heavier velvet ones closest to the gym, and it was among the folds of those gray curtains that Jim found Henry Somers and Tommy Jankovic, naked from the waist down, locked in a position that clearly revealed that the boys were engaging in an act of sodomy.

"Son of a bitch," he sighed.

At this point in Jim's life, few things should have surprised or shocked him. He had served four years in the army during World War II, several memorable months of combat in Italy, and figured he had pretty much seen and experienced all the crap he ever needed to see or experience in an entire lifetime. The army consisted of a cross section of boys and men (and boys in various stages of becoming men) from all walks of life, and during basic training, he had come across a guy in his unit who he privately thought *might* be a queer, and though this young soldier's unnatural tendencies and seemingly disgusting proclivities generally sickened Jim, it wasn't until he became an officer and had been shipped off to Italy that one of his own men schooled him about living life as a homosexual.

After a particularly bloody and gruesome struggle to cross Arno River, Ted Ambrose, a "regular guy," they had all agreed later, had been caught in a homosexual act with another soldier, a soldier who had eluded capture by fleeing in the moonless Tuscan darkness leaving Ambrose, the recipient of the escaping soldier's affections, literally caught with his pants down.

As salacious as the incident was at the time, it was only after the initial dust had settled that Jim actually began to put together just what it might mean to be a homosexual. In college, he had known plenty of fruits, guys who were light in the loafers, limp wristed as hell, and may as well have been wearing a sandwich board announcing to the entire world just how queer they were.

But this guy, this soldier, this brave man who had fought beside him and his men, a guy who wasn't afraid

72

of anything—a guy who had smoked cigarette after cigarette alongside of them in mud-soaked trenches, slept beside them in bivouacs, pissed inside of his helmet, spit in it, wiped it out then filled it up with C-rations—the same guy who had watched in horror as some of his own buddies were blown to shit by mortar fire—this guy, this "regular" guy, was actually a queer.

Before he was to turn himself in, Jim had pulled the man aside and in order to satisfy his own curiosity, he asked Ted Ambrose about his preference for men with as much tact as he could muster under the circumstances. After all, it wasn't that long ago that the two of them had considered themselves friends. After questioning him once again about this partner of his who apparently didn't have the balls to stick around and take his punishment like a man, Jim had asked, "Look, pal, I'm not trying to be an asshole here or anything, but I've always wanted to know something and never knew who I could ask." Jim had taken a deep breath, not sure how he was going to ask this former soldier, this friend of his, such a personal question that he never thought he'd have had the opportunity to ask, not in a million lifetimes. "What's it like? I mean, being queer. What's it like being a queer? You seem like such a normal guy. I gotta say, I'm shocked. We're all shocked. You're one of us, Ted. You act so normal. No one would ever in a lifetime peg you as a fairy. We're all

73

just kind of wondering why you would choose to throw your whole life away — over a — a *blow* job."

The hapless soldier looked at Jim for a long time before answering. Finally, he took a deep breath and began speaking, steadily and carefully, as if he had thought about this very thing for a long time. "This is not something I have *chosen* to be, Lieutenant. Why would anyone choose to live like this? Do you think this is what I *want* to be? Lemme ask *you* something, Lieutenant, and I mean no disrespect here: How would you like it if you had to serve beside women day in and day out — you had to eat with them, sleep beside them, take a shit next to them, dress in front of them — how do you think you'd react? You'd go out of your fucking mind, Lieutenant. Out of your fucking mind, I tell you. I'm almost glad I got caught. Trust me, Lieutenant, I wouldn't wish this on my worst enemy."

And with that, Corporal Ted Ambrose had educated Second Lieutenant Jim Adamson on the reality of being a homosexual. That conversation with Ted Ambrose had changed something in Jim — it gave him the unique ability to see the world through another's eyes, and that was a skill that would serve him well in the profession that he had chosen and, indeed, for the rest of his life. The problems of the world were no longer divided into right or wrong, black or white. No, after thinking about Ted

74

Ambrose for a long time, Jim had grudgingly concluded that life was full of gray areas.

Jim Adamson was not a complicated man, at least he didn't think of himself as a complicated man, but he certainly did not fit into any particular category when it came to type. A physical force to be reckoned with, he would enjoy the youthfulness of a thick head of blond hair well into the autumn of his life. He was tall, big-boned, barrel chested and strong. Over the   past several years, though, the body he had honed to perfection while playing high school basketball, then college football, basketball, and baseball, had begun to go to fat. He liked to eat, he liked to drink — a lot — he smoked about a pack of cigarettes a day, his blood pressure was too high, his heart was too large, he suffered from paralyzing nightmares the likes of which he would never have wished on his worst enemy, and he was the fifty-one year old husband of a beautiful thirty-six year old wife with three elementary school-aged children who were the absolute best thing that had ever happened to him.

Jim considered himself more street smart than book smart, although his academic resume ran counter to this perception of himself. Though he did not consider *himself* a deep thinker, he actually was a man who weighed every thought, every decision, and every action with the utmost consideration. He was well read, well versed, and, though he seldom looked the part, his knowledge of the complexities of the twentieth century world around him was the unexpected by-product of his upbringing. He would rather that others see him as an old farm boy, a country bumpkin, just an ordinary man trying to make his way in the world instead of the brooding deep thinker that he was, the man who took sarcasm and bigotry to a whole new level when called upon to do so, but could also surprisingly join ranks with the hippies protesting against the Vietnam War. A life-long Republican, he had unapologetically voted for Kennedy in 1960, but railed against Johnson and his 'Great Society' a short time later.

Remembering that long ago conversation with Ted Ambrose, Jim now had a choice to make regarding these two young boys who, after shamefully scrambling to their feet and pulling up their pants, stood in front of him, the bigger boy crying quietly — not talking, not asking Mr. A. for any kind of leniency, but simply crying. The boy hung his head low on his chest, his large shoulders heaving. His name was Henry Somers, and Jim knew him well from basketball season and his involvement in Future Farmers of America; the other boy, the one who wasn't crying and who looked to be in some kind of shock, was Tommy Jankovic.

The surreal nature of the tableau he had just witnessed would require some processing, some type of debriefing

76

on his part. Jim needed some time to think about what to do with this, whatever *this* was, so he told the boys to get the hell out of there and go on home. He knew something would have to be done, but what that something was still preyed on Jim's mind nearly twenty-four hours later. Somehow, the crisis above him in Doris Pennycroft's third period home economics class did not register as a priority. And where was Betty with that damn dessert?

It's not as if Jim condoned the boys' behavior, and indeed, both boys were probably sick to their stomachs today waiting for Mr. A. to deliver their fate. Recalling Ted Ambrose and his life-changing conversation with him, Jim thought that at the very least he had to tell the boys' parents. But Jim knew Henry Somers' father, Henry Sr., and Henry Sr. was a mean son-of-a-bitch who would undoubtedly beat the living shit out of young Henry if he didn't outright kill him. Tommy Jankovic was another matter. Tommy and his parents lived about as far west as anyone could and still live within the Commonwealth of Pennsylvania and the Mercyville attendance area. Jim had been out there once a couple of summers ago trying to find someone who could fix his hot water heater cheap, and he saw Tommy and his mother in the garden. He had pulled over to the side of the road and asked Tommy if he knew where Mel Banks' house was located. Tommy had cheerfully given Jim directions, and when Jim had thanked both Tommy and his mother for their time, Mrs. Jankovic had simply looked at him with a blank stare and returned to weeding her row of peppers. Jim did not relish a discussion with either her or Tommy's father, wherever he might be hiding, but it was probably inevitable.

Jim hollered for Ruthie to come into his office. He had hired Ruthie Stone right out of high school—her excellent typing, shorthand, and unparalleled organizational skills were chief among her best qualities, but it was her overall plainness, her awkward appearance, and her unexcitable and even-tempered personality that ultimately made her a good school secretary. Nearly as tall as Jim's six foot two frame and damn near as big as he, Jim had figured when he hired her that Ruthie's prospects for marriage and a family were somewhat remote. Ruthie was an only child, and given her devotion to her aging parents, he reckoned he could count on her to be around for a while. That was 1956, and here she still was, thirteen years later—she would, in fact, remain the principal's secretary throughout the rest of the millennium and beyond.

Ruthie lumbered in and raised her eyebrows in response to his somewhat unorthodox manner of summoning her—not that she was offended, since a certain relationship existed between the two that made the need for words rather superfluous; her raised eyebrows were her way of saying, "Yes?"

"Come on in and shut the door behind you. We have a problem."

Jim proceeded to tell Ruthie, in as delicate a manner as was befitting a middle-aged man to his younger, albeit older-souled secretary about his discovery on the stage the previous evening. He left out the more salacious details of the boys' coupling, but somehow he supposed that Ruthie, who, like many students and former students who had grown up on a farm, knew exactly what had transpired between the two. Ruthie listened, her countenance belying no reaction one way or another, and waited for him to finish.

"So, given Henry's dad's volatility and the fact that Tommy's parents probably wouldn't know a queer from a hole in the ground, what do you think we should do?"

Ruthie thought for a moment before speaking. "Mercy. That's a tough one, Mr. A. I've known Mr. Somers most of my life, and you're right: it don't take much to set him off. He may come after *you*, you know. As for Tommy's parents, I don't know as much about them, except that they don't have a telephone or a television set, there's no hot water in the house, and neither of them are too good with the English, if you know what I mean."

"I know all that, Ruthie. I'm just asking you what *you*

79

think I should do."

"Who else knows about this? Did you tell Mrs. A?"

"No, we didn't have a chance to talk last night. We had to go into that goddamn Erie television station. Julie was supposed to be on TV. Some kiddie show. She pissed her pants right at the beginning of the taping, and we left." He turned and looked out the window, squinting though there was no sun, then continued, "Carol was in no mood to talk when we finally got home. I thought she was going to kill that child," he said, shaking his head, remembering the events of last evening. What he did not share with Ruthie was that he purposefully avoided telling Carol about the two boys. Carol was famous for taking a crisis and turning it into her personal crusade. Something like this would have her bringing the two boys together to "talk it out" or worse yet, it might inspire her to seek out other students with the same tendencies and become their life coach—the very person that would turn them around and lead them away from the darkness of homosexuality. It was one of her more endearing traits, this need to help people, especially the students at the school, and he would not have wanted her to be any other way. It's just that this was an entirely new area for him, and he did not need her intervening until he knew all of the facts.

He returned to look at Ruthie. "And to answer your first question, no, I haven't told anyone else, just you. And you know I'm counting on you to keep this between us."

That Jim had confided in her, Ruthie, before telling his own wife (a teacher, and someone far more qualified to weigh in on such a delicate matter), did not surprise Ruthie. She was used to Mr. A. using her as a sounding board and he knew he could trust her to keep her mouth shut. Mercyville was a small town, and gossip was one of its favorite spectator sports. Moreover, it was common knowledge among the staff that, though Mrs. A. had unusually high expectations, she was also sympathetic to a fault. If a student was in trouble, she would make it her mission to remedy the problem, even if it meant violating a confidence if she felt it was in the best interest of the student. It was not out of the ordinary for her to publically shame a boy into marrying some poor girl he impregnated, regardless of what that girl or her family thought about the situation. She would ferret out the most obnoxious boys and make them her right-hand men, especially during Gym Show time. She often took it upon herself to make sure that the kids who felt left out, bullied, or shunned for whatever reason were included in some kind of activity at the school; in short, she felt it was her calling as a teacher, a mentor, and a mother to do what she felt best for all of the students at Mercyville. Oftentimes, this meant that her *own* children (especially Julie) were left to their own devices.

The Gym Show

The Adamson children spent much of their after-school time at the high school, so the staff had plenty of opportunities to interact with the youngsters and found them, at least the older two, delightful, polite, well dressed, and handsome little ambassadors for their parents. After all, the children had plenty of practice interacting with adults. Poor little Julie, though, either had not yet adopted the older two children's manners, or would remain awkward, shy, and mousy in contrast to the blond "Dick and Jane" looks of her older brother and sister. Few could resist Jenny's ebullient personality and brightness, and Jimmy's maturity and well-mannered demeanor were difficult standards for little Julie to aspire to. As the youngest, Julie somehow always managed to say and do the wrong thing at the wrong time.

Once, when Julie was nearly four, she was perched upon the high counter in the school's outer office coloring with crayons as she waited for her mother to finish her meeting with the varsity cheerleaders. Mrs. A. had assumed that among her many duties that Ruthie wouldn't mind keeping an eye on Julie. Ruthie *didn't* mind; she thought the little girl was cute in a kind of awkward way, but she didn't like Mrs. A. always making the assumption that, in addition to serving as her husband's Girl Friday, she was also a babysitter. As Julie sat coloring, Ruthie decided to engage her in a little conversation. She asked her what her favorite colors were, she asked her if she was excited to start school in a couple of years like her big brother and sister, and then she asked her, "What kinds of things do your mummy and daddy do when all of you are at home?"

Julie put down her crayons, looked Ruthie straight in the eye and said very seriously, "Dad only wears his underwear when he's home, and he and Mum fight a lot about whiskey."

Ruthie didn't have time to fully digest the little girl's revelation when she suddenly heard the heavy sound of a chair scrape away from his desk, and, as big as he was, Mr. A. had managed to fly out of his office with a speed more commonly reserved for someone half his size. Without a word, he scooped up his youngest child, crayons scattering the floor, and, carrying her like a football, marched with her out into the hallway and into the direction of Mrs. A.'s office outside of the girls' locker room.

And now, picturing Mrs. A.'s fit of rage the previous evening over Julie's embarrassing television debut, Ruthie fought back a grin. In all fairness to her boss' wife, Ruthie supposed that, as busy as she was all of the time, Mrs. A. probably didn't have as much time to mold her little one into a perfect child as she did with Jimmy and Jenny. It seemed, too, that Mr. And Mrs. A. didn't have that much time to themselves, either—all the more reason that Jim relied on Ruthie for counsel.

"I don't know, Mr. A. You're kind of in a pickle. If you ignore what happened, you're really saying to those boys that you think it's okay that they were doing...whatever you call it what they were doing. That kind of stuff isn't natural, Mr. A. It says so right in the Bible. On the other hand, if you tell their parents, chances are one of them, probably Henry, is going to wind up with a broken jaw or a black eye. Maybe both."

Jim agreed. Unfortunately, Ruthie's insight did little to provide him with a solution to this rather unusual predicament. Over the years as a teacher and then principal, he had caught various couples—girls and boys—in compromising situations, but *never* two boys. It was Ted Ambrose all over again, and that poor bastard was eventually court martialed.

Jim sighed. "Well, at any rate, get me both boys' phone numbers—oh, that's right, you said Jankovics didn't have a phone. I guess I'll have to drive out there and talk with them."

Ruthie returned to the outer office and began flipping through the Rolodex on her desk looking for a phone number for Henry Somers. Jim sighed and sat back in his chair, lit another cigarette, and tried to put together a script that would help him explain to these boys' parents

84

what exactly it was they were doing on the stage yesterday after school.

Carol stopped by her little office in front of the girls' locker room to touch up her hair and makeup before her next class. Ever mindful of her appearance, she kept hairspray and extra makeup in the small bathroom off to the side of her office; it would be unseemly to appear disheveled in front of a classroom full of senior girls. Her first three periods were spent in the gym—well, half the gym—and the next three periods she was in the classroom teaching health. She preferred the gym; she felt more at home and more in control there. A large net and vinyl curtain hung in the middle of the gym dividing it into the girls' side and the boys' side for physical education classes. At that time, combining a class of boys and girls for something so visceral as exercise was unheard of. The divided gymnasium suited Carol just fine since she could hardly stand to be in the same school let alone the same gym and breathe the same air as Vincent Tagliaburro, the boys' physical education teacher. To Carol, Vincent was a lecherous pig she had been acquainted with back in college at Slippery Rock, a man notorious for seducing unsuspecting girls, ruining their formerly pristine and virginal reputations then dumping them, just in time to take on his next female conquest. When Carol was first hired to teach at Mercyville, she was appalled to discover that Vinnie also worked at Mercyville High School and became even more ill at ease when she learned that she actually had to share her space with him. She could not imagine why Jim had ever hired him.

Jim, for his part, had found Vinnie to be likable, and even though privately he pegged Vinnie as an oily guinea, the guy interviewed well and seemed to fit the exact profile that Jim was looking for in a boys' physical education teacher. Vinnie was never late to work, he took care of his own issues with regard to student discipline, and besides, he had hired Tag a full year before he had even met, let alone hired, Carol.

Like Jim, Vinnie was on his second wife, but to Carol, that is where the similarities between the two men ended. Dreama Marciano was a co-ed the still-married Vinnie had met four years earlier during an alumni weekend at Slippery Rock, which was largely spent slumming and engaging in all manner of debauchery. At the time, Dreama was a senior with a somewhat casual attitude toward morality and virtue—one who either didn't care about Vinnie's missing wedding ring (made visible by the clear indentation below his hairy knuckle) or was too dumb to notice it. After what Carol could only imagine was a bacchanalian sex and drug-filled weekend, it didn't take long for Vinnie—Mr. Tag to his students—to unceremoniously dump his long-suffering wife and take up with Dreama.

Whether it was because she felt sorry for her for being married to Vinnie, or whether it was that they both had small children, Carol had made friends with Vinnie's first wife Tammy, Vinnie's high school sweetheart. After being publicly humiliated by Vinnie's departure from their marriage, though, Tammy quietly tucked her tail between her legs and returned, kids in tow, back to Pittsburgh to live with her parents. Tammy's seemingly shameful departure had made Carol despise Vinnie even more. Clearly, Vinnie was the one who should have left.

Now it was Vinnie and Dreama who occupied the two-bedroom bungalow that used to be the happy little home of which Tammy was so proud. Dreama resembled nothing of the sweetness that was Tammy Fox Tagliaburro. Dreama's long, black, straight hair, the crown of which was forever teased into a puffed up pompadour, and her severe-looking features, her too-thin frame that was clad in an outrageous wardrobe, not to mention the talon-like fingernails lacquered a frosted pink were a stark contrast to Tammy's round and subtle softness.

Moreover, Dreama was delighted in making her presence known. She talked loudly, she laughed loudly, and she played the rock and roll music in her car — a used

Mustang convertible that Vinnie had bought her before the ink was dry on his divorce decree—so loudly that there was little question when Dreama was in the vicinity.

But to Carol, the most irritating and ingratiating thing about Dreama was that she had a teaching degree, and because she had a teaching degree, and because she was a willing subject with a new husband who was also on the staff, Carol's husband felt as if he *had* to hire her as a permanent substitute teacher at Mercyville. Substitute teaching was not high on too many prospective teachers' list of desirable jobs, but every once in a while, a substitute teacher, if he or she was good at it, could slide into a teaching position when a retirement came up. The trouble was, at Mercyville, the attrition rate for teachers was remarkably low. Jim was adept at *mentally* separating the cream from the milk, but he lacked the motivation to actually remove any staff member who fell below his standards (all that paperwork!), so the only chance a new teacher had to become part of the permanent staff at Mercyville was a retirement or a maternity leave that would turn into an actual teaching gig. This was, incidentally, how Carol herself had come to be hired for her position.

Beginning with this school year, Dreama had weaseled her way into the Mercyville High School culture by taking any substituting opportunities that came her way, and in doing so, she now felt ensconced as a regular staff member and wished to be treated as such, even though she might only be there one out of five days. Regardless of the number of days she was actually working, she obviously was out to prove to Jim and to others that she was there to stay; if not as a permanent teacher at Mercyville, as Vinnie's permanent wife. Dreama was also confident in the knowledge that the students at Mercyville were fascinated by her exotic looks, her over-the-top wardrobe, which varied from cheaply made Pucci-style mini-dresses to hippie skirts and beaded jewelry. She asked that the students call her 'Mrs. Tag' just as they called Vinnie 'Mr. Tag'. So hip. To the kids, Mrs. Tag represented their generation — she understood the divide between them and authority. Mrs. Tag was cool. She was one of them.

Carol's loathing for the couple reached a pinnacle that particular morning. After homeroom and before his boys were to enter the gym for their warm ups, Vinnie had breached the vinyl divide between his and Carol's respective domains and had, in his smoothly slick voice, heavily laced with that western Pennsylvania phenomenon called "Pittsburghese," where every question ended in an annoying downward inflection, approached Carol with an idea that she found so preposterous, so unbelievably audacious and bold of him,

89

that she considered just ignoring it altogether.

Vinnie wanted to put boys in the Gym Show.

"Look, Cupcake, I know this is kinda' your thing an' all, but I was thinkin' that, well, it might look good if some a my boys were included the Gym Show, uh? Yinz girls are havin' all the fun, you know? How's 'bout we add some men to the mix — you know, muscle it up an' all. Ya' see, Dreama an' I, we was talkin' about it last night, you know, and she's the one who brought it up. She's got some real good ideas, you know? She'd be a real help to you, an' at."

Carol had looked at him as if he had just proposed that they lift the vinyl curtain between the two halves of the gym, invite all of their students in to sit in a circle, smoke marijuana, strip bare naked, and have a love-in. Was he out of his goddamn mind?

The whole reason Carol had even conceived of the idea of the Gym Show in the first place was that she felt the girls at Mercyville were being shortchanged. The boys had basketball and baseball; the girls had volleyball and cheerleading. The volleyball program, under Carol's control as well, was successful — in fact, last week the team had won the Lake County Championship trophy by beating Mercyville's bitter rival Iroquois Lake. To Carol's utmost delight, the Iroquois Lake coach had refused to accept the second place trophy and had marched her team off the floor in a fury of bad sportsmanship. Another feather in Carol's cap! However good their little girls' volleyball team was, though, volleyball had never drawn the crowds of spectators that boys basketball did. Carol had always intended that the Gym Show remain the possession of Mercyville's girls. No boys allowed! How dare Vinnie Tagliaburro try to steal her show!

She couldn't see Jim agreeing to include Vinnie's boys in the 1970 Gym Show, so she put the whole ridiculous mess out of her mind for now, and like Scarlett O'Hara, her favorite character from film and literature, she vowed to think about it tomorrow. She was late for class, and that, too, would be unseemly for her.

The Gym Show

V

Tommy Jankovic was having trouble keeping his eyes open during world history with Mr. Owens. He had slept little the night before and, to the delight and surprise of his mother, he had risen early and asked if he could take the truck into town so he could go to 7 o'clock mass at Immaculate Heart. He assured her he would be back in time to catch the bus to school.

Tommy wasn't one to stand out at Mercyville and he preferred it that way because it afforded him more time to devote to those things that were important to him, like academics and music. He was known as a quiet kid, he usually kept to himself, and he had only a few friends, mostly girls in band with him and with whom he shared a love for music. Tommy was only one of seven boys in Mercyville's band—either the other boys who might, in another school, have joined band must have thought that participation in the school's small but dedicated group of musicians wasn't a cool enough or manly enough activity to be a part of, or perhaps their families simply couldn't afford the rental fees for the instruments. Tommy's parents couldn't afford the rental fees either, but Tommy was lucky that his parents had brought with them from

Europe a French horn that, though battered looking, was perfectly tuned and sounded much brighter than the Selmer-Bundy instruments the rest of the band played. They may not have hot water in their house, but they owned a beautifully crafted and well-cared-for French horn, an instrument that Tommy played brilliantly and beautifully. Until yesterday after school, Tommy Jankovic had been a happy kid.

Tommy used all of his powers of concentration to suppress the freakishly inexplicable events of yesterday afternoon, but despite his best efforts, yesterday's incident kept worming its way into his consciousness like a slithering serpent. Tommy invoked every prayer he knew, prayers to wash the shame from his soul, fervent prayers to the Blessed Mother to intercede on his behalf to restore his ravaged heart to one that was righteous and good. Then he would squeeze his eyes shut and think of anything else—the otherworldly smell of the incense during mass, the thrill of playing his instrument, the quiet conversations and light-hearted laughter at night between his parents—anything other than the image that retold the story of how Henry Somers had grabbed hold of his belt and ripped down his pants, the feel of Henry's weight on his back, the sweet, sweaty stench of Henry's dirty hand clamped over his mouth, and the shockingly painful and humiliating act that followed—an act he didn't even have a name for. That's when Tommy knew that what had happened yesterday was real, but the memory of it was something that knew he must keep under control. He was determined to keep pushing, keep shoving, and lock away those awful images so they would be forever erased from his pained memory.

It was now fourth period, almost lunchtime, and Mr. A. had not yet called for him. Earlier that morning, he considered the almost unforgivable act of lying to his mother and telling her that he was sick so that he wouldn't have to come to school today, but he knew he had to go to mass in the morning if for no other reason than to ask Our Lady to intercede on his behalf, beg forgiveness without entering the sanctum of the confessional, and remind himself that he was still a good, decent, and moral person. Besides, his mother might become suspicious that something was amiss if he was well enough to attend mass but feigned illness to get out of school. Something amiss — never in a million lifetimes would she ever know or understand just how amiss things were.

Tommy hardly knew Henry Somers. He was a big boy, a farmer's son, and the only contact he had ever had with him was last year when they were both in the photography club with Mr. Snyder. Tommy declined to join photography this year — something about what his brother George had told him last summer about the club didn't set right with him, and besides, he didn't want to take more time away from his studies. He was determined to maintain his perfect 4.0 average and spend more time with his horn.

Then yesterday, between lunch and sixth period, Henry had approached Tommy and told him to meet him in the gym after school—not to worry about catching the bus; he'd give him a ride home. Tommy was puzzled; he couldn't imagine what Henry would want with him since the two could not have had less in common. Seeing his confusion, Henry, looking to his left and right to see if anyone might be listening, whispered, "Okay, it's about a girl," he explained, taking a step forward closer to Tommy. "A girl you know in band. I got a couple a questions about her, and I don't want to ask you here in front of everybody."

That seemed plausible enough, so Tommy had waited for Henry in the gym after school, trying to figure out which one of his friends Henry was interested in getting to know. As he was running through the short list of girls he knew, then filtering out those that he knew Henry couldn't possibly be interested in, he had narrowed that list to three. By that time, Henry had appeared on the stage, whispered, "Psst!" and motioned for Tommy to join him. He must really like this girl, Tommy had thought at the time. He jumped up on the stage and followed Henry

96

behind the curtains.

That is when all the awfulness began.

There was nothing consensual about their coupling, but Tommy was too shocked and horrified to utter a sound—he wouldn't have been able to anyway since Henry's ham-sized hand had covered his mouth and the portion of one of his nostrils. He could hardly breathe and felt he was going to pass out. Then there was the feeling of his body ripping apart, that awful feeling of defilement, the pain of which remained yet today. How long it had actually gone on was unknown to Tommy—it could have been thirty seconds, it could have been three hours. At one point, Tommy thought he may have blacked out; that is until Mr. A. came up on the stage and interrupted Henry's assault. After scrambling to his feet and pulling up his trousers, Tommy had dropped his head on his chest in an effort to obliterate that look that Mr. A. had given them, but he never cried, not even from the searing pain, the shock, and the utter humiliation of what had just occurred. What had just occurred? The idea of trying to explain what happened to him--to Mr. A. or to anyone-- was nearly as horrifying as the act itself. He just wanted to block it all out. Once Mr. A. had told them to get out of there, Tommy ran as fast as he could out of the building and into the dusk. As painful as it was, he would walk home that night but later not remember how it was that he had arrived at his front door. The shaking didn't begin until that night when he was alone in his bed.

Mercifully, he had not seen Henry at school today, and he did not know what he would do when he eventually did run into him. They had no classes together, thankfully, but Mercyville was a small school, everyone knew everyone else, knew who their brothers and sisters were, what their dads did for a living, and where they lived. Tommy lived in the country, as did Henry, but on opposite ends of town. Quitting school was not an option, and besides, Mr. Bixby, the guidance counselor, had told him that because of his excellent grades, there was a good chance that he could earn a scholarship to attend college. When Tommy told his parents this, they had wept with pride, and from then on, the idea of Tommy doing anything to prevent him from going to college was unheard of. Tommy's father even eased up on his chores so he had more time to study at night. What would his parents do if they found out what Henry had done to him?

The bell rang, signaling the end of fourth period. He had fifth period lunch, and dreaded the idea of coming face to face with Henry, but he needn't have worried. Henry was not in his usual spot with the other guys from the FFA club. Maybe he, too, was scared of what Mr. A. was going to do. However small his relief at not seeing Henry, he nearly threw up when he saw Mr. A. walk into the cafeteria and approach him.

"Tommy, after school, I don't want you getting on the bus. Come to my office. I'll take you home." Mr. A. turned and walked back out of the cafeteria. Tommy wordlessly put his tray down. He was soon joined by some of his fellow band members at their usual table, but he paid no attention to them or to their inane chatter; his friends, in turn, didn't notice anything particularly out of the ordinary with Tommy. The entire lunch period went by as Tommy, with a white, hot roar in his ears, choked down what he could of his lunch, too afraid that whatever small amounts he managed to swallow would soon come back up. He simply couldn't imagine why Mr. A. would want to take him home unless he was going to tell his parents what he saw Henry doing to him yesterday afternoon. His life, as he knew it, was over.

The more Jim had thought about it, the more he figured that what he witnessed between Tommy and Henry Somers was probably Henry Somers' idea. Tommy, from what little he knew of him, was a quiet kid, had only a few friends and these were females, and most likely was blindsided by Henry's sometimes obnoxious personality and brute strength. Henry, Jim had surmised, had probably run out of farm animals to violate and decided to pick the low hanging fruit that was Tommy.

99

That's why he decided he wanted to talk with Tommy first.

On his way to his office, Carol ran into him, grabbed his arm, and hissed, "I need to talk to you, now!"

Jim saw that determined look in his wife's face – the look that usually cleared his agenda of any other pressing matters. Carol had a persistence that was unparalleled, but today just might be the day that he matched that persistence. He drew in a breath and decided that every single time she got her panties into a twist he simply would not be forced to cave in and give her his undivided attention. "Carol, I've got a real shitstorm brewing here. Can it wait?"

"No! I have my own shitstorm brewing! Vinnie cornered me this morning. He wants to put boys in the Gym Show!" she proclaimed, waiting for her husband to share her outrage.

While he always tried to be on Carol's side in all things, or, at least appear to have her best interest first, this revelation of hers wasn't exactly surprising to him. Vinnie had already talked with him nearly a month ago about putting some of his boys in the show. Since the Gym Show wasn't until May with preparations beginning in January, he had already forgotten that particular conversation. However, it would be idiotic to let Carol know that he and Vinnie had already chatted.

100

"Boys, huh. Would that be a huge problem?"

Carol cocked her head like a beagle puppy and looked at her husband wide eyed, as if he had gone insane. Jim inwardly recoiled. He knew Carol's prurient hatred of anything having to do with Vinnie (and secretly wondered if there were not more to the stories she had told Jim about Vinnie's collegiate escapades). Right away, he knew he had said the wrong thing.

"Yes. Yes, James, it would. It would be a problem of astronomic proportions." Carol was fond of using space metaphors when she was trying to make an important point. "The Gym Show is for the girls, Jim. It's for the girls only! That's the whole reason I created it. Boys have enough to become involved in. I'm late. We'll talk tonight."

You mean it's for you, Carol, Jim silently corrected.

Short of stamping her foot and throwing a tantrum, Carol had definitely made her point. This would be a conversation that would best take place after Jim had absorbed a sufficient amount of alcohol in order to dull the verbal onslaught that Carol was sure to ignite once ensconced in the privacy of their home.

The Gym Show

VI

Mercyville, for all of its supposed artlessness, was actually a small tourist town, at least from Memorial Day through Labor Day. Each Saturday of Memorial Day weekend heralded the official start of summer, and the beaches and campgrounds of Shenango Lake unfurled themselves from the winter's gloom and spring's muddy wetness in time for another season of swimming, fishing, and camping. After Labor Day, Mercyville and Shenango said goodbye to its summer explosion of visitors, exhaled, then folded inward onto itself, returning to attach to the high school as the epicenter for what passed as bustle and activity — much like most little towns in the 60s and 70s.

Summer in Mercyville was unique if only because of the assortment of people who landed there from the working class steel cities south of Shenango — an array of out-of-towners who, whether it was for a week, a weekend, or for the entire the season, straggled into the area towing their sleek campers and state-of-the-art fishing boats behind rusted out pickup trucks and patched station wagons. Along with the townies, these summer folks ate breakfast at the Driftwood Restaurant, played pinball and shopped for sundries at Collins' cut rate, bought Coleman lanterns and replacement propane tanks

103

at Tabor's hardware, pawed through the musty assortment of tents and used camping supplies at Morrison's army surplus, purchased cokes and Saegertown ginger ale at Woodard's grocery store, stopped in to Isaly's to stock up on chip-chop ham, and wandered through the three cramped aisles of the Five & Ten for penny candy, plastic kiddie toys, and, of course, stepped next door to Betty's Bait to prepare for the day's fishing. The summertime shower of out-of-towners were well aware that Mercyville lacked the charm of more commercial tourist towns, towns like Put-in-Bay, in Ohio or Mackanaw Island, in Michigan; nonetheless, for a working class family from Pittsburgh or Youngstown or Kittanning, a camping or fishing trip to Mercyville was a chance to break free from the grit of the city, breathe in some fresh air, and drink Iron City beer and roast wieners alongside other working class folks from Youngstown, Pittsburgh, or Kittanning.

If Mercyville laid claim to Shenango Lake, its neighbor to the east, the Town of Iroquois Lake, boasted its pride and joy and its namesake--Iroquois Lake. Town-wise, there wasn't a whole lot of difference between Mercyville and the town of Iroquois Lake, but an unspoken and solid reality existed: Iroquois Lake, and the Town of Iroquois Lake which sat right to its south, featured a captivating measure of vacation magic that made it much more alluring to tourists, especially those with more capital than Mercyville's summertime flotsam and jetsam. If Mercyville was a bologna sandwich on white bread, Iroquois Lake was steak and lobster.

Though the lake itself was smaller, Iroquois Lake, unlike its bigger brother Shenango, was a clear, crisp, spring-fed glacier-made body of water that had existed long before the Iroquois Indians had inhabited the deciduous forest surrounding it. Its main attraction, its crowning glory, and, for many families, the pinnacle of their summer vacation was a magical day spent at Iroquois Lake Park, an historic turn-of-the-century amusement park featuring an exciting assortment of rides, its own charming boardwalk overlooking the entire lake, the popular nighttime hangout The Lake Club, the stately and prestigious Hotel Iroquois, an impressive and historic midway, and one of the country's oldest and most thrilling wooden roller coasters, The Wild Indian. If one was looking for magic in this little corner of northwestern Pennsylvania, it could certainly be found at Iroquois Lake Park. The entire park was gushing with enchantment, charm, and its own Fairytale Forest, a sweet addendum located across the road from the main park, which showcased exotic creatures nested in a storybook setting — an added attraction for smaller children and animal lovers. That the establishment's resident chimpanzee was notorious for angrily flinging fresh feces at its gawkers, and the hapless bear was suffering from some type of mange did not detract from the number of delighted visitors flocking to Fairytale Forest for a calm respite following the bustle of the park.

A mere ten miles to the west lay the vast and steady shores of Shenango, with its safely benign ten horsepower motor limit and profusion of flat-bottomed outboard fishing boats and fat pontoons teeming with life-jacketed retirees. Shenango was a "fisherman's paradise"; its main attraction the Spillway, an asphalt funnel about twenty feet in diameter where fish that were bred and hatched at the upper lake's fish hatchery would gather in such profusion (before being sucked through the funnel and ferried under the causeway's bridge to the lower lake) that it became a favorite stop for visitors who liked to throw bread over the rail and watch the fish devour it. Though a variety of fish were bred at the hatchery, the Spillway's most frequent guests were carp, — big, bloated oversized goldfish that bullied themselves over to the Spillway because in some corner of their paraphyletic brains, they learned that food was being proffered. Then, once the area's ducks and geese discovered that human visitors were actually casting entire loaves of stale bread into the Spillway to feed the bloated goldfish, these fowl were savvy enough to learn how to walk on the backs of those same fish in order to snatch the bread before it was consumed by the gaping, sucking mouths of the greedy carp. Thus, Mercyville became known as the town "Where the Ducks Walk on the Fish." Most first-time visitors to the area thought the moniker was a clever slogan made up by the Chamber of Commerce to entice hunters and fishermen to the area, but once initiated into the reality that is the Spillway, they soon discovered that the ducks do indeed walk on the fish in order to nick some bread—or empty beer cans, or the twist ties from bread bags, or cigarette butts, or any other manner of detritus cruelly heaved at fish and fowl. Nearly fifteen years into the future, a college-aged Julie Adamson would find herself in a Penn State dorm room amidst a blue haze of cannabis smoke attempting to describe this very same phenomenon to the two Massapequa, Long Island boys whose weed she had just gulped into her lungs. Despite her uncharacteristically vivid and colorful explanation, however, she failed miserably to make the magic of the Spillway sound plausible to either of them. She concluded later that there wasn't enough weed on the entire eastern seaboard to make anyone believe that ducks could walk on fish.

Sadly, Iroquois Lake did not feature any category of pedestrian attraction equal to the evolutionary marvel that the Spillway represented. On Iroquois Lake, though, visitors could delight at the panorama of slick Chris Crafts and Ski Nautiques pulling bikinied water skiers eagerly waving to the bathers on Deer's Beach or on the docks of the private Iroquois Country Club, or better yet, witness a 'ski-by' past the park's boardwalk. Those who vacationed on Iroquois Lake could choose among a variety of fun and exciting water activities—speed boating, water skiing, floating endlessly on plump, brightly colored rafts, and could enjoy swimming with inflatable toys, beach balls, and other accessories such as fins and masks, while Shenango's water enthusiasts were left floating on grandpa's boat, fishing for walleye, or swimming at one of the state park's beaches notorious for their draconian rules (no inflatables!) that sucked all of the fun out of the swimming experience. This triggered envy among many of Shenango's vacationers. If, in the course of their trip, they had been unfortunate enough to peek at the excitement that Iroquois Lake had to offer—perhaps after spending a day at the park—these same folks might have longed for a more civilized holiday. Instead of a moldy army surplus tent or a musty pop up camper in which to sleep, they just might pine for the luxury of falling into deep Adirondack chairs perched on the manicured back lawn of their lakeside cottage while watching the twinkling array of boat lights on Iroquois Lake, their sunburnt children soothing their aching backs during a midnight swim off the cottage's private dock. Shenango's campers were the kids on the field trip to the Heinz ketchup factory; Iroquois Lake's tourists were at Disneyland. The younger the tourist, the more pleasure Iroquois Lake provided. It wasn't unusual on a Saturday or Sunday to find ten to twenty boats lashed together on the sandbar in Iroquois Lake's Harm's Bay, tethered coolers of beer floating between boats; the urine content of the bay most likely rendering the entire lake unsuitable for swimming. It was as if Iroquois Lake was the rich cousin with the expensive toys everyone wanted to play with and Shenango was the matron aunt with the comfortable lap and the stale breath that smelled like old people.

Curiously enough, this distinction often played out in the rivalry that existed between the townspeople of both Iroquois Lake and Mercyville. Iroquois Lake was hip, it was fun, it was where everyone wanted to be in the summer; Shenango, and its accompanying village of Mercyville, was like returning to something safe and quiet, earthy, and serene. Summertime cottages surrounded the shoreline of Iroquois Lake; Shenango's shoreline was protected wildlife areas — the entire reservoir and its surrounding wetlands were all part of the state park.

Those summertime cottages that dotted Iroquois Lake's shoreline were usually owned by wealthy folks from Pittsburgh; that is, they were wealthy by Mercyville's standards. Farther inland, the year round homes were either large family estates that had been broken up into smaller pieces of acreage and owned by locals, or were comprised of one or two acres upon which more modern mid-century ranch homes were built. Thus, not only did the summertime fun discrepancy between the two towns loom large, but also the differences in lifestyle among each town's inhabitants created an interesting dynamic when it came time to play each other in basketball.

The Adamson home, as well as the small farm where Jim had spent much of his youth, was situated between the town of Mercyville and the park. Carol's and the kids' summertime ritual included, ironically, daily trips to Shenango's End-of-the-Road beach, but few excursions included the park. As much as Carol liked to be around people, if only to show off her trim, petite, bikini-clad body, she preferred the atmosphere of the End-of-the-Road. Not surprisingly, as soon as Carol Adamson made the End-of-the-Road her "beach," others followed suit, and Carol smiled with satisfaction once she had realized that she had started Mercyville's own summertime trend.

As a youth, Jim Adamson had spent many summers working at the park, as well as hiring himself out as a day laborer to various farmers in the area, so his relationship with the park, the lake, and the surrounding area was bittersweet. While he appreciated that the park employed a large number of teenagers during the summer vacation months and that the taxes levied upon the summertime establishment meant more money for the school, he detested the onslaught of tourists that bottle-necked his precious country roads; moreover, he had little tolerance for the Pittsburghers who descended upon the area with their odd manner of speaking ("can yinz tell me where Err-uh-kwoy is?") and their invading campers and trailers and rude manners. That he himself was born in Pittsburgh was not germane to his opinion — these 412s (Pittsburgh's area code) were nothing like the quiet and cultured family from which he hailed, Pittsburgh or no Pittsburgh.

And so on this rainy November afternoon, Jim headed out in the station wagon toward Iroquois Lake to Henry Somers' farm, located just inside of the Mercyville attendance area and not too far from the park, but situated on a dirt road that bore little resemblance to the inviting tourist attraction. Though he had planned to speak with Tommy first, he had discovered that, oddly, Henry wasn't at school today, which was unusual, since the kid hadn't missed a day since the seventh grade. That is, Henry hadn't missed a day except for the start of deer season which began the Monday after Thanksgiving — a day where eighty-five percent of the male population, including teachers, were absent. Jim didn't count any

111

absences that first week of the season; it was one of the advantages of running a one-man show.

So, he thought he'd drive out to the Somers' place and check things out—talk to the old man, see what kind of home life the kid had before he ripped into him. Jim was not looking forward to the visit—not because he was afraid of Henry Sr.'s wrath—Jim's size, despite the extra weight, usually dissuaded even an angry farmer from trying to start something with him—but more because he did not quite know how he was going to tell the man that his son was a queer. Furthermore, he did not want to question Henry Jr. yet about yesterday afternoon's activities—something told him that he needed to hear Tommy's side of the story first. Jim sighed, thinking that this was the exact kind of situation when it would be to his advantage to have someone else to help him deal with matters like this, like an assistant principal. He had a loyal assistant in Ruthie—the girl was a good listener with sound instincts, but she wasn't as experienced with the nuances of adolescents and therefore not nearly wily enough play the good cop to Jim's bad cop when it came to how to deal with two boys engaged in sodomy. Sodomy. Christ almighty, none of his graduate school professors thought to teach their prospective high school administrators how to handle...buggering. Jim shuddered, remembering the image of Henry grinding

112

against poor, skinny little Tommy. Jesus.

While it might be a relief to share the burdens of meeting with parents, disciplining kids, and dealing with whining, bitching teachers like Doris Pennycroft, an assistant principal could prove to be an additional pain in the ass. Who else could get away with fudging the attendance register during deer season the way he did? No, he rather liked running his show by himself and doing things his own way, with only the half-assed elected school board to contend with.

On the way out to the Somers farm, Jim passed the Ettinger house. The Ettingers were the only black family who lived within the Mercyville attendance area. Pat and Freda had two sons, Damon and Dwayne — superb young men, both strong athletes, and seemingly untouched by the broiling civil rights movement that had recently swept through the nation. It may have been the combined athletic prowess of the Ettinger brothers, their good looks, and their polite and friendly manner that made them among the more popular kids in the school. Both boys would go on to play college baseball and eventually make their way back to the Mercyville area to raise their respective families and run successful businesses. All of this would be accomplished as if being the only colored family in an all-white town in the 1960s was just a minor postscript in an otherwise ordinary life.

113

If the Ettinger family ever felt like outsiders or out of place—strangers in a strange land—they never indicated it, and even if they did, Jim knew that Pat and Freda, as well as both boys, were too polite and respectful to ever think of mentioning it. He waved at Pat who was loading the last of his wet, raked leaves into a large aluminum garbage can, his tidy lawn a veritable showpiece compared to many of the ragged looking landscapes surrounding it. Pat tipped his hound's-tooth newsboy cap back at Jim, a wry smile wrinkling the corner of his mouth. The easy relationship that currently existed between the Ettingers and the rest of the community was one of those rare pieces of serendipity seldom enjoyed by a high school principal.

Jim wished that instead of this dreaded task in front of him that he could stop in at Ettingers and he and Pat could sit on their front porch enclosure talking baseball over a couple of beers, but unfortunately, he needed to get this damn home visit over with and get back to school. Jim began running through the various scenarios that he could possibly use to illustrate to Henry Sr. exactly what had transpired on the stage the previous afternoon. He knew better than to outright accuse Henry of being the aggressor, and it could be that Henry Sr. already had some inkling of his son's proclivities. Hell, maybe the old man was a flit, too, though he sure didn't fit the profile. He was small, and bull-like, with huge hands that Jim remembered from a certain basketball game last year when Henry had fouled out during the last few minutes of a close contest and Jim had to hold back the old man from beating the hell out of the ref. No, it wasn't likely that the elder Somers was queer, (though who would have thought that Ted Ambrose was queer, either?) But Jim still couldn't quite picture how he was going to approach this particular problem with someone as unpredictable as Henry Somers, Sr.

Jim pulled the Falcon into the muddy, rutted drive. He more than likely would find Mr. Somers in the barn on a rainy day, but he thought, out of respect, he that he would first knock on the front door. No cars were parked among the farm implements and scrap pieces of equipment scattering the yard, but that didn't mean that Mrs. Somers wasn't out somewhere. Remembering her husband's demeanor and associating that to Jim's perceived notion about how he probably treated his wife, he figured it wasn't likely that Henry Sr. was one to let the little woman drive anywhere.

Not surprisingly, Jim's knock went unanswered.

He turned and made his way in the rain and muck toward the barn when he saw what appeared to be the Somers' hired man. The tall, painfully thin farmhand was of indeterminate age, filthy, and looked at Jim

115

suspiciously from one eye; the other eye torqued in the opposite direction and clouded over with a white film. His overalls were grease-stained with holes in the knees; his boots were caked with manure and mud, and his near-toothless mouth gaped open between a long, unkempt beard over what appeared to be a pronounced cleft lip.

"Who you? What you wan?" His nasally voice garbled, the man stood stock still while holding a menacing-looking pitchfork in his grimy right paw.

"Hello there," Jim held out his right hand, hoping the man would drop the pitchfork. He didn't. "I'm Jim Adamson. From the high school. Is Mr. Somers at home?"

"Theys all lef. Lef this mornin'. Baa to the ill. Ome. Theys in rubble wi the law, theys say. I don' know when theys comin' baa."

"Trouble with the law? May I ask what kind of trouble?"

The man bristled and puffed out what little chest he had. "I don' know misser, but ain anybody's business, now, is i? Theys baa to the ill! I was sumpin abou a girl Henry mess wi, and tha's all I'm gonna' tell ya."

"Henry the boy or Mr. Somers? I need to know,--er, what did you say your name was?"

"Niney Vol. M'name's Niney Vol."

"Ninety Volt," Jim repeated. "You mean like the battery?"

116

"Niney Vol! Now you nee to go on baa from where you came, misser. Theys ain gonna' lie that I was tallin' to ya."

Jim held up his hands in front of him an effort to prevent Ninety Volt from approaching him any further. "Fair enough, Mr. Volt. If the family happens to come back anytime soon, can you let them know that I was here today asking after Henry Jr.? Since he wasn't in school today, I felt that I ought to check up on him."

The hired man glared through him with his one good eye. Jim wasn't about to wait for an answer from Ninety Volt, even if he would have been able to understand him.

"Thank you for your time, Mr. Volt."

Well, that was a bust. Jim wasn't a detective, and he wasn't the law, and he knew something was amiss, but he had accomplished all he could for one day, and he was decidedly more relieved to get the hell out of there than to stand there trying to figure out what Ninety Volt had meant by "trouble with the law" — he knew better than to prod further a half-wit holding a pitchfork.

Safe inside the Falcon, he backed out of the farm's muddy drive. Once on the road, he thought again about Henry, the Somers family, and his stomach soured at the possibilities that "trouble with the law" could mean. He had a sick feeling that the layers of depravity surrounding this family were thicker and more numerous than the skin of an onion.

VII

A visibly shaking Tommy Jankovic arrived at Mr. A.'s office shortly after the dismissal bell. He knew that every aspect of normalcy was about to be permanently turned to shit by whatever was going to transpire within the next few hours, and he would have given his very life not to have to face Mr. A., his parents, or the fact that he had been a participant—albeit unwillingly—of such a sickeningly disgraceful and disgusting act. Before Tommy's brief encounter with Mr. A. in the cafeteria during lunch, which had reminded him about yesterday, well, he might have thought that the entire sordid episode was a figment of a twisted imagination, a truly horrible nightmare, or, at the very least, a sad, sick sentence in a larger paragraph that described the essence of Tommy's soul. Mr. A.'s unspoken acknowledgement of yesterday's encounter with Henry Somers now took on the form of a beastly, larger than life monster that was poised to devour Tommy whole and vomit out his sorry remains all the way into the ninth level of hell.

Mr. A. walked out of his office, his London Fog raincoat open and flapping about his prodigious belly, and motioned for Tommy to follow him. Tommy gathered in his thin, shaking arms his few books and his French horn case and nearly tripped over his own feet in an attempt to keep up with the formidable Mr. A. He followed behind the big man, hoping no one would see him and wonder why he was following Mr. A. to his car. Once inside Mr. A.'s station wagon, Tommy, for the very first time that day broke into convulsing sobs, which, to his surprise, proved to be cathartic. At least he didn't wet his pants like he did last night in bed while re-living earlier events. Mr. A. looked at him with a rare show of sympathy, touched his shoulder lightly, then removed his hand and started the car. He let the car warm up and the windshield to defrost, hung his large hands over the steering wheel by his wrists, and sighed heavily before he spoke.

"Tommy, son, this isn't easy for me, and I get the feeling that it isn't easy for you, either. I think it would be best if we talked a bit before heading out to your folks' so I can get an idea of your side of this story. So, I'm going to ask you some questions, and I want you to be honest — honest like your life depends upon it. This is a serious matter, son, and I want to make sure that it's handled fairly between all — uh — parties involved."

"Yes, sir," Tommy sniffled quietly.

"Tommy, I want you to tell me how you came to find yourself in that situation with Henry. Whose idea was it?"

Tommy continued shaking, but found his voice at last

and relayed to Mr. A. the brief conversation that Henry had initiated about wanting information from him about a girl in the band, and how he was supposed to meet Henry after school in the gym (why, why, why had he not just gotten on the bus and gone home? What had made him think that Henry Somers, a boy he had never spoken to in his life, a boy with whom he had nothing in common, actually wanted the scoop about a girl — a girl whose name he never even got a chance to discover?) Tommy relayed to Mr. A. that he never imagined that Henry was thinking about...about...that thing that he did to him. He must have sounded convincing, because Mr. A.'s face suddenly hardened.

"I see, Tommy. So you had no idea that Henry was wanting to...um...engage you in...uh...that activity, is that correct?"

Tommy turned and looked Mr. A. right in the eye and said, definitively, "Mr. A., I didn't even know that 'that activity' as you call it was even possible. I've never even heard of such a thing! Why would someone want to do that to another person in the first place? What is wrong with me that would make someone like Henry think that what he did was okay?"

Tommy could see that Mr. A. believed his side of this story, but that still did not alleviate the feeling that he was going to throw up all over the inside of Mr. A.'s car. They

121

still had to face his parents.

"Tommy, tell you what. I'll take you home, and I want to talk to your dad, alone. You don't even have to be in the room. Is he usually home this time in the afternoon?"

"Mr. A., unless you speak Serbian, you're not going to be able to make him understand a thing about this, and I'm not just saying that because I don't want you talking to him. Ask our neighbors. They'll tell you. He only speaks a little bit of English, and I don't know how you could even begin to explain to him what...what happened. Besides, Mr. A," Tommy dropped his head and looked away, "if he knew what happened to me yesterday, it would kill him. He's not very understanding in that kind of way. This would just kill him."

"Well, Tommy, if he can't speak English, how does he manage? Don't you all have a farm, or some kind of shop? What about your mother?"

"Oh, Mr. A., you can't say anything about this to my mother! Please, please don't say anything! She's really, really religious, and she just wouldn't understand! She would die if you said anything to her! She's not a strong person; she's, well, she's been through a lot! Please, Mr. A., I'm begging you. Please. Can you just drop me off at home and forget this ever happened? I can't have anyone find out about this, do you understand? Not only would it kill my parents, but nobody would ever understand that I didn't want this! I never wanted this! If you tell even one person, the whole town will know, and then," he lowered his voice to a whisper, "I'll have to kill myself. I've already thought about it, see, and that's what I would do if anyone found out. I've been picked on before—I won't stand to be picked on again. Now can't you please just drop me off at home and please, please forget this ever happened?"

Jim looked over at the thin, frightened boy and, at that moment, Jim knew that Tommy was sincere—he made his intent very clear. "I promise that I won't tell. And, yes, if that is what you want, we can forget that this ever happened."

Jim put the car in reverse. If only it was that easy, he thought.

It was a good night to tie one on, Jim thought. To him, "tying one on" involved a stop at the State Store where Fuzzy Jacobs would pull off the shelf a fifth of Seagram's 7 as soon as he saw Jim's car pull into the parking lot, sell it to Jim without a word, Jim would go home and, with the bottle still hidden in its brown paper bag, he would screw off the top, take a deep, long swig or two of the life-affirming elixir, hide the bottle on the top shelf of his closet (Carol couldn't reach that high without a stool, and besides, he had usually knocked it all off before she even realized he was drunk), and fall into a dreamless stupor until about four o'clock in the morning at which time he'd get up, shower, and make breakfast for the entire family, conveniently forgetting that he had drunk an entire fifth of whiskey.

If this bothered Carol, she seldom complained, and she understood why Jim had this need, every once in a while, to soothe himself in this way. Furthermore, Carol was usually so tired after school and wiped out by whatever practice she had going on at the time to even realize or care how much he'd had to drink, and the kids were conditioned to make their own supper with little help from him.

That dreamless sleep was the whole reason that Jim was compelled to anesthetize himself so destructively. He knew his increasing dependence upon alcohol was unhealthy and unproductive, but he would much rather have the habit of relying upon alcohol to keep the nightmares away than to lie awake each night, exhausted, trying desperately not to fall asleep for fear that the dreams would invade his soul, rendering him terrified, feeling helpless, and above all waking with an aching sadness that stayed with him throughout the day.

He could blame it on the war since most of his nightmares involved the real and present terror of combat that often turned his bowels to water and at times had him rooted in place, unable to move in order to escape the grisly visions of severed body parts, savagely disemboweled torsos, their contents spilling over into the filth of the ground where they lay, and then the macabre, surreal images of dead GIs lying in fresh muddy fields, dog tags propping open gaping mouths surrounded by flies, eyes staring blankly at nothing. Those reflections were real but when visited upon him in his dreams, the body parts lying on the rocky Italian terrain were his, and the hands desperate to contain his guts inside of his body were his, and the dog tags shoved into his mouth in order to identify his mangled body belonged to him.

But other times, his dreams were of growing up during the Depression, and of being hungry and cold, hungry all the time, cold all the time, of going out into the barn only to find the animals dead of starvation, he and his dad, sobbing, unable to find feed for them during the frigid months of winter, of his mother and sister shivering thinly by the stove in the kitchen, the only source of heat in their little house, of having to smash the frozen surface of the piss pot under his bed, the pot itself smashing to bits and the shame and revulsion of having to clean up his mess in the middle of the night which caused great, gulping sobs that carried over into his waking hours.

Jim would often wake himself when these cries of

terror ended his nightmares, or Carol, having been in a deep sleep herself, would awaken with her own screams to match Jim's, alarmed at the ferocity of his panicked cries — Jim, who ordinarily was the one who comforted others when they were scared

VIII

Julie's new classmate, this Stanley, this boy who had seen her at her absolute worst and most shameful and embarrassing, had yet to utter one word to her or to anyone else in the class since he was deposited, wide-eyed and confused, into Miss Marpy's classroom earlier that morning.

She shivered, remembering the horror of seeing him appear in the doorway with his teacher Mrs. Haines. Miss Marpy did not go into any details about why they now had a new classmate from the first grade; she just acted as if kids were moved from an upper grade to a lower grade *every* day at this school. This thought was quickly followed by another, more ingenious one: If this boy could move out of his classroom into hers, why couldn't she move from Miss Marpy's classroom into his? That would solve two of Julie's most pressing worries of the day—her embarrassment at the proximity of Miss Marpy (just being in the same room with her brought back the entire regrettable events of last night) and the fear that this Stanley boy was going to spill the beans about her pee pants episode at the television station. But so far, Stanley, either because he was too dull to realize how valuable this

127

nugget of information he had in his possession actually was (and how he could capitalize upon it), or because he was too polite to mention it, had not uttered a sound.

So, what had Stanley done to necessitate a move from one classroom to another, and how could she, Julie Adamson, accomplish this same feat? Moving up a grade was a notion that she did not know existed, but what she did know was that she was a teacher-pleaser, she had a solid band of gold stars after her name on the letter chart, and the adults in her life were always telling that she was smart, just like her sister and brother. So maybe, just maybe, if she quickly learned to read or to do the same kinds of arithmetic problems that she had seen Jenny and Jimmy doing each night, Miss Marpy would decide that her talents were being wasted here in the kindergarten wing and would be put to better use in grade one. But how was she going to impress Miss Marpy with her newfound skills if she was too embarrassed to even be in the same room with her? She would ponder that question after recess.

Every Thanksgiving, Jim's sister Millicent, "Aunt Pippa" to her brother's three children, hosted Thanksgiving dinner in the home where he, Millicent, and their parents had lived since moving to Mercyville during the worst years of the Great Depression and until Jim left for the service following his graduation from Clarion State Teachers' College. In the years before the family's relocation to Mercyville and the little farm, they had lived in Pittsburgh. James Sr. had worked for the P&LE Railroad, the couple owned and operated a general store, and in whatever time she had left in a day, Ida cleaned houses for several families living in Pittsburgh's Squirrel Hill neighborhood. It was Millicent's responsibility, therefore, to mind little Jim, and, as an older sister, she took her task very seriously. Jim had adored her sister then, and loved her dearly still, and Pippa was often more like a beloved grandmother to his children than an aunt — that 'aunt' rhyming, of course, with 'debutante'. Now that James Sr. had passed on and Ida was suffering from the early stages of dementia, Millicent and her husband lived at the Adamson homestead, deeded over to them in exchange for Millicent caring for their aging mother.

The Adamson's place was a small, two-story, two bedroom affair that Millicent's husband Bernard would add onto in the coming years, but for now, the home stood atop a dug out, rock-lined cellar. The house that James Sr. had purchased for a song was once empty and remote and had originally sat nearly a half a mile to the north in the thick of a wooded area that wasn't much use for farming. In his newfound country wisdom, Jim's father had decided to move it to a better location. Jim had never

129

discovered whether his father had bought the house or the land first, but at any rate, their new house had been lifted up on skids and hauled by a team of horses across Iroquois Creek via a makeshift bridge. It was then pulled even farther south to the parcel of farmland that James had purchased, plunking it atop the cellar, its foundation. Jim's father had then added a wide, columned verandah where, in the summertime, they usually took their meals and where now, Millicent, Bernard, and Ida, their mother, entertained.

Millicent, too, was an educator — first as an elementary teacher, then a music teacher, then as the headmistress of an all-girls' school catering to the families living along Philadelphia's Main Line, one of the bastions of east coast "old money." But for nearly an entire lifetime prior to her later career in education, Millicent had served as a governess for a professor from Temple University. His wife's frail health had continued deteriorating, so much so that Millicent's duties were extended far beyond her governess' obligations and she soon became the primary caretaker for the invalid mother of her three young charges.

After his wife's death, Millicent agreed to remain in Bernard Rosenberg's home as governess, nanny, and, once Bernard's three daughters grew older and moved on to lives of their own, secret companion to Bernard. By the time Millicent's relationship with Bernard was finally ready to go public, James Sr. had died, Ida had begun to show signs of memory loss, and Bernard and Millicent were married in a civil ceremony with Jim and Carol as witnesses. A year later, the two moved from Philadelphia into the home place.

Bernard had no family living aside from his daughters, who loved Millicent ferociously, so the question of combining two lives from two very different backgrounds did not factor at all in Bernard's decision to finally make Millicent his wife. Millicent's choice in a husband — and a Jewish one at that — would prove to be a fly in the ointment only for her brother Jim, though most of the time, he was able to keep his feelings to himself out of deference to his sister. It wasn't as if Jim was an anti-Semite per se; it was more the fact that Jim couldn't stand Bernard, Jew or no Jew, and so Jim used Bernard's Jewishness against him whenever he could. Jim detested Bernard's haughty personality, his affected manners, his pipe smoking, his pseudo-intellectual pronouncements concerning geopolitical issues such as the War in Vietnam — a subject Bernard delighted in demonstrating himself an expert in, even though the man had never served in the military and had never heard a shot fired in anger. Jim hated the way Bernard "looked down his big Jew nose" at Jim, at Jim's affinity for the outdoors,

131

farming, and sports. It seemed to Jim as if everything that he stood for and that Bernard did not ran counter to Bernard's sensibilities, and Jim felt as if Bernard placed himself in a social class above him. Therefore, Jim conveniently blamed these traits on Bernard's heritage.

Had Bernard been more like Jim, these detestable prejudices would have never reared their ugly heads. Jim wasn't a bigot until someone gave him a reason to become one, he figured. To wit, the reason that the Ettinger family was immune to Jim's racial stereotyping had everything to do with the fact that Pat Ettinger and Jim Adamson had quite a bit in common and genuinely liked each other.

Another of Bernard's more ingratiating traits was his habit of referring to himself in the third person, as a refined renaissance man of the twentieth century; Jim, more rough around the edges than most college-educated men, wanted to knock Bernard's yellowed teeth down his throat every time he waxed philosophical about himself. That Bernard was Millicent's husband and Jim's adoration of Millicent was unwavering was the only thing keeping Bernard from getting the verbal shit kicked out of him every time Jim (usually lubricated by a few pulls from his bottle) was forced to sit down to dinner with him.

Carol, however, adored Bernard. Bernard never failed to shower Carol with all manner of flattering praise, extolling her with various pronouncements about her beauty, her charm, her athleticism, and her three lovely children. It made Jim almost sick to his stomach to see how Carol would coo and giggle at nearly everything Bernard had to say, making Jim wonder just how many other women Bernard had wooed this way before, during, and after his arrangement with Millicent.

Following the Thanksgiving holiday, Bernard and Millicent, along with Ida and her diminishing memory, would close up the Mercyville home, the home that Bernard lovingly and affectively called "Thistle Dew" (prompting a pronounced eye-rolling from Jim and another reason for him to despise Bernard even more), and retire to Fort Myers, Florida, for the winter months. The trio would return in late April, always, so that Millicent could be in attendance at the Gym Show, usually to watch after Julie, Jenny, and Jimmy, but more so because she was so proud of her brother and his wife's involvement in and contributions to the small community. Bernard, not so much community minded as he was fond of himself, liked returning to "Thistle Dew" to lovingly tend to the ancient fruit orchard James Sr. had planted, to his small but unique assortment of bonsai trees (a hobby that necessitated the grudging assistance of Jim to monitor the sophisticated winter care setup for the bonsai that Bernard had created to keep the trees alive in his absence), to his burgeoning butterfly collection, to his model train hobby,

133

and most of all, to the baby grand piano that sat in the parlor at "Thistle Dew," an instrument purchased by the elder Adamsons for their children but only played by Millicent and now Bernard. In contrast, Jim's hobbies included his plowing his garden in the spring, tilling his garden during the summer, plowing under his garden in the fall, and drinking whiskey while doing all three.

Each summer afternoon, Bernard and Millicent hosted "cocktail hour" beginning around four o'clock and they invited Carol and Jim down to "Thistle Dew" for happy hour. Each day's happy hour included a new mixed cocktail of Bernard's concocting, the very idea of which made Jim sick to his stomach. Carol loved happy hour with Bernard and Millicent—she said it made her feel sophisticated and worldly. She'd don a sunny flowered dress, tie a scarf in her hair, and deck herself out in bangles and bracelets so she could hear them tinkle together every time she lifted her glass. Jim's idea of happy hour was he, alone, with a bottle of Seagram's 7 still in the bag from the State Store, taking a nip every now and then until there was nothing left and he could pass out for the night.

Thanksgiving, then, to Jim, was never the relaxing time spent with family that everyone else seemed to enjoy. To him, it was first a battle with Carol about what to wear. Carol preferred that the family dress up; Jim felt that since

134

it was *just* the family that he should be able to wear more casual attire — this from a man who shed his clothes down to his underwear every night after returning from work much like a snake sheds his skin, except that a snake still has something decent on after his molting ritual. With Jim in his skivvies, the rest of the family prayed that no visitors would appear winding their way up the long driveway because getting Jim back into his clothes proved time and again to be an arduous ordeal, usually accompanied by someone yelling, "Get Dad's pants!" No, he did not feel like dressing up in a suit for Thanksgiving dinner, only to have to unbutton his already tight trousers midway through the meal. Carol, on the other hand, used every opportunity to dress up, and today, she wore a camel colored wool jacketed dress, matching suede pumps, and her signature piece of jewelry — a charm bracelet that Jim had given her after Jimmy was born. Every time the two of them hit a milestone in their combined lives, Jim would add another charm to the bracelet; however, seeing it now reminded him that he had neglected to update the silver trinket in a long time.

Then there was the ritualistic manner in which his brother-in-law Bernard would conduct the meal as head of the "Thistle Dew" household, as if his proclamations and witty anecdotes were the keys to proper dinner party protocol. Jim couldn't conceive of any reason that this

135

Thanksgiving would be any different. Because of his parents' strict adherence to his upbringing, Jim's table manners, for all of his apparent rough around the edgedness, were as impeccable as Emily Post's; Bernard, however, insisted upon adding his own flair to the dining experience before each course was served. The guests would all have to repeat, in unison, some stupid saying, or solve some labyrinthine riddle that no one had the foggiest notion about except for Bernard, or the oldest child would have to recite a poem before the soup could be served — most annoying of all was the ceremonious homily that Bernard delivered while carving the turkey. By the time Bernard was finished dedicating his elegy to the departed fowl, the damn thing was cold.

What further infuriated Jim was the fact that Millicent was an extraordinary cook and an unparalleled hostess, and he felt as if Bernard's contributions to the meal further devalued his sister's efforts at lovingly preparing for it. As hostess, her preparations forever remained behind the scenes in the home's immaculate kitchen and were always timed perfectly so that any guests at her table would not feel as if she acted as the cook, the waiter, *and* the maître-d. She also insisted that Carol prepare nothing for the Thanksgiving meal, telling her lovingly that she had more than enough to keep her occupied with her teaching job and those three precious children that she needn't worry about baking a pie or bringing a covered dish. This was Millicent's gift to the busy family. That suited Carol just fine, as cooking, baking, and just about anything requiring her slavish devotion to the kitchen was well out of her wheelhouse. Dear Millicent was gracious to a fault, perfect in all of their eyes, and remained that adored older sister to Jim.

Jim loved Millicent unconditionally, and she him — it was only his drinking, or rather the *way* he drank that had Millicent troubled, though her distress was out of nothing but the purest and most tender love for her brother and her concern for his well-being and the well-being of his family. If he had been more of a social drinker, a more moderate drinker, she wouldn't have been so worried, but Jim tended to go off alone when he drank and his demeanor nearly always reflected a broodiness and foul temper that were uncharacteristic of him when he was sober.

There had been a few unfortunate occasions where the drunken version of Jim had displayed his contempt for Bernard in front of both Millicent and Bernard, which nearly broke Millicent's heart. He had made certain, loudly though not so clearly, that Bernard knew what an objectionable addition he was to their family, an affected and self-aggrandizing interloper who had weaseled his way into the hearts of these humble, unassuming, and rather modest people whom Jim loved best. He further intoned, using his most colorful language, that Bernard represented everything that he despised about those born to wealth (although Jim was never privy to what exactly was contained within the Rosenberg's portfolio) and his very existence was disrespectful to the saintly image Jim maintained of Millicent. For this very reason, Millicent had decided to limit the alcohol served at her table this Thanksgiving to the two bottles of vintage cabernet that she and Bernard had brought back from a rare trip to California. Jim might like to drink, but he hated wine.

And so, late on Thanksgiving morning, with the events of last week still weighing heavily on his mind, Jim, Carol, and the children drove down to "Thistle Dew" — a mere skip from their own driveway (and if they had been dressed more casually, they could have walked down and sang, "To Grandmother's house we go," but no, they were all dressed up like they were going to a funeral).

Jim had yet to tell Carol about the incident with the Somers and Jankovic boys — she was still seething, a week later, over Vinnie's threatened intrusion into her Gym Show. Henry Somers still had not returned to school, and though Jim had driven back out to the Somers farm twice after his first visit, it did not appear as if the Somers family had returned from wherever they had fled to avoid "the law." The second time he drove out, Ninety Volt had been sitting on the front porch looking as if he had taken ownership of the place. He did not move from the torn webbed lawn chair on which he was perched and Jim didn't have the energy for another encounter with the crazy old coot, so he simply gave him a wave and backed down the driveway.

"Jim, my good man; Carol, children! Happy Thanksgiving!" Bernard, dressed in a turtleneck and a checked jacket with those professorial felt patches on the elbows, herded the Adamsons into the parlor (what Jim and Carol privately called the "PAH-luh" in Bernard parlance). "Welcome to "Thistle Dew"! I trust your trip was satisfactory?" he chortled at his joke, the same witticism he repeated every time the family came to dinner.

"I'm not gonna' lie, Bernard, the trip here was a real pain in the ass," Jim said sarcastically, as Carol shot him a dirty look. "I didn't think we'd ever get here, what with the traffic, kids screaming in the backseat, and Carol having to stop and use the bathroom every fifteen minutes."

"Ah-ha! You are a quite the humorist, my man, truly a card! Come, Millicent has set out some hor d'oeuvres to get us started on this magnificent feast day. And what can I get you to drink?" he said ignoring Jim and turning to Carol. "Carol?"

139

"Oh, just a ginger-ale for Jim and me, Bernard, if you have it. Don't worry about the kids — they can have something with their dinner. Can I help Pippa in the kitchen?"

Millicent appeared at that moment, her brunette hair perfectly in place, makeup accentuating her unlined face, a brightly printed apron over her large frame. Julie, Jenny, and Jimmy adored their Aunt Pippa; to Julie, the aroma of Pippa — of Chanel no. 5 and Pears soap — would remain throughout her life as one of her most beloved scents. Millicent offered a cheek for Jim to kiss, gave Carol and each of the children a hug, and lovingly took Bernard's arm.

"We're so delighted you're here!" she crooned, as if the two families had not seen each other in months instead of the few days' span that usually marked their visits. "Jim, darling, Mother is in the kitchen with me — perhaps you could bring her out here to see the children. Carol, join me — you and I can chat about 'girl stuff' while I stuff the celery." She twittered at her little pun and turned to Jimmy, Jenny, and Julie. "Children, Grandmother has just been so excited for your visit! I know she can hardly wait to see you!" She shot Jim a knowing look. Ever since Ida had begun to forget things, the children had been somewhat scared of her sudden outbursts and the lack of recognition of the faces of her only three grandchildren.

Once engaged in a conversation, she could remember events from long, long ago, but then she would stop suddenly and look at her grandchildren asking, "And who are you?" Jimmy and Jenny would be taken aback, but Julie, her little mind not understanding that Grammy A. simply did not remember who Julie was, would be frighteningly puzzled. After one such episode, Julie once said, "Grammy, it's me, Julie! What's wrong with you? Are you drunk?" This sent Ida into a rage, and she would storm from the room muttering under her breath about the impertinence of these neighborhood children and something about a willow switch. Other times were actually funny, like when Julie or one of her siblings would sit with Grammy on hot summer evenings, watching her while she crocheted and listened to the NBC Nightly News. Grammy would nod off, still crocheting as she dozed, until David Brinkley would say, "Good night, from NBC news." Grammy would suddenly wake up and answer, "Good night, David! I'll see you again tomorrow" as if he was in the room with her.

Now Grammy A., on Jim's arm, looked even older and frailer than the last time she had seen her and this frightened Julie even more. She never knew her Pap-Pap, Jim's father, so she had no experience with death, but as frightening as Grammy was when she was forgetting who everyone was, the thought of her dying, to Julie, was downright terrifying.

"Let's have some music, Bernard, shall we?" Grammy, to Julie's relief, seemed to remember who Uncle Bernard was and remembered that he played the piano, so maybe this wouldn't be such an awkward and uncomfortable visit after all. Bernard sat at the piano, flipping back an imaginary set of tails, and, with a flourish, began to play a Chopin piece that clearly highlighted the man's musical prowess. It was when he switched to a Ragtime piece that Ida stood up and demanded that he stop playing.

"Mother, why on Earth don't you like this? I played it for you the other day, remember?"

"Oh, I remember all right," Ida said, nodding her head. "You played that at church last Wednesday night. I told you then and I'll tell you now—it sounds like you're the second shift piano player in a whorehouse!"

Jim damn near spurt ginger ale out of his nose trying to suppress his laughter. Carol, who had been shooed out of the kitchen by her sister-in-law and was just walking into the room, shot Jim the second evil look of the day, then turned and said to Ida, "Oh, Mother, I thought it was lovely. But, Bernard, maybe you could play something else. Go back to the Chopin piece."

Bernard complied and continued with the Chopin. Julie watched him in amazement. His hands glided over each of the keys as if he had developed a personal friendship with each one. He needed no music, his eyes were closed, and a sublime smile took over his face. Julie would have loved to have the ability to sit down and make such beautiful music. Maybe Mum would let Uncle Bernard give her piano lessons. Then she could play for Miss Marpy at school and Miss Marpy would recommend that she be moved up into the first grade. Julie made a little mental note in her five-year-old brain to remember to ask her mother.

Soon dinner was served; that is, the first course was laid out. Bernard deferred to Jim and Jim said a blessing over the meal, making sure to add, "In the name of our Lord Jesus Christ" at the end, if nothing else than to administer another dig at Bernard. Once Bernard made his first speech of the day and it appeared as if a lull in the conversation was about to finally take place, Jim turned to Millicent and asked, "Pippa, what do you know about the Somers family — the one that lives out on Geist Road?"

"Do you mean Henry Somers? The one who nearly beat that poor referee to death last year?"

"Well, yes, but no, he didn't get anywhere near the guy — I held him back. Yes, that same one."

To everyone's surprise, Ida, who had remained her typical quiet self since her 'whorehouse' remark, addressed the family.

143

"You stay away from Henry Somers, Jim, I'm warning you. You stay away from that man. He came in to the store the other day and threatened one of our best patrons, Mr. Kowalski. Threatened to kill him! Told him he was going to beat the Polack out of him and hang him from a tree! Bridie was there, she heard the whole thing—scared her witless, he did! Poor Mr. Kowalski, not a mean bone in his body, he'd never do anything to deserve to be spoken to—hollered at like that! Why would Henry Somers talk to him so? I should have called for the police. That's what I should have done. And if he ever comes in the store again, I will call for the police. That Henry Somers is an evil one, Jim. There's something not right with that whole family. Stay away from him. There's something utterly sinful in someone who would speak so to such a good man like Mr. Kowalski."

"Mother, you and Dad owned that store fifty years ago—back in Pittsburgh. We're in Mercyville, remember? This family I'm talking about is from this area, not Pittsburgh."

"That's what you know, Jim, but I know what I'm talking about. Mr. Kowalski is neighbors with Henry Somers up on Dobson Street. Henry married a Polish girl—you remember James, that Skalecki girl. We should probably do something! Oh, I should have rung up the police."

144

"Mother, I think you're confused," Millicent said gently, stretching her hand over Jenny's arms and patting her mother lightly. Jenny, who was sitting next to her grandmother, looked at both of her parents, wide-eyed. "And I don't think we should be talking of such things in front of the children. Jim will make sure that he doesn't run into Henry anytime soon, won't you Jim?"

Jim didn't answer his sister. He was suddenly reminded about something Ninety Volt had said that very first day he drove out to the farm to talk to Mr. Somers. Dobson Street was in Polish Hill, back in Pittsburgh.

"Baa to the ill."

IX

Dreama Tagliaburro was not officially working as a substitute teacher at Mercyville High School on that Monday after Thanksgiving, but she had decided to pay a visit to her husband during his lunch period anyway, a lunch period that Vinnie typically spent in his office eating a Snickers bar and smoking two or three cigarettes after having finished off the stale coffee left in teachers' room. Dreama had brought nothing for him to eat – she wasn't particularly fond of cooking and besides, sharing a meal with her husband was secondary to her real reason for meeting him at school on this cold Monday morning. Her ulterior motive, whether she consciously realized it or not, was to catch Carol Adamson flirting with her husband.

It may have been that Dreama had way too much time on her hands that led her to the erroneous conclusion that her husband was cheating on her with Carol Adamson or it may have been Dreama's natural tendency toward jealousy, but in either case, every day that Vinnie left for work meant that he was getting to spend the day with *her*. And that did not set will with Dreama.

Which is why her suggestion to Vinnie that he insist that boys be allowed to perform in the Gym Show was so

147

puzzling even to her — and that's when it hit her that it was Carol Adamson that she had the problem with, not Vinnie, *per se*. She wanted to be Carol. She wanted her job, she wanted her family — well, maybe not that old tub of a husband of hers, but he *was* a really nice man — and she wanted the attention that Carol Adamson gathered from the entire Mercyville community over her Gym Show — as if Carol Adamson had single-handedly invented the sport of gymnastics.

If Vinnie became part of the Gym Show, then she, Dreama, could insert herself as an assistant to him. By his side. Her handsome, desirable man. Dreama would be sure to be at every Gym Show practice and make sure that her particular brand of class and flair was stamped all over the Gym Show. After all, Dreama's measure of style was way more sophisticated and with-it than Carol's; just look at the differences in way the two of them dressed, wore their hair, and their taste in music (Carol listened to a new group The Carpenters and the panty collector Tom Jones; Dreama's record collection included hip artists like The Doors, Jimi Hendrix, Janis Joplin, and The Mamas and the Papas). Dreama had even made the trip to Woodstock with two of her college girlfriends that August while Vinnie was away at his mother's spending time with the kids, but Dreama and her girlfriends never got close enough to the music for her to really experience her own

148

"Summer of Love" thing—not only did the trio run out of cash, but the two hitch hikers they picked up (trading transportation for weed) were arrested by New York state troopers for possession of marijuana and LSD. The three girls, with money wired to her friend Linda from her rich daddy, left upstate New York and drove back to Pennsylvania without ever getting near the mud-caked masses. That was a trip Carol Adamson, in her safe, bourgeois bubble, would never have had the nerve to make. Carol was all Donna Reed and Doris Day and 'done up' hair, stockings, girdles, and padded bras—all those trappings that restricted a girl from being a true woman; never mind that Carol was a solid ten years older than Dreama. Dreama was a rebel, a child of the 60s, a trendsetter. She wasn't afraid of wearing short-short skirts, she was skilled at applying both false eyelashes and outrageous makeup (did Carol even wear makeup?), and she took every opportunity to go bra-less. The fascination with Dreama and her exotic and sultry looks already had most of the male staff at Mercyville wishing they could be Vinnie Tagliaburro, the lucky guy who had the privilege of crawling into bed every night with the gorgeous, sexy creature that was Dreama.

For today's luncheon date with Vinnie, Dreama had decided upon a pair of white vinyl go-go boots with a daisy applique on the ankle of each boot, a gauzy deep

149

purple mini-dress that, when properly arranged, would outline the dark saucers of her areola because it was, after all, another bra-less kind of day, and she tied a green leather braided cord around her head, her black hair left to flow freely across her shoulders and down her tall, slender body. She applied her makeup with uncharacteristic haste—the false eyelashes she had worn yesterday while at her mother's were still affixed to her eyelids, so just a bit of aquamarine eye shadow, some frosted pink lipstick, and voila—she would not only make Vinnie wish he had a cot in that stinky little office of his, more than likely, she would turn every male head in that building her way. God it was good to be young and beautiful. Beauty and youth were Dreama's instruments that she used almost daily to get just about anything she wanted.

Dreama entered the building just as Jim Adamson was walking back from the kitchen, a lunch tray filled to overflowing with today's leftover turkey, mashed potatoes and gravy, stuffing, and cold peaches perched atop a mound of cottage cheese. How revolting, Dreama thought. The man really does need to stop eating so much, but she smiled big at Jim, touched his elbow, and cooed, "Well, Mr. A., did you have a nice Thanksgiving weekend? Enjoy some time with the family and the little wifey?" She all but batted her artificially enhanced eyelashes at the man who she hoped would someday become her boss.

"Why yes, Dreama, we had a very relaxing weekend, how 'bout yourself?"

"Oh, I spent the weekend at my mother's. Got out of Hicksville for a change. Vinnie went to Pittsburgh to you-know-who's house to see the kids and ended up spending the rest of his weekend at his mum's place. But, all in all, it was fun. I'm just here to have lunch with Vinnie. Hope that's okay?"

"By all means, Dreama. Enjoy. Though, I'm not sure how Vinnie's going to like you treating him to lunch without, well, you know, bringing him anything to eat," Jim lifted his cafeteria tray in her direction and chuckled.

"Oh, I've got something other than lunch in mind, Mr. A," Dreama purred mysteriously. "See you later, Jim." She actually winked at Jim before taking off toward Vinnie's office but didn't take her eyes off Jim, then gave him a little wave, those frosty lacquered fingernails shimmering in the late morning light that shone through the small, glass-block portals to the outside, and moved, hips swaying, down the hallway.

Jesus, what a piece of work, Jim thought. Every time he saw Dreama, all he could think of was that she needed a good, hot bath. He really hoped no one would see her walking the hall like a prostitute; he had enough to worry about without a bunch of adolescent boys racing off to the

151

bathroom to rub one out after seeing her jiggling her way toward a rendezvous with that oily dago Vinnie.

It had been nearly two weeks since the "engage on the stage" as Jim had privately dubbed the Tommy Jankovic-Henry Somers fiasco. Henry was still not back at school, and Jim had yet to talk with Tommy's parents about the incident. He wasn't sure if he would ever get the chance — if what Tommy said was true, then sitting down to explain this very disturbing story to two naïve immigrants was not going to be very easy, and by now, he gave up any hope that Tommy might sit them down and tell them himself.

Tommy's threat to kill himself was something that Jim did not take lightly. He could only imagine that the kid's nerves were frazzled, and in that state, there was no telling what he would do. It was too bad he didn't have any other family close by. When they had sat in Jim's car that rainy afternoon following the incident, Jim had questioned Tommy about his family, hoping to get some perspective on how to proceed. Apparently, he had a brother in the army stationed at Fort Bragg; other than that, it was Tommy and his parents living in the small, old, but neatly cared for little house with the workshop in the back.

Tonight was the school board's monthly meeting, and though Jim only answered to the school's five members of the board, two of the school board members were female and one of those females was the wife of Fallowfield Orly, the preacher at the Pentecostal Holiness Church. Jim knew he needed to relay the salacious events to the board that night, but he had not decided whether to include the ladies in the discussion. Olive Orly, the preacher's wife, would probably keel over and die of abject embarrassment at his description of the two boys' coupling. Her contributions (if one could call them that) to the school board were limited to acting as judge and jury regarding student life at Mercyville. To Carol's horror and Jim's amusement, Olive famously waged an ongoing one-woman campaign to outlaw the Gym Show (those girls in those tight outfits bending and stretching in front of God and everybody!). As for Marilyn Gillespie, she was a little more cerebral and sensible, but he still did not look forward to relating these events to a woman — any woman, though it might, Jim thought in the more callously uproarious core of his brain, be entertaining to watch Olive squirm. It was one thing to share the details with Ruthie — he had faith that nothing surprised Ruthie, and he trusted her loyalty, more than he trusted the loyalty of his own wife if truth be told, but to share this kind of prurient information with two women, well, he just wasn't sure that they needed to know all of the facts.

Then there was his mother's outburst on Thanksgiving Day — that story about how, while in the store, Henry

Somers had threatened to kill one of her customers. Jim quickly did the math and realized that Henry Somers wouldn't have even been a twinkle in his old man's eye about the time Jim's parents had owned that store, and besides, Jim doubted that the Henry Somers from here in Mercyville was the same Henry Somers his mother was referencing. Chances are that Ida had been confused, but then again, she seldom forgot details about things that happened long ago — more likely, she was unable to remember who Jim was whenever he visited her or she'd ask why Millicent was not at school — things like that, not an incident where one of her favorite customers from the store was threatened with an unnatural death. That would have remained stored in her memory for a long time, he supposed. The Adamson's store was located in the Strip District in Pittsburgh, a sliver of the city that sat on the south side of the Allegheny River — Polish Hill, where apparently this Mr. Kowalski lived and where this Henry Somers haunted. This was actually fairly close to the Strip District, by streetcar, anyway. Could it possibly be that his mother knew something?

Waiting outside of his office door was Shirl Snyder, the art teacher. Shirl was something of an oddball, reminding him of a modern-day Ichabod Crane, with his tall, bony structure, prominent chin, jutting cheekbones, and deeply set steely eyes, but he seemed harmless — never

154

any complaints from students or parents, and he wasn't one to send kids to the office for stupid shit like eating crumbs—Jesus. Jim didn't know much about Snyder even though he, too, had grown up in Pittsburgh—Jim knew that Shirl had been married once but the wife had left him, he knew he did not care for Shirl's long hair (it was already touching his collar), but other than that, Shirl's tenure at the school was unremarkable.

"Mr. A., could I speak with you for a moment?" Shirl asked, knowing that he was probably going to have to sit through watching Jim eat his lunch.

"If you don't mind my eating while we chat. Sure. Come on in." Jim motioned for Shirl to take the seat across from his desk. "Door opened or closed?"

"Oh, opened. Thanks for seeing me. I just wanted to ask you if my budget for the photography club might include funds for a field trip. I thought I might take the youngsters to Pittsburgh over the Christmas holiday to the Carnegie. There's a small but rather powerful Warhol exhibit being featured for a limited time."

"What's the hell's a 'Warhol'?" Jim mumbled awkwardly, trying not to speak with his mouth full of mashed potatoes, but hungry nonetheless. Art, unless it was standard, conventional, and iconic, failed to strike a chord with Jim.

"Andy Warhol. Pittsburgh native? Phenomenal pop
155

artist. Did the Campbell's Soup can? Ring a bell?"

"Nope. But that doesn't mean much. I'm not that familiar with modern art." Jim took another bite of mashed potatoes, spearing a rubberized slice of turkey in the process. "It all looks like a monkey threw paint up against a white canvas then some son-of-a-bitch sold it for millions of dollars."

"You're thinking Jackson Pollock," Shirl said authoritatively, crossing one knee over the other, using the fingers of one large bony hand to gesticulate how Pollack's art has gained a vast following, now secure in the knowledge that he has presented himself as a true connoisseur of modern art. "No, Andy Warhol is a different type of genius." Snyder's eyes nearly glazed over thinking about the genius of this Andy Warhol. "This is an opportunity to view some amazingly stark and profound pieces. Few students would ever get this chance again."

Well hells bells, Jim thought sarcastically, who am I to stand in the way of the appreciation of amazingly stark and profound pieces of art? He almost laughed, but his mouth was still full. It wasn't as if any of these kids Snyder was planning to take on this trip would experience some sort of artsy epiphany just because they had a chance to gawk at a row of stupid looking paintings, not unless milk cows or basketballs were somehow woven into the leitmotif. "Sounds fine to me. Fill out the paperwork. You want a school bus or are you going to charter an Atherton?" Atherton was a local chartered bus service that the school sometimes used when traveling over fifty miles. Nice ride, made the kids feel important.

"An Atherton bus?" Shirl's eyes lit up at the prospect of traveling to Pittsburgh in style. "Why, yes! Fine, fine. Thank you, Mr. A. Yes, I'll get the paperwork to you."

"Thanks. Oh, and Shirl? Get me a list of who-all is going."

At once Shirl's mood shifted. The man who had so confidently imparted his intellectual wherewithal regarding the august subject of modern art suddenly appeared uncomfortable, which was rather odd given that Jim had just granted him permission to take his photography groupies to some fruity-assed exhibit. "Right," Shirl said, paused as if he was going to say something else, then turned and left Jim's office.

"That was just strange," Jim said quietly to himself.

The Gym Show

X

Stanley Czerniawski was hard at work coloring his picture of the moon landing. The class had been asked to draw a picture of something important to them or something interesting that had happened to them. Most of the thirty or so students were coloring pictures of Christmas trees, Christmas presents, and Santa Claus; a couple of students were drawing likenesses of their mommies, and one was drawing what appeared to be a calf hanging out of the back end of a cow. Stanley's moon landing tableau, in contrast, was a rather impressive montage of the lunar module, Neil Armstrong just as he was about to make that historic step onto the moon's surface, complete with a reflected image of Old Glory visible from his astronaut's helmet, and the iconic American flag which Stanley had taken great pains to copy with utmost precision from the silkscreened banner hanging above the door beside the printed alphabet that resided in the space above the chalkboard.

Julie's picture was of the May Queen court from the Gym Show. Two of Julie's favorite pastimes—and two things that she happened to be very, very good at—were drawing and coloring. Her pictures were well-planned,

159

balanced, showed depth and perspective, and the human expressions on the faces in her drawings showed quite a range of emotions. There was the brown haired, brown eyed queen, crying, of course, blue teardrops falling down her beautiful face and onto her dress, crying because she had just been crowned May Queen, her white dress with purple ruffles in the shape of a bell. Her escort, wearing a big smile and a white dinner jacket was tall with dark hair. The May Queen's court included three girls smiling but not crying on the queen's left — tiered in the order in which they ranked below the May Queen; thus the third girl on the lowest tier was not smiling as big as the one on the first tier since she was, technically, third in line to the throne—and three boys on the escort's right. The three boys were not smiling because they thought this was all dumb and they just wanted to take off their white dinner jackets and put on sweaters with big 'M's on them. Then there was the flower girl and this is where Julie really concentrated and took her time to make her likeness as close to Julie-ness as possible. It was a masterpiece. One more accomplishment to shove under Miss Marpy's nose (she had gradually fallen out of love with Miss Marpy — her quest to be moved into the first grade was now just a means of proving to herself that she was smart enough to be moved). Julie fashioned her flower-girl Julie's hair in a tall, brown beehive, nearly obscuring the not so smiling face of tier three girl, affixed an enormous blue bow on the back of flower-girl Julie's head—the ribbons of which were flowing visibly down the length of flower-girl Julie's back, dressed her in a sky blue frock with a white sash about the waist (again, bow and ribbon flowing freely behind her) with a white ruffled petticoat peeking from underneath, and, of course, the de rigueur black patent Mary Janes. A masterpiece.

Stanley, his tongue clenched between his teeth, never stopped sketching or coloring long enough to look up to see Julie's creation, but Julie couldn't help but steal glances at the complex artwork that Stanley was producing. This was not good. Artwork, Julie felt, was her métier, and to have what appeared to be another artist among the children in the class, well, that just wouldn't do. Somehow, she must keep the others, including Miss Marpy, from eyeing Stanley's picture in its present form. Julie had to admit that the tour de force that she was creating might not be judged as being as technically brilliant as Stanley's grudgingly piece of high quality kindergarten art.

So Julie took the opportunity, when Stanley was at a crucial point in the outlining stage of perfecting his illustration, to rise as if to retrieve the crayon she had just dropped on the floor and soundly bumped into Stanley's desk—so soundly that the noise of the desk's legs scraping

161

the checkered linoleum floor made everyone stop and look.

"Oops."

"Julie, what do you say?" Miss Marpy, busy trying to show Ronnie C. how to hold his crayon correctly, obviously did not see Julie's affected blunder.

"Sorry? Sorry, Stanley," Julie said as if bumping into Stanley was not the result of a deliberate and spiteful need to remain queen of the crayons.

"Julie Adamson, you messed up my picture," Stanley said, quietly, the first words, in fact, that Stanley had ever spoken to Julie. "See? Now you can't tell where Neil Armstrong's boot was." A plump, round teardrop plopped from behind Stanley's glasses and landed squarely on the American flag.

Julie froze. A sudden realization came over her. Stanley had called her by her first and last name, a practice not common among kindergarteners or even first graders. That meant that Stanley *must* remember her from the television station, since not even Miss Marpy used last names, just last initials if there happened to have been two 'Patty's or two 'Michael's in the class. She was the only Julie, so there was no need to call her 'Julie A.'; there was only one Stanley, but there were two 'Ronnie's, two 'Debbie's, and two 'Shelly's.

He knows me, Julie concluded. He knows me, and
162

he's never, ever said anything about when I peed my pants at the television station.

Now it was Julie's turn to cry. This was a new emotion—this little girl's remorse—and her stomach ached at the very idea that she had ruined this sad boy's picture because of her jealousy over his rather obvious artistic talents. What kind of person *was* she? She wasn't mean like her sister Jenny, she didn't like hurting people. Oh, why had she ruined Stanley's beautiful picture?

"I'm sorry," Julie whispered, hopefully loud enough for Stanley to hear but not loud enough for anyone else to wonder why she was crying over Stanley's work of art.

Stanley said nothing, but tried in vain to remedy the damage that Julie's jealousy had caused. This made Julie feel even worse.

"I'm sorry," Julie whispered louder, but still, Stanley said nothing and pitifully wet his index finger to try to erase the black mark that would forever linger on Neil Armstrong's boot.

"I'm *sorry!*" Julie gulped, but still Stanley did not look at her or acknowledge in any way that the remorse she felt was tearing her apart.

Then she had an idea, an idea so perfectly sensible, so profoundly gracious, and so precisely fitting that she stopped crying, smiled, stood up, turned to Stanley and announced to him and to the rest of the class that her

163

mother, Mrs. Carol Adamson, had just last night decided to choose Stanley Czerniawski to be the crown bearer in The 1971 Gym Show.

Finally, *finally*, Damon Ettinger was free of the constraints of sitting in a hot, nasty, boring classroom all day, jiggling his right foot, his left hand busily tapping the desk with his pen. He had been dying to be anywhere but cooped up in a smelly, stuffy, room with a bunch of punk-ass honkeys jockeying for a seat next to the black dude and at long last was able to savor the sweet, sweet feel of pulling on his whiter than white Converse high tops just in time for that shithead Danny Teague, Mercyville's own praying mantis and one of the ugliest mother fuckers alive, to slink by and hold out his right hand, not for a shake but for slappin' a brother, his cracker-assed nasally voice singing like a little girl, "What's *happenin'*, my man?"

Damon return-slapped the boy's bony hand and did his level best keep his cool. As the token "brother" on the boys' basketball team, Damon was used to being the repository of all things hip and black, and it no longer bothered him that he served as the very vehicle that made all the other guys on the team feel as if they were with it, cool cats, and down with the whole *Negro* thing, but he just couldn't stand it when white guys like Teague tried to act like they were black, too, as if Damon needed his teammates to make him feel better about being one of two black kids at Mercyville. Danny Teague, with his pasty-ass freckled face and ugly mother-fucking ginger hair wouldn't last an hour if some Martian up and abducted his narrow ass and dropped him off in the middle of Cleveland Heights, but Damon wasn't about to tell the boy how weak his shit was.

"Hey, man, what's up. Ready for this shit to start?"

"Hell yeah, Damon, ready to *roll*! We gonna' kick some mother fuckin' *ass* this year, *bro--tha*!"

"Yeah, sounds about right, dude." He almost "axed" Teague why he was ending his retarded-sounding sentences on an upward inflection, but thought better of it. Damon double-knotted his Chucks and grabbed the pinny that the team's manager had tossed his way. Damn, Damon thought as he watched Teague start to undress, I can't wait to wipe up the floor with this asshole.

The Damon Ettinger that Mercyville High School loved and revered was one person; the Damon Ettinger that existed in real life was an altogether different person. To Mercyville, Damon's academic achievements, his outrageous athletic ability, and his overall great-guy personality was the very reason that kept Damon, and to a lesser extent his little brother Dwayne, from waking up on any given morning to find a burning cross planted on their front lawn. There was no doubt that both Pat and Freda

165

Ettinger knew which side their bread was buttered on, and they had taught their sons well. But the Damon Ettinger that longed for an existence that included a hell of a lot more kids who looked like him—especially girls—was another person altogether. He had wisely accepted the condescending way that the staff and students at Mercyville treated him and Dwayne, as if the two of them were some kind of Civil Rights trophy boys won at a carnival that proved to the rest of the world that Mercyville wasn't some shitsville hick town with absolutely nothing to offer a brother. He accepted this, but that didn't mean he liked it.

Whenever he tried talking to his old man about how he felt, Pat was less than sympathetic. The whole reason the Ettingers lived here in Mercyville, he reminded his oldest son, was for the opportunities that they wouldn't have had if they remained in the declining neighborhood east of Cleveland where officials had begun to integrate the schools. Pat firmly believed that forcing white students into schools in black neighborhoods might *appear* to be a good idea to the white bureaucrats who designed the whole desegregation model, but in practice, he knew in his heart that it would prove to be a disaster. In fact, in later years, his sons would recognize, too, that the American experiment in desegregation would have devastating consequences on inner city schools all across

166

the nation. Pat felt, and history later proved him correct in this regard, that inner city schools were far better off when they were connected to the neighborhoods they served, be they black or white, and all that forced integration had accomplished was a marked disconnect between home and school.

Pat Ettinger counted among his many gifts the ability to see the handwriting on the wall. He decided it was time to leave the city and move somewhere that remained untouched and outwardly, at least, unaffected by the entire Civil Rights movement. A series of seemingly unrelated events landed the Ettingers in Mercyville with Pat appointed as a park ranger at Shenango; in fact, because he was college educated with a background in biology of all things, the county commissioner had slated Pat to become the park's game warden after old Jack Warren retired. That a black man in 1969 could ascend to the position of game warden for one of the Commonwealth's largest state parks was due in large part to Pat's nearly obsessive work ethic. Some may have believed that his appointment to such a prestigious position within the park was a result of affirmative action, and that may have been true, but Pat knew that in order to gain and keep the respect of his fellow rangers and of the community at large that he would have to work harder, smarter, and longer than his white counterparts. And so

167

he did.

His task now, his and Freda's, was to make sure that his two sons understood just two things: Being a black man could be the very worst thing to be in America, or being a black man could be the very best thing to be in America. Damon thought it was rather ironic that his father up and moved his family to an all-white town without even one black dot to be seen for miles and miles, but Pat's belief was that if his sons continued to keep out of trouble, continued making good grades in school, excelled at athletics, and toed that white line, they would be successful in this world regardless of the lack of diversity in the area. If they became reactionary, bitter, or resentful, it would be that much harder for them to make it. If Damon and Dwayne would simply trust their parents on this one, the world would be theirs for the taking.

Damon had this mantra preached to him almost daily, and he knew where the old man was coming from, but it was still hard to watch that shit on TV—race riots, Dr. King's assassination, the stereotypical images that dominated the news. Out of respect for his parents, and, well, because it seemed to be working for him for the time being, Damon toed that line, but knew that once he graduated and went off to college—and he *would* go to college because there was no way his black ass was getting sent off to Vietnam — the time would come when Damon would be his own man in his own way.

What *remained* working for him were these two things: basketball and baseball. There was no one in the entire Lake County league that could touch Damon Ettinger in either sport. People loved him — even the players and fans from other schools. There wasn't an adult out there who didn't know who Damon was, who didn't fight the after-game crowds just to shake his hand, who didn't revere the tall, good-looking, not-so-dark skinned young man with the clean cut hair (no Afro for him), and beautiful smile. And Damon was convinced that these same people would defend him from anyone on the outside who made disparaging remarks about him. It was true that he was blessed to be gifted athletically and to be so well liked by the community.

But Damon often wondered what some of these same fathers who pumped his hand after basketball games and cheered him on as he pitched another no-hitter out on the baseball diamond would react if he were to ask one of their daughters to the prom. See? There was the rub. There wasn't a girl at Mercyville or anywhere nearby whose daddy was going to let her go out on a date with a black dude. And he also realized all too well that life as he knew it would cease to exist if he ever so much as made a half-assed move toward any of these snowflakes from

169

Mercyville.

Damon picked himself off the locker room bench and proceeded out into the gym to that heavenly echo of bouncing basketballs, whistles, and the squeak of rubber Chuck Taylors against the lacquered gym floor. Time to shine, man.

XI

She had left him on a Friday morning. He was not sorry to see her go. While marriage to her was tolerable at best, at its worst, the time he spent as her husband further confirmed that he had no room in his life for women.

It had all begun with good intentions—Shirl Snyder had moved into the area from his family home in Pittsburgh shortly after the deaths of his parents, had bought a small farm, and soon realized that the culture of the tightly woven community coupled with his role as a teacher demanded that he take a wife. He had started attending the Methodist church in town and shortly thereafter, the pastor introduced him to Mary Esther, a widow with no children. Mary Esther's looks were anything but plain—she possessed a kind, cherubic face, bright blue eyes, and a comfortably plush and ample body, short on stature but long on warmth. However, for Shirl, though she showed promise as a hardworking farm wife, it would not be enough for man like him.

After a respectable courtship, they married quietly in the pastor's living room one Sunday afternoon, and Mary Esther moved herself and her cherished belongings from her small cottage in town into the old, drafty farmhouse

171

that Shirl owned. Shirl had watched somewhat unnervingly as she turned his once private and secretive bachelor quarters into an antimacassar-ed nightmare of femininity. The kitchen, pre-Mary Esther, had been without the modern conveniences of a working gas or electric stove, a refrigerator-freezer combination, or enough surface area on which to prepare a decent meal. In the space of a few weeks, however, Mary Esther had magically transformed the heart of the home into the warm and cozy source of all that makes a house welcoming and purposeful—bread baking, soup making, pie assembling. No man could have asked for a better homemaker. But then again, Shirl was no ordinary man.

His attempt at respectability and acceptance was, for him, a way to assuage his inner most desires, his proclivity for the prurient, and his unhealthy appetite for teenaged boys.

Ever since Shirl had been a student at Pittsburgh's Shady Side Academy, he had harbored an attraction to boys. This in itself was problematic in the era of post-war America, but as he grew older, his penchant for males remained focused on teenaged boys, all manner of teenaged boys. He liked them small and helpless, strong and muscled—he liked the effeminate boys and the masculine boys. The thought of sexual encounters with men his own age began to disgust him.

172

The Gym Show

In his way of thinking, becoming a teacher was the most likely career for a man who reveled in the company of young men, but too many folks in his small circle of acquaintances suspected, at the very least, that Shirl was "a confirmed bachelor." Remaining in Pittsburgh as a teacher would have placed Shirl in jeopardy of others finding him to be more than "attracted to men" — he would be in danger of others discovering his peculiar habit of seeking out school-aged boys. No, it was safer to move away.

Though farming had never been something that Shirl had ever though to embark upon, he saw an opportunity to supplement his meager teaching salary by collecting rent while at the same time reaping a profit from someone else's labor — all without getting his hands too dirty.

The Somers family was willing and even somewhat relieved to have Shirl as their new landowner — their previous landlord Otto Muller, while providing a house for them to live in, such as it was, mistrusted Henry and his hired man, forever hovering around them and getting in their way. Henry didn't care for Old Man Muller and his habit of always poking around in their business. Shirl seemed to be the type to let Henry alone to run things his own way.

Meanwhile, Shirl's position at Mercyville High School afforded him all kinds of access to boys, but he was

173

shrewd enough in the ways of teenagers to know how best to go about delivering them into his circle of lieges. Money was always an attraction. The promise of pornography, alcohol, and even marijuana also lured even the most recalcitrant of boys into his lair. Before Mary Esther, Shirl had exploited a legion of young boys, not just from Mercyville, but also from the surrounding communities—boys eager to play his games, drink his liquor, smoke his pot, and revel in his extensive library of avant-garde artwork that often led to an even more critical examination of his unusual and disturbing collection of photographic pornography. Even his decision to make Mary Esther his wife—for no other reason than self-preservation—did not prevent Shirl from engaging in his lustful affinity for boys, though once he had reluctantly allowed the widow to become a part of his life, these things had to be secreted away, stashed in a location only accessible by him.

His shrewdness, though, was no match for Mary Esther's fondness for organization and cleanliness. After her shocking discovery of his extensive hoard of homoerotic pornography, she began to put together the puzzle pieces of their marriage and came to the incorrect conclusion that she existed only to serve as her husband's foil for his homosexuality; she would never know that her husband was, in fact, *not* a homosexual but a pedophile.

174

The idea of Shirl, or anyone for that matter, living as a pedophile had never entered Mary Esther's imagination, but to regard him as a homosexual—well, now *that* began to make sense. The delayed consummation of their marriage—an act that would never have taken place at all had she not questioned him about it—had left her not only unsatisfied, but moderately disturbed at his lack of experience and his utter unfamiliarity with female anatomy. Her uncovering of Shirl's disturbing collection coupled with his lack of affection, his reluctance to confide in her, and his eventual mental and physical abuse ultimately led her to the decision to quietly leave him.

Once more, she packed her belongings. To get as far from him as possible, Mary Esther decided to retreat to her sister's home in Florida. The cancer that had resided dormant in her left breast until fairly recently would remain undetected for yet another year. Sadly, two years after leaving him, Mary Esther died quietly, having never revealed to anyone why she had left her second husband and never fully realizing why her marriage had been doomed from the start.

For his part, Shirl was not surprised to see her go. It seems that married women, no matter how homely they may be, longed for affection, despised abuse, both physical and mental, and had little tolerance for sexual depravity. He had delayed the consummation of their

175

marriage for as long as he could, but even when he did capitulate and manage to have intercourse with his wife, it sickened him to the point of nausea. Mary Esther was a female approaching middle age, and no amount of fantasizing could have provided for him what he truly desired and needed in a sexually gratifying experience. She held no attraction or desire for him whatsoever. She represented all that ran counter to his cravings.

Good riddance.

Now that he was able to practice his activities without the fear of his being discovered by Mary Esther, Shirl became even bolder in his scheming. He organized Mercyville's photography club and used the spacious cellar of his farmhouse as the club's darkroom. What better way to entice his young friends whom he dubbed "Old Sports" into his home than with the promise of producing original "works of art"?

Some boys were put off by their mentor's taste for them and their young bodies (unfortunately, not until it was too late), while others were all too eager to participate in their new friend Blade's games. And those boys who, after discovering their teacher's intentions, were reluctant to "play along" often did not make their feelings known to their teacher in time, for these boys, out of respect for his age, his position, and his willingness to include them, were hesitant to do anything to offend him. In short, their parents had brought them up to respect their elders, and their upbringing had conditioned them to politely accept anything that an adult suggested, no matter how disgusting or sinful it may have appeared. Shirl Snyder was an adult, and once he surreptitiously placed his stamp of approval upon their activities, the boys were at a loss as to how to say 'no'.

He knew just how to package his particular brand of affection—offer these boys a kindness, something that their own fathers were too "manly" to do, shower them with compliments, present them with things they couldn't access any other way—money, alcohol, pornography. Then once these boys eventually discovered the motives behind their teacher's actions, it was already too late, his ubiquitous camera would have already captured enough images of them smoking pot, drinking beer and liquor, nakedly engaging in lively wrestling matches, or playfully posing with arms furled, muscles bulging, penises erect. Their private parties with "Blade" would forever remain secret, buried, undiscussed, but everlasting nonetheless.

Oh, he had the goods on all of them.

For years, Shirl Snyder had operated in this manner—without fear of discovery, without fear of recrimination, and without mercy. He considered himself a mentor, a friend, and a confidante to these boys, and he most definitely was providing something that they wanted and

177

needed. To him, it was all part of the package—he was a teacher, wasn't he?

His gift to these boys, his harmless beneficence, satisfied his every desire, his every need, and acted as his life's blood. Though he knew that others would never understand nor accept this yearning of his, he reminded himself that he had never physically hurt any of these boys; thus, his conscience remained free of any guilt.

It was simply unfortunate that others might see things differently.

XII

Boots Malloy called the meeting to order, thinking that this regularly scheduled December board meeting would be nothing out of the ordinary. Jim Adamson, resolute in his decision to inform the board members about the stage incident, felt a weight in the pit of his stomach knowing that what he had to tell the group would be anything but ordinary. He waited it out until the call was given for new business. Once recognized, Jim took a deep breath and addressed the board, purposely avoiding Olive Orly's narrow-eyed stare in the process.

Once he finished telling the story of the two high school boys and the activity he had witnessed between the two of them on the stage, the room was silent and remained silent. Jim had no idea what kinds of thoughts were running through each of the five members' minds at that point until Boots Malloy finally stood up and cleared his phlegm ravaged throat three or four times and spoke directly to Jim.

"Jim, I don't have to tell you that what you've just shared with us is a very serious allegation, and it's not something we want 'out there' so to speak. How many other people know about this?"

179

"Just me," Jim lied. His confiding in Ruthie about the incident would serve no purpose, and besides, he knew for sure that the board would not understand the relationship that Jim shared with Ruthie in terms of using her as a sounding board.

"Did you tell Mrs. Adamson?" Marilyn Gillespie found her voice, and though she and Jim had always been cordial to each other, he really wasn't sure how she was reacting to this rather appalling disclosure.

"No, Marilyn. I wanted to share this first with the board and take any recommendations you might have about what to do next."

"You said that you've not talked to the boys' parents. Shouldn't that have been your first move?" Remy Paulson asked. "And by saying 'share this first', you aren't implying, Mr. Adamson, that you're going to tell anyone else about this, are you?"

"No, not yet. And as far as the boys' parents are concerned, as I stated before, the Jankovics speak very little English, and, according to Tommy, there would be no way that I would be able to make either of his parents understand the situation unless I spoke to them in their own language. Of course, I realize that this apparent lack of understanding is according to Tommy, but my gut tells me that he's telling the truth. As far as the Somers' family is concerned, they are out of town indefinitely, according to their hired man. I've gone out there three times to speak with Henry Sr. but no one has been at home."

Olive Orly finally spoke. "Mr. Adamson, the situation you've just described, isn't behavior like that — behavior that only farm animals and mongrel dogs would ever engage in — isn't that behavior illegal?"

"I'm not sure, Mrs. Orly. I haven't checked the statutes for this — ah — type of explicit behavior. I am going to leave that up to the justice of the peace. I wanted to address all of you, first, before I hand this over to a judge."

"Now wait just a minute there, Jim. Let's not be so hasty," Boots said. "Why are we getting the law involved here? This thing, well, it's a family matter, as far as I'm concerned, and I'll bet that the rest of the board agrees with me. Involving the law would invite all kinds of trouble. Besides, with *both* boys being minors, and if a law *was* broken — that is, if what you're telling us is true — well, I just don't think we need to go getting Frank Jenner involved in all of this."

"If what I'm telling you is true?" Jim said, incredulously. "Do you actually think I would make up something like this? Ladies, gentlemen," Jim pleaded, "Trust me. I've been sick over this, and I certainly don't want to be the only one with this incident on my hands! This is unchartered waters for me. This is precisely why I

181

am bringing the matter before the board. If a law has been broken, it is incumbent upon me to report it. If a law hasn't been broken, then, well, we're back to square one, but I'm not the one who can determine that. I'm not a lawyer, and like I said, I'm not familiar with the statute – if there is a statute – that addresses this crime, that is, if there was a crime. I tried to imagine what I would do if the two parties in question were a male and a female, and I'm still at a loss. But I do think that we need to turn this over to a judge. Now, after talking with Tommy, I can tell you that he isn't willing to talk about it to anyone, so where do we go with this if we don't bring the law into it?"

The members of the board looked at one another searching for some way to answer Jim. Olive Orly stared wide-eyed at Jim as if he had been the one who had caused this entire tragedy. Marilyn Gillespie, head down and to the side, appeared to be holding back tears. Remy Paulson just looked angry. Norm Snow, the fifth member of the board and the only one who had remained silent, also served as the mayor of Mercyville. Norm sat shaking his head, apparently unable to process this news and the possibility of some real distressing consequences to not only the school but to his beloved town of Mercyville. After about a minute's worth of silent contemplation, Boots Malloy stood up. "Mr. Adamson, you're excused from the rest of the meeting."

182

"What's that supposed to mean?" Jim asked.

"It means, Mr. Adamson, that we, the members of the board, as the very body that sets the precedents and policies for Mercyville High School, we need some time to discuss this matter without interference." Sensing that Jim was about to rear up like an angry bear, Boots softened somewhat, and tried unsuccessfully to affect a benign countenance in an effort to mollify a visibly disquieted Jim, "This is standard procedure, Jim; don't get your tail feathers all in a ruffle." Then, changing back the pitch of his voice to a more humorless tone, Boots continued, "We'll let you know our decision. In the meantime, you are not to divulge to anyone, and I mean *anyone* – not Frank Jenner, not the police, not your wife, you're to tell *no one* what happened on the afternoon of November 10, nor are you to discuss what has transpired here in this room tonight. That should go without saying."

With the scorching stares of five sets of eyes nearly burning a hole through his already heated face, Jim scraped his chair back away from the cafeteria table, gathered the papers stacked in front of him and placed them within his leather folder, returned the folder to his briefcase, and took his leave.

Never before had Jim wished to be anyone other than who he was – husband, father, school principal, the hand

183

on a shoulder, the sage to those who sought his advice and counsel, pillar of the community and credit to the upbringing that his parents sacrificed so much to provide for him and Millicent.

However, tonight he felt as if everything that he knew was true about himself was all a lie, a sham, that he was faking it at being the person that others thought he was and expected him to be. During the war, he had been awarded The Purple Heart after the seizure of the Po Valley, but he had never felt worthy of it—the wound in his hand was akin to a dog bite compared to the mangled and missing limbs, destroyed faces, blood, screams, and the sickening smell of decay he had experienced in that field hospital. He wasn't noble, he wasn't a hero, he was a sorry-assed drunk who didn't deserve to be married to a beautiful woman, a weak man who was a sad excuse of a father to the three children God had blessed him with, a man who had no right to live in a three bedroom split level home on ten acres of land his father had practically given him, and he sure as hell didn't have the balls to claim leadership of a school that, for many in Mercyville, represented everything that was sacred about their small, tightly knit community.

Jim sat for a long time in the parking lot of the school and for the first time since he said goodbye to his sister Millicent before boarding the ship that took him to Italy

184

and into the darkest depths of a manmade hell, he sobbed with ferocity that he didn't know he still possessed.

1970

The Gym Show

188

XIII

January 1970, Mercyville, Pennsylvania

The Fifth Dimension's "The Age of Aquarius" blasted from the record player's speakers until Peggy Huffington heard JoAnn Donaldson's shriek for her to turn it off. Not wanting listen to JoAnn's bitching any longer than she had to, Peggy hastily lifted the needle off the album.

"God, stop! That was awful! Beth, you gotta' turn when the other girls turn, and Debbie, that last part when you do the jazz square then plant your feet apart? Your feet are supposed to be *apart*, not crossed. Man. That was bad. Again."

Forty girls were crammed onto the stage, some sitting cross-legged on the wooden floor, some standing with arms folded in front of their leotard-clad bodies looking bored and wondering why Mrs. A. was forcing them to be there; only five of the forty were busy learning a dance that was supposed to be performed during the Gym Show between equipment changes. While it was true that this first week back after Christmas was the first solid week of preparations for the Gym Show, things were not boding well for JoAnn Donaldson and her troupe of amateur

189

dancers.

JoAnn had talked Mrs. A. into letting her take charge of the dancers in this year's Gym Show. She had been taking dance lessons from the venerable and demanding Miss Arita Lee Blair since she was seven, and thus considered herself far above anyone else in the dance milieu at Mercyville including Mrs. A. Since a dance milieu didn't exist at Mercyville, Carol was more than happy to let JoAnn (who displayed a rather poor showing during last year's floor exercise portion of the Gym Show) take over the dance part. Maybe then, Carol hoped, she wouldn't throw a tantrum when Carol broke the news to her that, no, JoAnn would not be performing a floor exercise this year. Carol didn't care if JoAnn was a senior—JoAnn, with her awkward un-pointed toes and bent knees—her tumbling was simply awful. She and her jazz hands could dance instead.

Once again, this year Carol was competing with the basketball coach Ken Montgomery for time in the gym. As far as Ken was concerned, Carol's little project ranked far, far below his quest for a Lake County championship in basketball (this could be the year) and so he had no problem telling Carol (and he didn't give a shit who she slept with every night) that during his practices, she and her girls could be on the stage with the curtains closed, as long as they kept the music down. As if anything would

190

have drowned out Ken Montgomery's particular brand of coaching vernacular, liberally laced with various four letter words designed to inspire his players to greatness.

Carol, for her part, would play her accompanying music as loud as she wished, and Ken Montgomery could stick it up his fat ass; in fact, she would tell him that very thing as soon as he was finished insulting Danny Teague's parentage and questioning the more personal details of the poor boy's anatomy. If he could scream like a lunatic and swear like a longshoreman, then she would play that damn record player as loud as the dial would take it, and if he didn't like it, here it is, mister, you can kiss my sweet little tushie. That would shut him up for a little while at least. Carol sighed. "Count to ten, Carol," she whispered to herself. She reminded herself that she   must be careful to avoid using her position as the boss' wife to leverage things in her favor—even *she* knew how devastatingly dangerous that could prove to be for both she and Jim — but every now and then, some folks needed reminding of their place in this school, and Ken was one of those people.

Pulling back the black velvet curtains and revealing herself to the entire basketball team, the coach, and the assistant coach resulted in a sudden halt to the verbal assault on poor, skinny Danny Teague (so pale and freckly, that one).

"Coach," Carol began, "we can hear you swearing all

the way up here on the stage, and I just wanted to remind you that the young ladies who are *so* hard at work preparing for this year's Gym Show really have no need to know the exact length of Danny's penis."

Luckily for most of the team members, they happened to be, at that moment, situated out of Coach Montgomery's range of sight, so Ken wasn't able to see the thumbs and forefingers estimating, in centimeters no less, just how small they knew Danny's little willy to be, and if Ken or Dan Baxter, the assistant coach, heard the teams' bubbling snickers, they chose to ignore them. Ken fumed at Carol.

"Mrs. Adamson, I'm surprised you can hear anything at all with all that goddamn hippie music playing. Now why don't you just go on back there, conduct your little practice, and let us finish ours. We play Iroquois Lake this Friday, and I would like for us to at least look like we've shown up."

"I, too, Coach Montgomery, want to do win this Friday. My cheerleaders, who also have had *no time in the gym*, have been practicing out in the cold lobby every night after school, and they've worked very hard to support your boys. I certainly do not want their hard work to have been in vain. Now, I will excuse myself and return to our Gym Show preparations, but please know," Carol glanced at the caged-in clock that hung on one wall of the gym, "that you have exactly eight more minutes left in which to practice in this gym. In eight minutes all forty or so of my girls will descend upon this floor and begin erecting the equipment necessary for them to, once again, draw a standing room only crowd come Friday, May 8, 1970. Oops," she said, looking down at her petite silver watch, "looks like you have seven minutes now."

Montgomery looked at Carol with pure hatred in his eyes, blew his whistle, and yelled at his players (who were painfully stifling themselves over Mrs. A. saying 'erecting') to the east end of the gym to begin running pro sprints. Carol turned and flung the velvet curtain aside with a dramatic flourish and returned to her girls.

Oh, that man. As if my girls, who don't *have* a basketball team to play on, deserve to be treated as second-class citizens simply because they're girls! This is precisely why Vinnie Tagliaburro and his asinine idea of putting boys in the Gym Show is about as fair as the way his wife gets to traipse all around this school dressed like a hooker even on days when she isn't substituting!

Much to Carol's continued distress (and her beleaguered husband's list of shit he had better take care of before his wife makes his life even more miserable), Vinnie Tagliaburro had been persistent in his quest for a male presence in this year's Gym Show. At the staff Christmas party, hosted every year by Carol and Jim, with

193

their three children spying wide-eyed and curious at the outrageous nighttime behavior of the usually staid and conservative faculty, Vinnie had made his move. Loosened up after several shots of Black Velvet, and feeling as if no woman present would be able to resist his charms, Vinnie had cornered Carol as she was digging through the garage freezer for more ice.

"Carol, come on, hun. What could you possibly have against having some ah...the more, you know, talented and athletic boys doin' a little something-something during the Gym Show? What, are all they're good for is moving mats and breaking down equipment, uh? Building that throne a yours for the May Queen? Come on. We could even think of some things they could do together — like build pyramids or something. Hey, my Dreama's got some really cool ideas — 'member she was on some dance squad or something like 'at back at Slippery Rock. She's got some good ideas for getting the boys involved, an' 'at. Whaddya say, uh? Come on, Cupcake, do me a favor — do all of us a favor--and just think about it, uh?"

What made it even worse, and what had nearly ruined Jim and Carol's much looked forward to and well-deserved two week Christmas vacation, was that while Carol brought up the subject nearly every day, Jim brushed her off. Whether he was buying time or whether

194

he was just hoping that Carol would move on to another crusade or campaign, he didn't really know. He was more bothered by the whole stage incident, the board's reaction to it, and his moral obligation to protect the students at Mercyville High School. Vinnie and Dreama Tagliaburro were way down on his list of priorities.

Dreama had continued to insert herself into life at the Mercyville High School, no doubt in an effort to bolster Vinnie's boys-in-the-Gym-Show campaign, and was now a regular at dropping by the school during Vinnie's "lunch." Even more infuriating to Carol was the fact that she began showing up early enough to catch Vinnie just as he was in the process of dismissing his class into the locker room to shower and change. Her appearance caused quite a stir among the boys in that particular pre-lunchtime class period, and after being dismissed, the comments and innuendos flying about the locker room (complete with accompanying pantomimes and sound effects) would have, had he heard any of this, unleashed a rage in Vinnie that would probably have ended in someone leaving the premises in a body bag, but because they were horny high school boys, they simply couldn't resist.

If Vinnie had ever indicated to Dreama that her presence and especially her rather provocative attire was a disruption, it sure didn't appear that way to anyone who was paying attention. Vinnie and Dreama would quietly retreat into his little office adjacent to the boys' locker room, the frosted glass obscuring any activities within that happened to be taking place between the two. It was almost as if Vinnie enjoyed the attention that he knew his young wife drew from those hormone-ravaged adolescent boys, but on the other hand, had any of them ever so much as looked her way, they were dead. As for Dreama, she instinctively knew that whenever she made an appearance, the aura surrounding her was positively electric. Her natural born instinct for and ensuing years of practice in the art of allure was made manifest in the attention she so reveled in. Beauty was power.

On the days when she was 'Mrs. Tag,' she managed to tone down her sexual magnetism to a lesser degree, but any earlier visions of her wearing a short skirt with those long, long legs had already been burned into the collective retinas of about 250 boys, not to mention the other males on the staff. In those days, separate teachers' rooms existed for men and women, as if to ridiculously prevent some type of desperate coupling in between classes and during lunch. Since Vinnie was occupied in his office keeping company with his wife, the men of the staff, much like the boys in the locker room, were free to, although a bit more subtly and with better vocabulary, discuss the finer details of Mrs. Tag's more attractively proportioned and beautifully defined attributes.

Had Carol been privy to the conversations taking place among the men, she would have become even more enraged at the presence of Dreama at the school. Most of the male staff were married with families, and so if Carol would have had *any* inkling of what went on inside of their heads (and, in some cases, inside of their trousers), well, that was just one more reason to despise Dreama, and to a certain extent Vinnie for bringing her to Mercyville in the first place.

The women's lounge, in predictable contrast, cackled with outrageous rhetoric concerning the second Mrs. Tagliaburro. All manner of assumptions and opinions were proffered, and most of the women agreed with Carol about the questionable virtue of Mercyville's sexiest part-time staff member. Dreama was smart enough, on the days when she was substituting, to avoid the catty chatter that dominated the conversations in the women's lounge; however, the knowledge that these dried up old biddies and jealous women with their sagging breasts and thickening middles talked about her behind her back emboldened her, whereas most women would be bothered by such vicious gossip.

Carol and her girls were scurrying around the basketball-free gym, now able to practice and prepare in earnest, the Gym Show returning to occupy center stage

197

amid Carol's deepening foreboding about the future of the all-girls' endeavor. She decided to think about Vinnie and his boys tomorrow — there was way too much work to do with these budding gymnasts, JoAnn's pitiful dance troupe, and the knowledge that, as of now, the Gym Show remained hers and hers alone.

XIV

Damon Ettinger had rolled his ankle during Wednesday night's practice — not too seriously, but it was serious enough that Coach Montgomery had recommended that he get the ankle taped up before practice after school on Thursday. In the days before schools mandated athletic trainers to be present to keep athletes healthy and injury-free, players would have to rely on someone, usually the gym teacher or the school nurse, to minister to them. Ankle taping was more than just wrapping white canvas-backed tape around a swollen joint; there were several considerations to be made that required someone with skill to properly tape the ankle so that the support provided did not impede the joint's movement or flexibility.

Damon checked with Ruthie in the main office to see when Mr. Tag, the closest thing to a qualified ankle taper he could think of, was available. It was lunchtime, and Mr. Tag had apparently already had his prep, so Ruthie directed Damon over to the boys' P.E. office where Vinnie usually could be found during his lunch period.

Damon approached the closed door of Mr. Tag's office, knocked twice, and was surprised a few moments

199

later when Mrs. Tag answered, wearing a seductive grin, tousled hair, and stood before him, draping her long, curving body provocatively along the length of the door, her painted fingernails tapping languidly on the door's frame. "Well hello, Mr. Ettinger. Here to see me?"

Embarrassed by Dreama's overt suggestiveness, Damon swallowed, "Uh, no ma'am. I'm here to see Mr. Tag. I was wondering if he had time to tape up my ankle before practice this afternoon."

"Well, he's in the little boys' room right now," she waved her hand in the direction of the small lavatory in the back of the office. She sang out, "Vin—um—Mr. Tag," she paused and giggled superfluously, "You have a visitor." Then, slowly returning her eyes to Damon's six and a half foot frame, she smiled enticingly and said in a low breathy whisper, "Come on in Damon," though why she was whispering was a mystery to Damon. He sat down on the only other chair in the office that wasn't heaped with papers, folders, and binders, and waited awkwardly for what seemed like an eternity while Mrs. Tag leaned up against her husband's cluttered mess of a desk, its surface obscured with even more papers, clipboards, magazines, a dirty jockstrap, and an old first aid kit. Dreama posed seductively, tossing back her long, black hair so that her breasts, unencumbered by the restraints of a bra, were visible, and stared at Damon,

200

appreciating the vision of this young man who sat before her, rather awkwardly but elegantly nonetheless, the poor boy trying to look anywhere in the office except at her. It was true that Damon was a handsome young man, tall, muscular, perfectly proportioned, and with skin the color of rich caramel and eyes the most unusual hue of deepest amber. Finally, and much to Damon's relief, Mr. Tag walked out of the john, wiping his hands on a paper towel.

Not taking her eyes off of Damon, Dreama addressed her husband. "Damon needs you to fix a boo-boo, Vin. And I need to go. See you tonight," Dreama stepped forward toward Vinnie, grasped her husband's fleshy chin that was just beginning to show the signs of an impending middle age and a bit of hard drinking, and kissed him full on the mouth. Damon stared at the floor, but couldn't help but witness Vinnie's playfully slapping at his wife's behind before she giggled her way out of the office.

Vinnie drew in a deep breath and turned toward the young man sitting uncomfortably on a chair that appeared way too small for his large but graceful form. "Ah, Damon, it's great to be young an' 'at, uh? Hey, you gotta' girlfriend Damon?" He laughed, feigning embarrassment, but unmistakably his motives were clear. "Uh-oh. Sorry, that was a dumb question, of course you don't, at least not one here. No colored girls here at Mercyville, uh?"

"No, sir. Look, I can come back—"

201

"Nah, nah, nah, this'll only take a minute." Vinnie pawed through the chaos on his desk and produced a roll of athletic tape. "Here we go. So, you got a girl back in — where're you from? Detroit? Cleveland? You got a little brown sugar back 'ere?"

Damon deftly removed the shoe and sock from his left ankle and presented it to Vinnie. "Cleveland, sir, and no, no girl. I'm pretty busy with school and basketball right now. Maybe when I'm in college."

"College, yeah. Probably play some basketball in college, uh? Lotta' colored kids play basketball in college — good for 'um. Keeps 'um outa' trouble an' 'at." Vinnie, ripping strips of athletic tape from the roll with his teeth, began placing the strips on the corner of his cluttered desk. Damon willed him to shut up and start taping.

"Well, don't know about that, sir. I'd rather play baseball."

"Baseball, uh? Jackie Robinson, uh? Thought all a yinz colored boys were into basketball — Lew Alcindor, Wilt Chamberlain and 'em."

"Well, yes, but I think I have a better shot at baseball than I do basketball. But right now, I'm just focused on this season — well, really our first game against Iroquois Lake on Friday — and school. I wasn't quite prepared for how hard physics is, so, you know…" Christ, get me out of here, now, Damon prayed.

"Physics? What the hell you taking physics for, uh? Thought you wanted to be a baseball player—don't need physics to throw a baseball, unless you're into all that trajectory shit. Hell, I never even took physics! Why you taking physics—you plan on bein' an astronaut? First colored astronaut and all?"

"Well no, I mean, yes, I do want to play baseball, but I doubt I'll make a career out of it."

"Career, uh? You want a career. Well, you know, you could always be a teacher. World needs colored teachers too, uh?"

Damon smiled, lowered his eyes, and nodded his head, finally realizing that a conversation with this goomba was about to go south real fast. And the man wore the city of Pittsburgh like a white sheet with all of his "'an 'at's" and downward inflections at the ends of his asinine questions.

While nearly all of the teachers and students at Mercyville genuinely liked and respected Damon, there was always going to be someone—his father had cautioned him, no matter where he was or who he hung out with—who just couldn't handle the whole black thing. "Get used to it, son," his dad had told him. "Just 'cause they're white and act like they like you don't guarantee that they have any damn sense."

203

Damon imagined how his father would have reacted to Mrs. Tag's lack of damn sense during that earlier and oh-so-obvious display of seduction she performed in front of him. It was bad enough that she acted that way in front of Mr. Tag (Damon nearly laughed out loud imagining his own mother acting like that), and realized that, once again, his old man was right. Tag finished his tape job, and Damon put his sock and shoe back on, stood, and offered his hand to Vinnie, "Thanks, Mr. Tag. Feels much better. I appreciate your time."

Vinnie, somewhat taken aback by Damon's beyond-his-years maturity, returned the handshake, and said slowly, a marked difference from his earlier tone, "Any time, Damon. I'm free any time you need that ankle taped up. Glad to do it. Take care a that ankle, uh?"

Relieved to finally be free of the non-so-enlightened and bigoted creature that was Vinnie Tagliaburro, Damon nodded and turned to leave the cluttered little office. Jesus, he thought to himself, I hope he doesn't slap me on the ass.

Shirl Snyder was sitting at his table at the front of the empty art room flipping through what appeared to be a large portfolio that presumably contained student work when Jim Adamson passed by his open door. Jim backed up, cocked his head, and decided to go on in and pay Shirl a little visit.

"Shirl. How're you doing? How was your Carnegie trip?" Jim looked around the room to make sure that no stray students happened to be lurking about.

Surprised by this impromptu visit, Shirl closed the portfolio, laid down his wax pencil, and answered, "We had a fine time. Weather was good—no snow, nice bus ride, and I really think the kids gained a new appreciation for modern art. Why do you ask?"

"Oh, just curious, that's all." Jim paused for a beat. "You know, I never did get that list of kids who were going on the trip—did you ever put that in my mailbox?"

"Why, I gave it to Ruthie. Didn't she give it to you?"

"No, no—but the trip's come and gone, so don't worry about it, I guess." He paused again, then dove in. "Say, Shirl, are you thinking about getting a haircut any time soon?"

Shirl's brow furrowed in an obvious display of bemusement, "No. I have not scheduled a haircut for any time soon. Is there a problem?"

"Oh, I don't know," Jim decided to take a more lighthearted tact, "but pretty soon, you'll have to climb a tree just to take a piss. Are you going for a 'Rasputin' look?" He laughed, but Shirl Snyder was anything but amused.

"Mr. Adamson," Shirl said formally, dispensing with
205

the typical 'Mr. A.' sobriquet that nearly everyone else used, unless they just called him 'Jim', "the contract between the board of education and the Mercyville Education Association is devoid of any language addressing the length or style of a teacher's hair. Nor does it mandate a particular dress code."

Jim sighed. In his experience, when a teacher chose to invoke a paragraph from the teachers' contract in any discussion with him, a simple request, or a suggestion proffered concerning the teacher's behavior, teaching methods, or outward appearance often turned into a verbal tug-of-war. Jim believed this was about to get ugly unless he could summon enough tact laced with humor to get his point across. "I realize that, Shirl, but come on. That's like the kid who gets in trouble for peeing in the chalk tray then tries to tell me that there's no rule that exists that says he can't pee in the chalk tray. It's common sense. And after all, I doubt either the board or the teacher's union ever imagined that a male teacher would start growing his hair long enough to start looking like some damn hippie. Come on."

Shirl stood his ground. "If you are telling me that my employment here at Mercyville High School is contingent upon the length of my hair, then I shall have to meet with one of our association representatives and request a formal meeting among the three of us to discuss this. Now, if you'll excuse me, I did promise my Honors Art students that I would deliver their graded work to them no later than tomorrow at dismissal."

Jim sighed. So that was how this was going to be played. "Fair enough, Shirl, grow out your hair. Hell, wear it in a goddamn ponytail and tie it in a pink ribbon, I could give a shit. Just remember, Shirl, every teacher here at Mercyville serves as a model for the kids here. Think about this if you were a parent—how would *you* expect *your* kids' teachers to conduct themselves?"

For the first time, Jim saw a flash of something other than contempt in Snyder's eyes. It wasn't an angry look like he would have expected, but something else, something akin to fear—and not a fear of losing his job over the issue of a middle aged man growing his hair long in order to hang onto his youth and vanity, but more like a fear of a man who had something to hide.

I need a drink, Jim thought to himself.

XV

Mr. Cubby lowered his band director's baton and placed it gently on the black music stand waiting patiently for the horns to empty their spit valves before resuming the measure. The band director cum music teacher, a new addition to the staff at Mercyville High School, was a chance for a fresh start for the floundering department. Cubby's predecessor was Mr. Mack, a man who apparently had taken a page from Harold Hill's playbook. Charged with the task of collecting rental money for the instruments purchased years earlier by the school using a secret line of credit (arranged by Mercyville's new principal Jim Adamson and craftily hidden from the Commonwealth's board of accounts), Mr. Mack had decided to help himself to the kitty — money collected from his eager band members' parents — folks who had undoubtedly scraped together the funds needed to rent that trombone or flute or other musical instrument after having been convinced by the flamboyant Mr. Mack that playing an instrument would skyrocket their children into the stratosphere of musical and academic greatness.

Once it came time to pay on the note, it didn't take much detective work on Jim's part — thanks to Ruthie's impeccable bookkeeping skills — to finger the music man for his part in the crime, since Mack, to his credit, had made a very poor burglar. Mack shamefacedly returned the money in exchange for surrendering his teaching license, tendering his resignation, and getting the hell out of town — all without losing the burgeoning popularity of the music program and keeping that line of credit from being discovered.

Once established as Mercyville's new band director, Barry Cubby nearly trembled with girlish excitement when he imagined the wonderful performances he would direct as Mercyville's fresh baby-faced musical genius. He had great plans for his tiny band of troubadours. This year, the band would not only perform at their annual Spring Concert — in the past an affair usually only attended by those parents wishing to see the fruits of their sacrifice and the odd grandparent or two — but would augment their performance schedule by offering their musical talents to the Gym Show. Barry Cubby was excited about the Gym Show that he had heard so much about if only to witness the majesty and magnificence of its director, Mrs. Carol Adamson. He simply had to find a way for his band to be invited to the Show.

Barry had a hopeless crush on Carol Adamson, a safe crush made all the sweeter since he knew that never in a million lifetimes would he be called upon to act on his obsession. Barry was not a handsome man, and he possessed some serious social anxieties, especially when it came to women, so harboring a secret crush on a beautiful woman, —a woman married to the man who had hired him and a woman who may have casually greeted Barry once or twice since the school year started — was a perfect situation for a man who had never once taken a girl on a date and, just like a character plucked from Central Casting, still lived with his mother.

Most band directors do not grow up dreaming to be band directors, but Barry Cubby did. His days as a youth in Pittsburgh where he proudly served as a Fightin' Titan with the Shaler Township High School marching band were the happiest of his young life, and he wanted to recreate that magic here at Mercyville. So eager was he to become a band director, he accepted the job before discovering, sadly, that Mercyville High School had neither a football team nor a marching band.

Not to be deterred, Barry set about finding ways to first earn money for marching band uniforms and, regardless of the band's lack of military style attire, began preparing his small but mighty troupe of musicians to march in formation so at least they could participate in some local parades. Musically, the group was talented, but whether they could walk and play at the same time remained to be seen. Barry had confidence, though, that

211

his young musicians would rise to the occasion and prove to all at Mercyville that the Mercyville High Marching and Concert band under the direction of Mr. Barry Cubby might be small, but would soon prove itself a dynamic musical gift to Mercyville, and could even, perhaps, compel the school board to begin a football program. Barry relished the idea of being the school's first and most influential marching band director, almost as much as he dreamed about the elusive but oh-so-beautiful and charming Carol Adamson.

Barry's best and most accomplished musician, without a doubt, was Tommy Jankovic. The French horn was one of the most challenging of all instruments to master, but Tommy had obviously been born with a natural talent for music; however, his skill at the piano was even more impressive. Barry had spent some time at the school's library last evening—open late on school nights when it became the Mercyville Public Library—and did some research into the sport of gymnastics. There wasn't much literature available at the library's small collection of fiction, non-fiction, and reference materials, except for a couple of how-to picture books and the general entries in the World Book and Encyclopedia Britannica, but he was able to glean some facts about the music used during the floor exercise portion of a gymnastics competition, and he learned that the floor exercise must be accompanied by

212

live piano. If he could convince Carol Adamson that
Tommy Jankovic would be a perfect pianist to accompany
her graceful gymnasts — why, that would go a long way
toward encouraging her to also consider adding to the
Show a small ensemble of musicians as well.

He could then dream about a future where he and
Carol would produce the Gym Show together — music,
dance, and gymnastics all wrapped up in one beautifully
presented package. In his dream world, he could picture
the two of them walking to the center of the gym floor
after the Show's finale, he in a tuxedo and tails and bow
tie; she in a long evening gown complemented with white,
opera-length gloves, each of them with matching
boutonniere and corsage — carnations and babies' breath —
bowing and waving to an adoring and grateful audience,
cascades of flowers tossed at their feet.

"Mr. Cubby?" Tommy Jankovic interrupted Barry's
sweet reverie, "should we..."

"Oh, yes. Horns up! And..."

This guy's dreaming about something weird, thought
Tommy, watching only Cubby's baton, having already
memorized the piece they were in the midst of putting
together. This thought further convinced him about his
newly discovered ability to read minds. Several times
during the school day, he found himself looking into
others' eyes — teachers, classmates, the lunch lady, the

school nurse—and being able to tell exactly what they were thinking. And always, always these people were thinking about Tommy, taking inventory of his soul, telling themselves that this skinny boy with the thick black hair and dark eyes, this boy who was unremarkable until a month ago, had been violated in the most disgustingly embarrassing and horrific manner. They knew. And Tommy could read this in their minds.

This new skill of his had manifested itself shortly after "the incident" as he referred to it in his mind, and though he knew on a logical and scientific level that this ability to peek into the contents of another's thoughts was the stuff of science fiction, on another, more primal level Tommy was convinced that people, even people he hardly knew, were aware that he had been attacked and his body *entered* by Henry Somers. Furthermore, these same people thought of him as having asked for it, as if somehow Tommy had programmed Henry Somers into making the decision to wrestle him to the floor that day and...and...

Much to Tommy's continued relief, Henry Somers had not returned to school after "the incident" and, aside from the conversation that he was forced to have with Mr. A., not a word had been said about "the incident" since. But the damage to Tommy's psyche would be as everlasting as the memory of what had been done to him. His mind reading ability simply rendered him more paralyzed with

214

the fear of being discovered as a...whatever the kind of a person was called who allowed such things to be done to him.

One such mind reading incident occurred during his Honors Art class. As Mr. Snyder was handing back his latest charcoal sketch, he put a bony hand on his shoulder and said, "You know, Tommy, I'm disappointed you're no longer in the photography club. We had a marvelous field trip to the Carnegie Museum over Christmas break. We saw the Warhol exhibit. You would have found it fascinating, I'm sure."

He knows too, Tommy thought, the bile rising in his throat. He might not know exactly what happened, but he knows that I had something done to me. The constant murmur of Snyder's voice long after this encounter further convinced him that not only did people know that he had engaged in something hideous with Henry Somers, but every time someone encountered Tommy, the thoughts about "the incident" ran like a continuously playing movie in their minds. That's what he heard — the everlasting dialogue running through the minds of everyone he had any contact with at Mercyville.

Then, too, Tommy was reminded about the conversation he had had with his brother this past summer. The last time Tommy's saw George before he had left for Fort Bragg, the two of them had sat on the

215

back stoop of the family home trying to catch a breeze off of the lake, their father working in the hot, stuffy shed, and their mother in the small kitchen preparing a feast in order to send George off with poignant memories of what a home-cooked meal was like. George, rolling a joint, sat beside his little brother as Tommy watched with cautious fascination George's deft fingers work the thin paper that would envelope the small, but apparently powerful pinch of marijuana.

"What if Mama sees you doing that?" Tommy said, both mesmerized by his brother's bold openness with his stash of pot and horrified that his brother couldn't have cared less about what their parents might say about George's new habit.

"Don't worry about it. Who gives a shit, and besides, I'll just tell them I'm rolling a cigarette. So, tell me brat," cleverly changing the subject by using the Serbian translation for 'brother', "what kinds of things are you planning to do to keep yourself from going loony here in Hicksville? Still playing the horn? Practicing your piano?" George playfully elbowed the brother of whom he was secretly proud; nevertheless, he felt it his duty to give the little punk a hard time about something.

"Well, that, and school, and photography club. Weren't you in the photography club when you were at Mercyville?"

George stopped rolling, looked out onto the rows of field corn planted adjacent to their property, the corn already at its expected height of knee high by the Fourth of July and said flatly, "Don't do that. Not this year. Just don't."

"How come?" Now Tommy was curious. It wasn't like George to get so serious all of the sudden. Did he think it was un-manly of him to be in the photography club? And if so, why? George had been in the club for his last four years at Mercyville, though he didn't really do much with whatever he learned about photography. The only camera the family owned was an old Brownie that never had any film in it, so pictures at the Jankovic house were usually only taken on special occasions—First Communions, Confirmations, graduation.

"Trust me, just don't. You don't need to be in that mix. Snyder is a freak. He's an asshole. He—he's never called you 'Old Sport', has he? Nah, forget I said that. Just don't do it, okay? Just..." He didn't finish, but stood, put the joint between his lips, pulled out a Zippo lighter and lit it.

"Can I...?" Tommy began.

"No. Not now, not yet. Grow a little hair on your pud first."

Recalling that strange conversation with George, Tommy began to wonder if there wasn't something

217

bizarre about Mr. Snyder that George wasn't telling him —
something that he didn't think he would understand. All
this thinking, this mind reading, and this overwhelming
and paralyzing fear that others knew something about
what had been done to him was truly beginning to unravel
him.

"Ruthie, did Shirl Snyder ever give you a list of those
kids who were going on the Pittsburgh field trip to the
Carnegie Museum — the one they took over Christmas
break?"

"Yes, he did. He said that you had asked that I have a
copy for the club's file. Did you want to see it? I have it
right here." Ruthie rose and opened the tall filing cabinet
next to her desk.

I asked him to give the list to Ruthie? Interesting, Jim
thought. "So he never said anything like, 'Give this to Jim'
or never made an attempt to put it in my mailbox?"

"No. I just assumed that you just wanted me to file it
with the other paperwork for the field trip. Here it is."

Ruthie handed Jim the list. On it were about a dozen
names. "So this is the photography club," he said more to
himself than to Ruthie.

"Is there a problem?" Ruthie asked.

"No. Listen, I'm going to be unavailable for a few
minutes…"

"Before you go back into your office, Henry Somers' teachers are wondering what to do with his Semester I grades," Ruthie said, hoping that she would be able to take care of this now so that she could get back to her other work and leave on time for a change.

"In a minute."

Jim retreated into his office, pulled out the 1969 edition of "The Walleye," Mercyville's student yearbook. He flipped through the pages until he found the 'Organizations and Clubs'. Mercyville had a Future Homemakers of America club, a Future Farmers of America chapter — one of the school's largest organizations — the Tri-Hi-Y, a girls service club, a French and a German club, various musically themed clubs. He reached the end of the 'Organizations and Clubs' section, but there was no photography club included. He looked again. Then he looked at the list of photography club members still clutched in his big hand.

All boys.

Jim sat down behind his desk. Something was not right with all of this, and Jim's sense of foreboding, a trait of his that had served him well in the past, was telling him that Shirl Snyder was up to something foul. He looked again at the list of boys' names — boys who had been slated to go on the Pittsburgh field trip. Henry Somers' name was on the list, but since he still had yet to reappear after the incident on the stage, he obviously did not accompany the rest of the boys. Jim tried to find some connection with the names, but there was nothing that the boys on the list had in common—some were athletes, some were FFA members, some were in the band, but there was not one particular defining attribute that linked these boys together. All boys. Just what kind of fucked up freak was Shirl Snyder?

That Shirl Snyder had referenced a paragraph from the Teachers' Association's agreement with the Board of Education about something so meaningless as the length of his hair made Jim wonder suspiciously if Snyder had consulted his copy of the agreement that covered the dismissal of teachers. Ever since the mid-1960s and the rise in the number of teachers organizing themselves into 'Associations'—unions, really, but don't say 'union' around them—that fine line that Jim had to walk concerning appropriate teacher behavior was never as prominently shoved under his nose as it was now. In a show of comradeship, even his own wife had joined the Association, if for no other reason than to assure her colleagues that she was one of them even though she was married to the boss. Most teachers never felt the need to cite passages in the agreement to Jim since, generally, a good working relationship existed between him and the staff—he took care of his teachers, and they, in turn,

220

remained loyal to him. He defended them against angry parents, against students who wanted to argue about too much homework or a grade awarded unfairly, and against any in the community who railed against the amount of money teachers made "just for working nine months out of the year." This, though, this feeling he had — and for now it was just a feeling — that Shirl Snyder might be violating one or more boys in the most disgusting way imaginable rendered Jim nearly apoplectic.

But it was just a feeling. He had no proof. He had no allegations. But Henry Somers' name on that list jumped out at him as what he felt was a sure sign from God that what Henry had done to Tommy Jankovic on the stage that November afternoon was somehow tied to that sick son-of-a-bitch upstairs in the art room.

He looked at the list again. "And I gave that bastard the green light to take these boys all the way to Pittsburgh on a chartered bus. Jesus Christ," Jim whispered to himself, beginning to feel his heart thud in his chest, a cold sweat break out on his forehead.

Jim walked back out into the outer office, looked around to see if anyone else was there, and addressed Ruthie. "Ruthie, were you aware that every student on this list is male? Does that seem odd to you?"

"Well, yes, and no. Yes, because I think girls might be more interested in photography if Mr. Snyder would ask

221

them to be a part of the club, and no, because once they see how many boys are in the club, they might be scared the boys will make fun of them. Does that make sense?"

"I suppose," Jim said, trying to ease the pressure in his chest. "I noticed that Henry Somers' name is on the list. He doesn't look like the type of kid who'd be interested in photography — in fact, I can't see what any of the boys on the list have in common, except they're in this all-boys club."

"Oh, I'm sure Henry's in the club because Mr. Snyder is his father's landlord out there on Geist Road. Mr. Snyder owns all that property that Mr. Somers farms."

"You don't say." Jim at once saw black spots in front of his eyes and felt as if he was going to throw up.

XVI

Every Sunday morning, Carol dressed up her three kids in their Sunday best, donned a modestly cut dress or a skirt and blouse, draped a lace mantilla piously over her blond curls, and dragged the four of them off to mass at Immaculate Heart of Mary. When Jim and Carol married—quietly, nearly in secret, in a small, non-denominational chapel in Winchester, Virginia, with two witnesses pulled romantically off the sidewalk as if they were in a Gregory Peck and Audrey Hepburn film—Jim had already agreed to raise any children they might have in the Catholic faith in which Carol grew up. Carol did not consider herself a devout Catholic—she practiced birth control the minute the pill hit the market, she married a non-Catholic who only attended mass on Christmas Eve, Easter, and the children's First Communions, and she often released her tension in the form of a litany of swear words that would have made a sailor blush. But she was steadfast in her mission to raise her three children in the faith, and if Jim didn't go to mass with them each Sunday, he did, at least, manage to start dinner and throw in a load of laundry while she was gone.

Carol was nearly militant with regard to cleanliness

223

and neatness, and prior to the start of this school year, Jim
had finally caved in and hired a woman to come every
Friday to clean the house. Before this uncharacteristic
financial sacrifice on Jim's part, their Saturdays had been
spent with Carol, her nightgown tucked up into the elastic
legs of her panties, flying through the bedrooms changing
sheets, dusting, running the Electrolux, barking orders to
the kids about straightening up their closets, their
drawers, and furiously mopping floors, scrubbing the
kitchen, and cleaning the bathroom. Seldom was the
family finished with all of the cleaning on Saturday, so the
housekeeping ritual would continue on Sunday afternoons
after mass. The weekends soon became Jim's least favorite
days of the week, and he knew if he was going to keep his
blood pressure in check and his heart from launching him
into another cardiac arrest, or most importantly (to him),
maintain his sanity, that he would have to hire someone
to come in and clean the house. It wasn't a perfect
solution to Carol's obsession with cleanliness—she still
insisted that no one could clean her house as well as she
could—but at least dear Aggie cleaned well enough for
Carol to grudgingly admit that the cleaning lady was at
least up to scratch.

Thus, Sundays for Jim became a peaceful island in an
otherwise crowded sea of duties, obligations, problems,
and headaches. He certainly did not miss the Sunday

ritual of church; using the time, instead, to read the entire edition of the Erie Times, spending a considerable chunk of that time perched on the toilet, free from the intrusion of three kids clamoring for either his attention or the use of the bathroom.

Jim had grown up in the Methodist church and his parents, seeing the practice of their faith as a duty, an obligation, and a ticket to everlasting life, dragged little Jim to church and Sunday school. Jim was vocal about his disdain for organized religion—effectively paralyzing his parents with a real fear that Jim would grow into a heathen like the Chinese people their church took such great pains to convert to Christianity through their overseas missions. Jim's parents simply could not understand why their second born, their otherwise compliant and perfectly behaved young man, would so stubbornly resist the quiet calm of the sanctuary. Millicent, ever the example of piety and spiritual conformity, had faithfully continued her family's tradition even into her adulthood, now without Bernard, of course, and often substituted for the organist at the Methodist Church in Mercyville. Jim was content to let Carol be in charge of their children's spiritual life, though—it was something she was good at— as long as he didn't have to get dressed and squeeze his heaving bulk into a pew at Immaculate Heart of Mary each Sunday and risk breaking the kneeler in front of him with his football-ravaged knees.

It was on one of those Sunday mornings in early January after mass as Carol and the children were shivering in the car waiting for the windshield to defrost that Carol had announced to the three kids, but mostly to her youngest, "Guess what I'm doing tomorrow?"

Jimmy and Jenny, brows furrowed, looked at each other, but Julie knew exactly what her mother would be doing tomorrow, and she had been dreading what was about to become the worst Sunday of her life ever since she had announced to her entire kindergarten class that Stanley Czerniawski was to be her date for The 1970 Gym Show.

"Julie, I'm coming over to your school tomorrow to visit the kindergarten classrooms. I think you already know that I picked you, my little bugaboo, to be the flower girl, but who do you think I'm going to pick to be the crown bearer?"

Jenny began naming various boys from the two kindergarten classes that she, in her experienced opinion, would make good crown bearers; Jimmy could not have cared less.

Julie found her voice and proactively spoke. "Mummy, there's only one boy who I want to be the crown bearer. He's my best friend. He was there at the show—'member, the show I was on with the clown?"

Julie, painfully blocking out the memory of the cowboy on whose boots she had splattered urine all over, tried to begin to set the framework for her justification of Stanley's appointment as crown bearer, but all this bold move on Julie's part did was to cause Jenny to erupt in hysterical laughter.

"Oh, you mean the show that *I* was on with the cowboy and the show where *you* peed your pants? That show?" Jenny convulsed in the backseat, clutching her belly and wiping fake tears from her big, green eyes.

"Who are you talking about, Julie? I was thinking about that nice boy Ronnie Crawley — or, or, what about Tommy Lindstrom?" Carol said, still blissfully unaware that her plan for Gym Show perfection was about to have the first of several monkey wrenches thrown into it.

"His name is Stanley, and I want him." Julie lowered her head and said once more, in a whisper, "I want him."

"Well, Julie, when I come over to your classroom tomorrow, you can quietly point him out to me, and we'll go from there. How's 'bout that, honeybun? But remember, the final decision is Mummy's."

I want him, Julie thought to herself.

Jim used his time alone while Carol and the kids were at church to sort through his thoughts. He had already decided the previous Friday, before the glorious victory that the basketball team had delivered upon the evil Iroquois Lake Warriors (despite Coach Montgomery's lament that his expected big man — Henry Somers, the horse he was counting on for pulling down rebounds — was mysteriously, not part of the team), that he would pay a visit on Monday to the school's attorney, his friend Gordon Agnew.

Gordon was one of those "regular guys" Jim could sit down with and have a beer. Both Gordon and Jim had been the first two lucky guys to be conscripted from Lake County in 1941 prior to their entre into the European Theatre of World War II and did their basic training together, so the two of them had enjoyed a rare and uncommon bond that seldom existed between two "regular guys" in post-war life. Once both of them had returned relatively unscathed and began their respective careers, Jim had recommended Gordon be named as the school's attorney shortly after Gordon had graduated from law school at Pitt. Gordon had handled Jim's divorce gratis; thus, an easily exchanged camaraderie existed between the two.

Two years ago, Gordon's wife Ginny had been diagnosed with breast cancer, and after several painful surgeries and two agonizing rounds of chemotherapy, Gordon had announced to Jim that Ginny was in the 'all clear'. Somehow, the threat of Jim losing his own wife in such a devastating way had made him treasure his friendship with Gordon that much more. He and Gordon had recently gone to a rare lunch together at The Boat Club in Iroquois Lake last summer — a lunch that turned into a nearly two-day bender. Once the lunch ended, the two men, drunk and full of themselves, had driven up to Gordon's fishing camp in Tionesta to continue their drunken reminiscing. They returned to civilization the next morning. Jim, sheepish, disheveled, and painfully hung over, came home to a wife who sat waiting for him in the living room, a packed suitcase foreshadowing one of the nastiest fights either of them had ever had. The battle between the two of them had ended only when Jim had finally confessed to Carol that the thought of ever losing her had made him nearly lose his mind.

Despite Boots Malloy's dire threat about revealing to anyone the wretched details of this sordid business, Jim's plan was to lay it all out for Gordon — the stage incident, the board's stalemate concerning the stage incident, and, most recently, Jim's gut feeling that Shirl Snyder had something to do with not only the stage incident but might just be perpetuating his lust for boys by sponsoring the only club at Mercyville that was populated by an all-male roster. Add to that Jim's recent discovery, thanks to the revelation provided by his loyal minion Ruthie, that Henry Somers' farm was not owned by Henry Somers but was, in fact, owned by none other than Shirl Snyder, who served as Henry Somers' landlord.

When Jim was in elementary school in Pittsburgh — Brookline Elementary, one of the country's more progressive grammar schools at the time — his teacher had administered to him an Alfred Binet IQ test. Jim, usually not one to give much thought to what the adults in his life asked him to do (unless it was church) complied, and, apparently, the results of this IQ test revealed that Jim fell into the category of 'genius'.

While that in itself was meaningless to Jim, what was even more preposterous was that the teacher who had administered the test took things a step further and asked that she enter him into a study at the University of Pittsburgh, presumably to be subjected to even more horror movie-like tests in order to gauge whether his "genius" was a natural consequence of his upbringing and genetics or a reflection upon Brookline Elementary. Though lacking formal education themselves, both of Jim's parents had no interest in their son becoming a guinea pig for some nascent research on giftedness, nor did any of this interest young Jim, and he had taken the 'genius' title with the proverbial grain of salt. That was where his recognized 'genius' had ended.

Over the course of the ensuing years, however, Jim did begin to realize that, among other things like a
230

photographic memory, an almost otherworldly facility with numbers, and the gift for reading volumes of text in the time it took most folks to read one chapter, the one talent he possessed that was the most valuable to him was his innate ability for ferreting out the wheat from the chaff. Carol, who he often suspected was much smarter than he was on just about every level, had appropriately named this skill his "bullshit detector."

Well, that bullshit detector was on red alert, and it was blinking in rapid succession thanks to Jim's ever-increasing belief that Shirl Snyder was molesting boys at Mercyville High School.

"Julie, I don't understand," Carol said evenly, her fork poised mid-air hoping against hope that her youngest daughter had not taken it upon herself to make such a monumental decision all by herself. "What do you mean *you've* already picked the crown bearer?"

Julie's five-but-soon-to-be-six year old self drew upon every sense of little girl logic that she could muster and explained how, in her mind, that it was only fitting of her to have asked Stanley to be the crown bearer since he had so gallantly refrained from mentioning her shame that had resulted from the night she wet her pants so spectacularly at the television station. Years later, Julie would give herself way more credit for her conscious decision to

231

reward Stanley for his chivalry and discretion than her mother had at the time—the very same virtues that Stanley himself would not recognize he possessed until years later as the CEO of a successful and very lucrative software company he founded employing hundreds of talented designers and engineers. No, at this moment, Julie could only foresee in her future a spanking, one delivered soundly and painfully, with Carol utilizing, as usual, one of her own size five Puma tennis shoes as a substitute for her rather small right hand.

The ensuing silence at the dinner table was broken only by Jenny's request to be excused. Jim granted her leave then asked that Jimmy excuse himself from the table so that he and Carol could talk with Julie and find out just how deeply she had dug this hole.

"Julie Anne, I want you to tell me exactly what you said to this Stanley boy. Do I even *know* him? What's his last name?" Carol was becoming increasingly angry with her youngest, and Julie began to regret her decision to honor Stanley, even though she knew that her newfound loyalty to him would be everlasting.

"I can't say his last name, but it starts with a 'C'. He's Stanley C."

Jim interjected his point of view as gently as possible, tiptoeing that fine line between pissing off his wife and watching his youngest child suffer through her own

232

heartbreak. "I think that you had a very good reason for wanting to pick this boy, Julie. That shows what a nice little girl you are. You obviously are a good friend, and that's important. What Mummy is trying to get you to understand, though, is that this was supposed to have been *her* decision, not yours. Did you ever tell Mummy that you wanted Stanley to be the crown bearer?"

"No. Mummy's been busy with Gym Show and cheerleading."

"Oh for Christ's sake, Julie, you've had plenty of opportunities to talk to me." She turned in frustration to her husband, her voice beginning to crescendo. "I can't believe this, Jim. As if I don't have enough problems going on, what with Vinnie and his teenaged wife poking their dago noses into my business. This is my show, Jim! Mine! And now this." Carol was close to tears.

Julie knew this discussion was not over, and she dreaded the rest of the day and the next day when Carol would either pick someone that she herself had deemed worthy enough to be the crown bearer, thus humiliating Julie and devastating poor Stanley, or would accept Julie's appointment of Stanley as the Captain Nelson to her Jeannie, the Darren to her Samantha, her special boy who would hold her hand as she scattered rose petals across the gym floor to herald the entrance of the May Queen and her dashing escort.

233

It's about to get much worse, my dear, Jim thought. If Carol was at sixes and sevens over some little boy her daughter had picked to be her May Queen escort, wait until she sees who shows up for Gym Show practice tomorrow after school. Friday morning Jim had given Vinnie the green light to include a small number of boys in this year's Show.

Should have probably mentioned this to Carol earlier, Jim said to himself. Guess it slipped my mind.

XVII

Cathy Snow finished tying her signature baby pink satin ribbon in her nearly white shoulder-length hair, securing it on the sides with matching nearly-white bobby pins, grabbed a can of Aqua Net hairspray, and lacquered her coif with a copious halo of hydrocarbons. Satisfied that her 'do was going nowhere, she sat before her vanity, straightened her brush, comb, and mirror set, tidied up the variety of other tools used to enhance her already flawless gorgeousness, and smiled as she thought about the day ahead.

Unlike most students who woke in the dark, cold, wintry dawn of January dreading the thought of leaving cozy beds piled high with quilts and wool blankets, Cathy looked forward to school today with an enthusiasm that was rather uncommon among girls her age. Every day was a good day to be Cathy Snow, but today, in particular, she was eager to get to school, to be seen, to talk with her friends, whispering behind a cupped hand some little bit of harmless gossip, to bat her baby-blues at her teachers, both male and female, resulting in their continued admiration for her — this gorgeous creature who was so polite, so energetic, and so attentive and engaging during class, to flirt with the boys in her classes, though they and she knew that nothing would ever come of her overtures, and, in short beguile everyone who passed her way. Her campaign was about to begin, and though she might be the only girl at Mercyville who secretly electioneered for the title of May Queen, she knew, also, that her eventual selection would serve as the cherry on top of the ice cream sundae that represented the enchanted life she was privileged to lead.

She untied the outer layer of her peignoir set, allowing the gossamer garment to float lazily on top of her already made bed while she herself floated on kitten-heeled marabou mules across her spacious and lushly carpeted bedroom. She approached her large walk-in closet and surveyed her vast array of wintertime outfits. Today she would have to dress for the weather, so that included boots, but she most definitely would wear one of her wool skirts, shortened to a length that was short enough to be fashionable, but not so short that her virtue would ever be in question. Her long legs in knee high boots, short wool checked skirt...what to wear on the top, to increase the collection of stares at her two favorite assets? A pink, angora sweater set would enhance the lovely line of her long neck while accentuating her generously large but perfectly round breasts. She accessorized with a silver necklace, a cheerleader's megaphone charm dangling at the end, a gold circle pin, and Biff's oversized class ring wrapped in the exact shade of angora as her sweater. Perfection.

Cathy Snow was Mercyville's pampered princess, the only cheerleader who had managed to charm Ken Montgomery into allowing her and the rest of the varsity cheerleaders to sit with the players during the bus ride back from away basketball games on the odd nights when Mrs. A. drove herself home from the venue—the same Mrs. A. who would *never*, when she was present, have allowed such potentially immoral behavior among her girls. Charming Coach Montgomery was only one of many tricks Cathy Snow had in her arsenal of feminine wiles. Cathy had the distinct ability to make anyone in her midst fall hopelessly in love with her, though her rate of reciprocity did not match the ferociousness of her conquests. Not satisfied with the assortment of boys at Mercyville, Cathy chose instead to look afield for her prince and so she dated the quintessential boyfriend Biff Lord, a popular boy from a neighboring school--a gifted athlete who served as the quarterback for Fairlyville High School's winning football team and was slated this fall to don the blue and white for Joe Paterno at Penn State.

Cathy was a senior, and after graduation, she would become a flight attendant—not a "stewardess"! She was actively learning a foreign language in order to enhance

237

her job prospects with her newly acquired high school French. Her plan was to work as a flight attendant for Pan Am or TWA, travel to Paris, maybe even live there until Biff graduated from Penn State, and then she would return home to marry Biff, who would, by then, have become a professional football player, hopefully for the Pittsburgh Steelers so that Cathy could remain nearby. If he didn't play football, her plan was for Biff to become a doctor or a lawyer, in which case she would simply continue flying the friendly skies until he was ready to support her, and *then* they would get married. Either way, she had no plans to live anywhere permanently but in western Pennsylvania. Her parents meant *everything* to her, and she couldn't imagine living far away from them for very long. As the only child of Norm and Ruthie Snow, Cathy wanted for nothing and was accustomed to having everything.

The world as she knew it belonged to Cathy and, as her father had reminded her on more than one occasion, "You are special, remember that. You're a 'Snow'. You're my Snow Princess! And nothing is too good for my Snow Princess!" Cathy's presence created magic wherever she happened to be—cheering on the Mercyville Anglers in her green wool cheerleader's sweater and pleated green and white skirt while showcasing her long, smooth legs, or in her classes where she held court, each of her teachers

238

safely tucked in the palm of her delicate hand with the perfectly groomed nails, or as the daughter of the town's mayor living in the closest thing that Mercyville had to a grand home, the Snow Palace, perched on a hill and set back from Main Street, it's Victorian façade, leaded glass windows, and wrap around porch making it well-deserving of its title. Even her French teacher, Monsieur Schmidt, who often broke out in hives, a cold sweat, and a raging erection whenever Cathy's strikingly blond hair, beautifully assembled visage, and oh-so lovely form (oh, those breasts!) graced the cinder block walls of his classroom, had gushingly declared once that "Votre français est impeccable!" She was loved, she was adored, and how could any student at Mercyville High School possibly wish for *anyone* but Cathy Snow to reign as their May Queen?

While it was true that Cathy walked in sunshine, she did have one particular secret—a crush on someone who was really everything that Cathy could ever want in a boyfriend--tall, devastatingly handsome, athletic, smart. During the two classes that she had with him, all she could do was stare at him, watch him move, listen to his smooth voice. He possessed the same attributes as her boyfriend Biff Lord, but that wasn't the reason for her obsession with him, and besides, she wasn't *really* in love-love with Biff. She was, however, hopelessly in love with her crush.

239

There was just one problem.

Her father and everyone else in the town of Mercyville would shit a gold brick if they knew that her crush was Damon Ettinger.

Jim hung up the phone, leaned back in his chair, and clasped his hands behind his head. He had just spoken to Gordon Agnew's secretary, and the news that Gordon and Ginny were on their way to the Cleveland Clinic and wouldn't be back for a few days was bothersome — selfishly, it meant that Jim wouldn't have the opportunity to bend Gordon's ear about this whole business with Shirl Snyder and his possible connection with the Henry Somers incident, but even more ominous was that though Gordon's secretary Sally gave no indication that this was the case, Jim had detected a rather fearful tone in her voice that led Jim to believe that this trip of Gordon's to take his wife to the Cleveland Clinic was not routine, nor was it planned.

Well, at least I can keep my promise to the board not to run my mouth about all of this, Jim thought. Damn. It was only ten in the morning, and this was the second bit of news he could have lived without; the first was his wife's declaration to him that he was, indeed, the world's biggest shithead, that she couldn't believe that she had married him, and that he had better get used to sleeping on the couch for a while. To say that she did not take the news of Jim's approval for Vinnie's additions to the Gym Show well was a gross understatement. It was a good thing the guns he kept in the house weren't loaded.

So much for taming that shrew, Jim thought. She'll just have to get used to it. Jim could think of no good reason to deny Vinnie his request; in fact, had he told Vinnie 'no', the fallout would have been a hell of a lot worse than the prospect of sleeping on the couch. Yes, Carol would get over it, and in time, when the dust settled, she'd be pissed that she hadn't come up with the idea herself a long time ago.

Carol was high strung, she was emotional, and she was used to getting her way. If he knew anything about Carol, he knew this: It may have been Vinnie's idea initially, but he had better step back, because the man had no idea what he was in for. It wouldn't be long, Jim thought, until Carol put her little stamp on the entire Show — boys and all. That, or she would end up murdering Vinnie Tagliaburro, which, if that was the case, they were all screwed. Oh, hell. In his experience, these things had a way of working themselves out, and who knows? It might prove beneficial to the entire Show if some testosterone was injected into the whole thing.

Reaching for his cigarettes, Jim looked up at the chart hanging above his credenza to see when Shirl Snyder had his prep period. He may not have any proof that Snyder was buggering boys, but he sure as hell was going to stop him from carrying on with this all-male photography club of his. The yearbook would just have to make do without the services of Mr. Snyder and his merry (or not so merry) band of budding photojournalists or whatever-the-hell Snyder thought he was preparing these boys to do. Hell, Jim thought, if I have to hire photographers out of my own pocket I will before I'll let that twisted up fuck do any more damage.

"Good," Jim whispered to himself. "He's free right now. '"The time has come," the walrus said'."

"I'm afraid I don't understand. What does this have to do with...with... girls?" Shirl Snyder sat before him massaging his bony chin with his thumb and forefinger; wrinkling his long nose at the word 'girls' as if he had just smelled something foul. Jim wanted to shove the palm of his hand upward into the man's septum, driving the ethmoid bones into his skull thus rendering him brain dead, but he resisted the urge.

"It's all about fairness, Shirl. You know, it won't be long before we'll have to start offering girls the opportunity to play sports—you know, like basketball, softball. I just think having an all-boys club is kind of, well, out of touch with today's generation."

242

"The FFA is an all-boys' club. Are you going to suspend their club privileges as well? What about the FHA — that, Mr. Adamson, is an all-*girls* club." Again, he wrinkled his nose as if a foul odor had wafted through the office. "Will they, too, suffer the same indignities that you're imposing upon the photography club? And the Gym Show." Snyder's eyes narrowed, he removed his hand from his bony chin, and pointed at Jim with one, long, bony finger. It was all Jim could do not to grab that finger and snap it in half like the dead limb of a tree. "Certainly, you wouldn't risk your own wife's ire by revoking her right to assemble her girls every night after school in preparation for that ridiculously expensive and nearly pornographic parade of half nude adolescents flopping all over the gym floor?"

Fuck you, you son-of-a-bitch, don't you dare make any reference to my wife you sick-ass, sorry excuse for a man. "Funny you should mention that, Shirl. Just this morning, Carol and Vinnie decided together that, for the very first time, boys will be included in the Gym Show — a tradition that I'm sure will carry on throughout the coming years. You know, that same Gym Show--that ridiculous parade of half nude adolescents..."

Shirl interrupted, "Does this have anything at all to do with our earlier conversation regarding the length of my hair? I believe I made myself clear when I referenced the portion of..."

Jim wondered just how much more of this faggot-assed fuck he was going to be able to stand. "Wear a goddamn dress to school tomorrow, Shirl, I don't give a shit. All I'm telling you is that, as of this moment, your all-boys' photography club is no longer part of the organizational repertoire of Mercyville High School. Do you want to tell the boys or do you want me to tell them?"

Snyder blew a billow of hot air out of his ugly dragon nose and rose to leave. "This isn't over, Mr. Adamson. I have every right to..."

"Oh, it is over, Shirl. It is most *decidedly* over."

Jim stood as well, because the sooner Snyder left his office, the healthier it was going to be for the son-of-a-bitch, and for himself as well. Both men became startled, though, as Ruthie burst into the room, a commotion of girls' high-pitched babble in the outer office the apparent reason for her interruption. "We need you, Mr. A. Some of the girls from Mrs. Pennycroft's class are here. There's something wrong with Mrs. Pennycroft."

Jim moved out from behind his desk as fast as his three-hundred pounds would allow him, shoved past that prick Snyder, and ran as best he could out of the office and toward the stairway. On the way, he skidded to a halt at Connie Silver's door. The school nurse was using a long pair of tweezers to pick out the lice from some poor seventh grade girl's long, stringy hair. "We need you, Connie. Upstairs — Doris' room."

Connie Silver dropped the tweezers and followed a surprisingly expeditious Jim upstairs where they were met with a gaggle of scared, sniffling girls outside of the Home Ec. room. Both Jim and Connie had stopped short at the doorway, Jim heaving and out of breath and Connie sighing audibly.

Doris Pennycroft, her head slumped awkwardly upon her desk with her mouth agape and sitting in a pool of her own urine and feces, had decided to retire after all.

The Gym Show

XVIII

Carol sat quietly while Vinnie, who was obviously serious about this idea of his and had apparently given a great deal of thought to his plan, described for her how the boys he was planning to include in the Gym Show would fit into the overall program. Knowing there was little she could do to put a stop to this nonsense—Jim had seen to that—she sat, sphinx- like, and let him blather away.

"Well? Whaddya' think? We end the whole shebang with a finale where the boys an' the girls build, I don't know, some sorta pyramid structure," Vinnie's hands were flying all around his head in an effort to illustrate his great idea. "The boys can lift up the girls and they can do some sorta pose or somethin' like 'at, y'know, real pretty-like, and…"

"Have you thought about attire? What the boys will wear? I'm not sure there's money in the budget for more uniforms. Would they wear white stirrup trousers, suspenders? I suppose they can wear white tank t-shirts. And footwear…"

"Yeah, we got time, don't you worry. Listen, Cupcake…"

"Vinnie, if we're going to work together on this, do
247

not call me 'Cupcake'."

"Sorry, hun." Vinnie tried looking sheepish; Carol all but rolled her eyes. What a chauvinistic pig. He made her blood boil.

"So, Carol...we're okay? You're okay with this?"

"I don't have much of a choice, Vinnie, do I? I'll tell you what, though, whatever you do, — whatever *we* do together, it has to be *perfect*. The Show is much more than just a bunch of girls prancing and tumbling across the gym. And the thought and planning that goes into it is much, much more than anyone here at Mercyville realizes. It's our way of showcasing the talents of our girls — and now our boys — to not only Mercyville, but to the surrounding communities. It is, most decidedly, what sets us apart from other schools. It's special." Carol's voice lowered nearly to a whisper. "I want the Gym Show to become a tradition that remains the cornerstone of student life here at Mercyville for generations to come."

"Whoa! Damn, Carol. Well, okay! I get it. Yeah, yeah." He clapped his hands together and continued, "So, I've already lined up about a dozen or so boys, an' 'at, who're interested, and, well, we'll be at practice tonight. We'll go from there, uh?"

"Okay, well, there are some things you should know before practice tonight. First, the younger girls are going to be shy around all those boys. They'll be self-conscious

248

about being seen in their gym suits, and they'll be awkward when they do their tumbling passes down the mats. Could you please talk to your boys about this — try to get them to understand that I will have no one making fun of any of my girls? I want this to be a smooth modification in our practice routine. No snide remarks, no locker room language, and no swearing. Secondly, the older girls are going to act like fools around all those boys and probably won't get much accomplished unless we stay on them. They're going to flirt; they're going to act coy. Let *me* handle them. I will have no hogging around during our practice time. Now, the younger girls, believe it or not, are going to be the better gymnasts — they've not yet grown into their bodies…"

"Yeah, yeah, Carol, I know all about boobs and asses, what else?"

Jesus, Carol sighed.

"Jim, what a nice surprise!" Millicent was not used to hearing from her brother long distance. "It's Jim!" he heard Millicent whisper to Bernard who was probably sitting in his leather wing chair in front of a fake Florida fireplace reading some bullshit existentialist crap by Nietzsche himself and smoking a goddamn pipe.

"Actually, Pippa, I want to keep this private, between us," he said then quickly explained once he imagined the look of alarm on her face. "It's nothing bad—it's just about that thing that Mother had said at the dinner table at Thanksgiving."

"Well of course. Let me walk into the lanai and talk," She called out to Bernard, "Dear, could you keep an eye on Mother? Jim wants to go over some details with me about the trust."

The trust, Jim thought. Oh, that. Dearest Millicent, who had never been blessed with children of her own, had, out of the generosity of her heart and her love for Jim and Carol's children, set up a trust for each of Jim and Carol's kids; nothing too large, but she had wanted to do something special when Jimmy was born, and, in typical Millicent fashion, she wanted her gift to be lasting, practical, and of some significance, so she, with Jim's blessing, set about to form a trust that would pay for Jimmy's college education. Once Jenny was born, she did the same for her.

The sticking point, of course, was Bernard. Money was not an issue for Bernard; his family left him very comfortably well off, but he somehow felt that whatever part of the estate that Millicent would inherit from her parents should go to both of them in exchange for their caring for Ida in her declining years.

Millicent, however, wished to keep *her* money within her family of origin since she and Bernard had no children

250

together—just Bernard's three daughters from his marriage to the invalid. Bernard's daughters had married well, and Millicent was happy for them—each lived comfortable lives in large, well- appointed homes, and their children-- Bernard's grandchildren-- were privately educated. Millicent, however, wanted something of her own, so she wished to gift her nephew and nieces with a college education, and if Bernard disagreed with her, well, he would just have to learn to live with it.

The problem arose when Millicent had attempted to re-structure the trust after Julie's birth. Bernard had put his foot down at that point, saying that it was ridiculous that Carol was still having children with a nearly elderly husband, and what if they had even more? He had refused to sign his portion of the agreement. To date, the matter was still in the hands of Millicent and Bernard's lawyer. The issue of the trust remained the one wave that threatened to capsize the otherwise unsinkable boat of Bernard and Millicent's marriage.

"So first, tell me what's new. How are Carol and the children enjoying the snowy weather?"

Jim filled Millicent in on how the kids were doing in school, their sled riding parties they had begun organizing with the neighborhood kids after school with him in charge of making enough hot chocolate to keep them all from freezing to death. He had even, one Sunday, used an

251

old pallet to build a ramp wedged into the steep hill behind the house, had poured water over it, and let it freeze over, creating a dangerously slick but wildly popular addition to the whole sledding experience. This was the same hill where, in a few years' time, he would attempt to replicate his father's fruit orchard, but for now, it served as the neighborhood kids' after school entertainment. This kept 'J Cubed', as he had started calling his three squirrelly offspring, out of his hair while Carol was at cheerleading and Gym Show practice after school.

He also told Millicent of Doris Pennycroft's dramatic exit from this life, complete with gory details, and how Vinnie Tagliaburro's wife Dreama was now planted, for the time being, in Doris' place in Room 212 and would remain until the rest of the school year or until he could find another Home Ec. teacher. Home Ec. teachers were rather difficult to find since fewer girls of this generation were satisfied with becoming women who appreciated the fine art of homemaking, so it looked like Dreama was here to stay—for now.

"But what I really want to ask you is about that thing that Mother had said—remember? At Thanksgiving?"

"Yes, I remember. What do you think she meant by all of that? Do you think it's possible that the Somers' may have had some relatives living by us back in Pittsburgh?"

252

"That's what I'm thinking. I wish there was someone who *wasn't* losing her mind who we could ask..."

At once Millicent gasped, "Jim, I know who we can ask! Bridie Rooney, only that's not her married name; it's Bridie Hannigan. She was our shop girl, remember? Oh, you probably don't remember, you were much too young, but she worked for us for a number of years, a nice Irish girl. We exchange Christmas cards each year; in fact, I have hers right...oh, I'll find it. Yes, she's still living in that area of Pittsburgh. I could write to her and ask what she knows about the Somers'."

"Would you? That would be helpful, Pippa." He considered whether he should tell her anything else; Millicent, having been the headmistress at an all-girls' school in Philadelphia knew about the need for confidentiality regarding student matters, but maybe if she knew the whole sordid tale she would have some insight into how he should proceed.

"Look, Pippa, you're probably wondering why I'm so anxious about this —"

"Jim, I do wonder, but I also know that it isn't always appropriate to share information; that is, unless there's anything I could do to help."

So Jim did what he had hoped to do during a meeting with Gordon Agnew — he told her everything from start to finish, even the gruesome details about the incident,

253

which, the more he thought about it, the more he was beginning to believe that it was indeed a rape.

Millicent listened without interrupting, and when Jim was finished, he heard her sigh deeply and sorrowfully.

"First of all, I am so sorry that you have to deal with this, Jim. I can't even imagine how tortured you must be over this—this, whatever 'this' is. Secondly, Jim, I think what you're doing is wise; however, I would not share with anyone what you've just told me. And third and most disturbing of all, that boy, Jim, that poor boy—what did you say his name was? Tommy? That poor child is going to need some help getting over this. I'm not sure what kind of help—maybe he could talk to the guidance counselor or maybe there's a psychiatrist in Erie or somewhere—even in Pittsburgh—with whom he could talk this through—I don't know, and I don't even know how you'd arrange something like that. I'm just trying to think about what I would do in your place, but I've only dealt with girls. Bless his heart...bless his poor heart." It was entirely possible that Jim's tale had brought Millicent to tears, but he couldn't be sure. He heard her draw in a deep breath and continue, "But for now, I'll write to Bridie, and as soon as I hear back from you, I'll forward whatever information she provides, all right? I love you, brother. Please take care of yourself."

"And you do the same, Pippa. Thank you," Jim nearly

The Gym Show

choked back a sob he loved his sister so much.

The Gym Show

XIX

The hired man climbed to the top of the corn silo only after he had checked to see that the fans used to dry the corn were working properly. He was checking to make sure that corn had not caked up the sides of the silo, and if it had, he was going to have to auger it down. It was a dangerous job, climbing up the silo's side, especially now with thick ice caking the iron rungs, but to him, it was second nature, and for some strange reason, he got a thrill out of being up that high. Any work involving the silo was usually a two-man job, especially now, but the man knew what he was doing, and besides, he was starting to get used to being on his own.

The farm was technically owned by Shirl Snyder, but Henry Somers leased acreage from Snyder and along with his son and the hired man, farmed the rest for Snyder for what, at the time, was a ridiculously low rate, but nonetheless, as long as none of the Somers' bothered Snyder, he usually stayed out of their way with regard to the farming and let them run things the way they wanted—that is until the last couple of years. The Somers' were actually little more than sharecroppers, but there was a house on the property for them to live in, such as it was,

257

and it gave the hired man somewhere to live and work where no one questioned his provenance.

Things had started to go wrong with the Somers' well before the trouble with the gypsies. Once the boy had started in that school, Shirl Snyder had begun sniffing around their place asking after young Henry. Told Somers and his wife that he would start taking young Henry into school with him on cold winter mornings so he didn't have to wait for the bus. Somers let young Henry go on with Snyder--it wasn't like *he* was going to ever drive him to school, and besides, Snyder was their landlord. That's why Somers didn't give much thought to the whole thing — not until young Henry started acting out at home. Kid started sassing both his mum *and* Somers. Refusing to do his chores, things like that. Well, Henry Somers wasn't one to spare the rod, and on several occasions, young Henry found himself on the business end of a belt or his dad's big fists. When that happened, it wasn't unusual for young Henry to trot off to Snyder's place just to get away from his old man, which only made things worse.

The business with the gypsies made things much worse for all of them, the hired man thought. Then, on that rainy afternoon in November when young Henry had come home and told his father everything that had been happening to him and who it had been happening with, it was only the remarkably uncommon strength of the hired man and his equally unusual gift for putting into perspective this rather volatile state of affairs that prevented another murder from happening that night.

Once the hired man had managed to apply the Balm of Gilead, he and Somers had talked it out, made a plan, and together they decided that it would do no good to confront Snyder—it would be their word against his, and with his being a teacher and all, folks most likely would side with Snyder; furthermore, Snyder had the goods on Henry, he did. Add to that the fact Henry Somers was not popular among the community. Nor would it do to go to the authorities for much of the same reasons, and besides, they had, at present, no other way to make an income, but a potential for doing more than breaking even next year *if they kept their wits about them.*

That was when the hired man had concocted the story that the he would tell anyone who happened to come around and ask. Young Henry had gotten himself in a spot of girl trouble—no need to go into details and no need to name any names—and the family decided to leave town. The hired man would stay behind and run things and try, for at least this season, to generate an income from what had actually been a rather good year. After spring, they'd take inventory and figure out what to do next, though the hired man had it in his mind to end this foolishness once and for all.

For all of the wrong reasons, the hired man was enjoying being the one in charge. He was actually doing a fair job of running things with Somers away. What he found most amusing was that he wasn't the sorry-assed, booger-eating half-wit that he made himself out to be. He might have trouble with his speech, he wasn't much for writing and reading, and he was a fairly frightening creature to look at, but his mind was a steel trap. His days alone working the farm had given him plenty of opportunities to plan his final act of loyalty to Henry Somers.

"Ms. Tag, the water's boiling now. Should we put the Jello into the pan with the water or do we put the Jello into a bowl and then pour the water over it?"

Dreama Tagliaburro, the newly minted 'Ms. Tag', was finally a staff member at Mercyville High School; however, she was wondering if she had made a huge mistake in agreeing to take over for the now deceased Doris Pennycroft by teaching Home Economics. Housewife stuff just wasn't her thing. She knew how to make coffee, mix a daiquiri, and a Tom Collins, and occasionally she might heat up a Swanson's TV dinner in the oven, but that is where her skill as a homemaker ended. Dreama ate very little as it was, preferring to exist largely on Tab and cigarettes, and Vinnie didn't seem to be bothered by eating take-out pizza, dinner from the Dairy Isle when it was open in the summer, or the array of Swanson's Dinners in the freezer that Dreama had stocked up on for the months when the Dairy Isle wasn't open. How the hell should she know how to make Jello?

"What does the box say? Did you read the directions?"

What was worse was that, in addition to playing Betty Crocker every day, she also had to take over the sponsorship of the Future Homemakers of America. What a joke. First, she had no homemaker skills to share with these young girls who were so eagerly and pathetically sentencing themselves for a life filled with the burdens of marriage and motherhood, and secondly, her jadedness about the whole wifey-mommy thing had only intensified ever since Vinnie's kids had spent a week with them in Mercyville over the Christmas holiday. That was a disaster. She had half a mind to schedule a doctor's appointment to get her tubes tied after that week of hell, which had begun with a trip to the emergency room (stitches) and ended with all five of them throwing up from the stomach flu. Add to that Dreama's burgeoning interest in equal rights and women's liberation. Why should she tie herself down with kids when she had so much potential—so many things she wanted to conquer,

261

so much she knew she could do with the God-given looks and body she knew she possessed—why, she was just getting started! Dreama never wanted to have children, and she hoped that Vinnie felt the same, though they had never really talked about it—they never really talked much about anything of substance, come to think of it. Three stepchildren for her were quite enough, thank you, and besides, she had no desire to end up with sagging boobs, stretch marks, and a huge ass just so she could squeeze out a smelly, squalling replica of Vinnie. Who was she to be telling a roomful of impressionistic girls that marriage and motherhood were the grooviest things they could ever aspire to?

Did she share with these young girls the disgust she felt when she had to wake up every morning to the sight of Vinnie's fur-covered back? Or how romantic it was to listen to Vinnie fart and scratch his balls in the middle of the night? Or, or, wait, maybe it was the little collection of toenails he left for her to pick up on the dirty tiled bathroom floor after he had sat on the toilet for good solid hour, got bored, and decided to (finally!) clip his toenails? And his breath—ugh! His hot, smelly, cigarettes and onion breath, so sexy and alluring, was especially strong when he first woke up in the morning and started rubbing the front of his shit-stained white briefs against the small of her back thinking it was enticing to her to feel the hard, hot bulge within as he lifted her nightie and began blowing his warm, stinky breath over her shoulder and onto her breasts. Yes, that was it. That was the true essence of love and marriage.

Don't get me wrong, Dreama would say, Vinnie is sexy, he's handsome, and I do love him, but for Christ's sake, let's not make more of him, okay?

Carol's first few practices with Vinnie and his boys were nothing spectacular; the fifteen boys that Vinnie had recruited to be a part of the Show were just as self-conscious as the little girls in seventh and eighth grade. Carol, using one of her better tumblers to demonstrate, showed the boys the progression of stunts they would learn—from forward roll to back extensions. Surprisingly, they were quick learners, strong, and though their form was hideous—arm and legs akimbo, toes splayed all over the place—at least the foundation was there, and she soon began to feel *somewhat* better about this addition to the program.

Her girls, at least the more skilled gymnasts, went about their business with a seriousness that proved to be a pleasant surprise to Carol, and so she and Vinnie slowly forged a tenuous partnership—his boys, once schooled on the setting up and tearing down of the unevens, the beam, the high bar, horse, parallel bars, and Swedish box—could shave almost a half hour off the time it took Carol and the girls to maneuver all of that apparatus.

A roughly sketched outline of the Gym Show's program, then, began to take shape. It looked something like this:

Welcome

Introductory Dance

Introduction of the May Queen Court

Crowning of the May Queen

Seventh and Eighth Grade Girls' Tumbling

Seventh and Eighth Grade Boys' Tumbling

Senior High Boys' Tumbling

Boys' Apparatus

Rings

Bars

High Bar

Horse

Intermission

Girls' Apparatus and Rhythmic Dance

Beam

Uneven Bars

Rhythmic Dance

Girls' Floor Exercise

Vault with the Swedish Box

Finale with All Gymnasts

264

The Saturday night performance would be the same with the exception of the May Queen Crowning.

However, as Carol could have predicted, the honeymoon soon ended, and, at least in her mind, things began unraveling. That very morning, the little strange man-boy Barry Cubby who had taken over the music department had accosted Carol, almost backing her up against the hallway walls with his stuttering and fumbling through some diatribe about playing music during the Gym Show. He was saying something about a jazz ensemble and using a real-live piano player to accompany the gymnasts during their floor exercise. She didn't quite get all of what he was saying—he appeared to be all nervous and giggly around her for some reason, but Carol had managed to wrangle her way out of the conversation by smiling a lot, thanking him profusely, and telling him that, yes, she would definitely think about it.

Then, just as she had predicted, Dreama made an appearance at practice yesterday after school and tried unsuccessfully to take over the dance portion of the practice from JoAnn Donaldson, who tearfully pulled Carol aside (and through the dark hallway by the girls' locker room and into the supply room) and cried that she, JoAnn, had already been promised the dance thing, and why was Mrs. Tag here anyway? Carol had calmed the

265

girl by telling her that Mrs. Tag, or 'Ms. Tag' —the name she was now asking to be called — was just trying to help, but then Dreama herself appeared in the supply room, intervened, and began cooing and petting JoAnn, telling her that it was going to be all right, and Carol was all but brushed aside.

And the May Queen Court. If Cathy Snow was any more overtly positioning herself to be nominated to the court, she'd be walking through the halls bare-naked. Most senior girls who felt that their popularity and looks might garner them a seat on the court were modest, self-effacing, and genuinely surprised if they found themselves nominated to the Court, but not Cathy. She made it obvious with her overly extroverted maneuvers with both students and staff, since teachers did have a vote, too. "Stuck up Cathy" was turning into "Suck up Cathy," Carol mused.

Her own little daughter Julie's bold decision to select her own escort continued to bother Carol, not so much that this boy Stanley appeared to be somewhat backward, but that Julie took it upon herself to make that decision. Where did she get that kind of cheek? What next, she'd start dictating how she was going to wear her hair that night or what color of dress she was going to wear or what kind of flowers she was going to hold? And why him? Stanley was not a handsome little boy, by any stretch of the imagination, and why Julie thought he was an appropriate choice for such an important role was beyond Carol's comprehension. The kid had a smattering of graying teeth that Carol prayed would fall out before the Show — at least then people could *imagine* that he would have had nice teeth if they had grown in in time — and there was no way, judging from how he was dressed in school the day that Carol went over to the kindergarten classroom to see what he looked like, that he would ever be able to pull off a little man suit and tie. She just needed to concede that the flower girl-crown bearer portion of this year's Show was not going to result in the audible gasps from the crowd and the hands over hearts with all of the women in the audience murmuring, "How sweet, " no, it would be a disastrous and embarrassing stifling of laughter. Oh, how could Julie have done this to her? While it is true that Carol could have nixed Julie's choice right then and there, the awful discovery that it was Stanley's own mother Aggie who was cleaning her house every Friday made it impossible to choose someone else. She had run home during her prep period last Friday to leave a check for Aggie that she had forgotten to leave that morning — something that Jim usually did — and when she asked Aggie to spell her last name, the realization that this middle-aged woman who spoke heavily accented English was her daughter's escort's own mother. Oh, shit.

"Mrs. Adamson, I so happy you choose my Stanley, he such a good boy, and handsome, ya?"

Carol took a deep breath and replied, "Oh, yes, Aggie. I didn't realize what a good-looking little man your son is. He'll just be perfect."

"He make First Communion in April. He wear da same suit I buy him, ya?"

"Yes, Aggie that would be — well, that would be just swell."

Carol was beginning to wonder if her personal quest to leave her mark on Mercyville High School was worth all of this trouble.

XX

Damon shut his locker just in time to see that, once again, Ms. Tag was on the other side of his locker door waiting for him to close it, smiling seductively at him, her black hair flowing loosely over her shoulders, and, on this day, wearing an uncharacteristically modest mini-dress that accentuated her long curves.

"Hey there, Damon. How's that ankle?"

"Fine, Ms. Tag." He had already been coached in the transformation of 'Mrs. Tag' to the more liberated form 'Ms. Tag'. "Mr. Tag does a great job taping it up before practice. I'm really grateful he takes the time..."

"Oh, Damon, for you? He'd do anything. He thinks the world of you, you know, and so do I. So," she continued, changing her tact in order not to scare him away again like she did yesterday when she made her deliberate attempt to run into him, "basketball's going well, I see. Looks like you're the star player, huh? Who do you guys play this week?"

As if her blind ass couldn't see all of the cheerleaders' signs hanging in the hallways that said, "Go Anglers, Beat the Tigers!" and "Mercyville, Show NO Mercy! Beat Englewood!"

269

"Englewood — away." Damon attempted to look anywhere but directly at her in case he turned into stone or something. He was trying not to be rude, but he was so uncomfortable and so afraid that people were looking at him that he knew he needed to end this — whatever *this* was — fast. "They're pretty good, but I think we're better," Damon moved to the right, hopefully signaling to her that he had to be on his way.

"You mean *you're* pretty good." She sighed softly, running out of her usual litany of chitchat. She ran her green eyes up and down Damon's body, appraising the way his navy blue sweater fit over those broad shoulders, how his pressed slacks hung perfectly from slim hips. "You take care of that ankle now. We can't afford to have you sitting on the bench."

"No, ma'am. Thank you." Damon said abruptly, smiled awkwardly, and moved along. That was a dumb thing to say, Damon thought to himself. What the hell was he thanking her for? He just wanted her to leave him alone — well, most of the time. Unfortunately, the woman had gotten into his head. He hated to admit to himself that in the darkness of his bedroom at night he replayed every encounter with her in his mind like a bad movie, a movie that ended with her succumbing to his brute strength, his untapped sexuality, and his raw desire. God! He was embarrassed just thinking about it. Stop! Damon

270

fought back the overwhelming urge to paint that picture of her while he was here at school—it was a dangerous fantasy, one that would certainly end badly if he ever even thought about acting upon it.

There was no doubt that Ms. Tag was attractive for a white lady, and Damon, in another time and place would love nothing more than to tear apart that fine-looking ass of hers, but he knew better than to even think of acting upon any those fantasies he might harbor in the sanctuary of his bedroom while he was here at school, trying like hell to remain the all-American kid he had worked so hard to become.

Tommy sat next to Damon Ettinger in fourth period physics, and though the two had never spoken to each other, Tommy was certain that he could read what was in Damon's mind. He knows, Tommy said to himself. Damon knows that Henry Somers had molested Tommy, though Damon had never bothered talking to Tommy, ever. It doesn't matter, thought Tommy. I can tell he knows. The tense look on his face gives it away. He's thinking about what Henry did and wondering if I might try to do the same thing to him. He'd probably kill me, Tommy thought, almost feeling a sense of relief. Maybe I'd be better off. On the other hand, maybe I should just leave this earth on my own terms.

271

The Gym Show

Tommy thought about death a lot these days. His continued paranoia over the fact that he could read minds and the people whose minds he could read could also read his. His rational side knew this was impossible, but lately, the paranoia had been swallowing his rational thoughts. As a result, he guardedly walked the halls of Mercyville High School every day believing that everyone knew. They all knew—everybody who could read his mind knew of Tommy's shame. This line of thinking was beginning to take its toll, and sometimes, Tommy felt as if death would be a blessing. These voices wouldn't be able to drill inside of his brain if he wasn't here to receive them—voices that were constantly babbling, babbling, and there was little Tommy could do to make them stop.

To add to his constant state of anxiety, Tommy was worried about his mother. She had been sick—going on for about three weeks now, and though Dr. DeKreif had been kind enough to come out to the house to see her, she didn't appear to be getting any better. It had started out like a cold, but soon, it had turned into some kind of pneumonia-like illness—Tommy had looked it up in the encyclopedia during his lunchtime. He worried about her dying. What if she never recovered from this?

He had taken to hiding out in the library during lunch, since he wasn't hungry that much anymore, so he had time to look up whatever it was that his mother was apparently suffering from.

The only thing keeping Tommy from completely coming unraveled was music. Mr. Cubby was about to bust out of his bow-tied buttoned-up self he was so excited at the prospect of not only Tommy providing the piano accompaniment for the Gym Show's floor exercise, but about the jazz ensemble that he was forming that would provide the music during all of the other parts of the program. Mr. Cubby told Tommy of staying up until all hours of the night scoring music, trying to find the right combinations to splice together—what he did not tell Tommy was that all of this was in an effort to delight and impress Carol Adamson, and to the near detriment of the rest of the music program, Barry had begun to devote himself solely toward making an everlasting impression on the woman he secretly loved.

Tommy had proof that he could read minds, because he could clearly see that every time Mr. Cubby mentioned Mrs. A. in connection with the Gym Show the band director's voice would raise half an octave and his face would get all red and shiny, proof that the man had a wild attraction to Mrs. A. Whether or not Mr. Cubby thought about Tommy or was disgusted by Tommy's shame, though, remained to be seen—he had a hard time divining that portion of Mr. Cubby's mind it was so cluttered with this sloppy obsession of his.

273

Damon had leaned over to Tommy. "Man, are you deaf? Mr. Harvey's talking to you," Damon whispered, trying to break through Tommy's reverie.

"Mr. Jankovic, your homework?" Mr. Harvey strode toward Tommy, his hand outstretched.

"Oh, I'm sorry. Um, no, I mean, yeah, here it is. It's not all done—I mean, I don't think it's..." Mr. Harvey looked down at Tommy, a junior for whom he had gone to bat to get him into Advanced Physics and now appeared to be regretting his decision.

Damon jumped in. "Mr. Harvey, I think what Tommy's trying to say here is that while you were assigning the last four problems yesterday he was helping me with that stuff on page seventy-two, remember? I was having a hard time understanding it." Damon was pulling this shit out of his ass, he realized, but he also knew that Mr. Harvey sort of worshipped him, and that any load of crap that Damon concocted Harvey would believe. "That's why Tommy didn't finish—I don't think he heard you yesterday when you assigned the rest of the page. It's my fault." He turned to Tommy, "It's my fault, man, sorry 'bout that."

Mr. Harvey softened somewhat. "That's all right, Damon. It happens. Thomas, why don't you give me what you have and then Damon here can help you finish the other problems. Thank you, Damon for being such a help." God, thought Damon, the guy is truly a dipshit.

Once Mr. Harvey was back at his desk helping another hapless student understand the intricate nature of last night's homework, Tommy turned to Damon and asked, "Why did you do that?"

"Save your ass? Uh, a simple 'thank you' might be nice, man." Damon returned to the textbook he had been leafing through.

"Thank you," Tommy whispered. Maybe he doesn't know. Maybe he doesn't.

The letter from Millicent arrived in Saturday's mail, and Jim, in his haste, almost destroyed the envelope — a rare deviation from his usual obsessive rule that all envelopes must be slit open with either a pocketknife (which Jim always carried in the right pocket of his trousers) or a letter opener.

The first part of the letter contained, in Millicent's perfect Palmer penmanship, the obligatory greetings and queries about his, Carol's, and the children's health then retold the story told to her by Bridie Hannigan, nee Rooney, what she knew about the Somers' family and its relationship to the incident in the Adamson's store all those decades ago.

When I described in my letter to Bridie about Mother's

interjection during our Thanksgiving dinner, she told me as much as she could recall of the story to which Mother had been referring. To make sense of all of this, understand that there are four generations of Henry Somers' — from Henry Sr. all the way down to your young student.

You were right in your suspicion that Mother was telling a true story. The fuss to which Mother was referring and that Bridie wrote of all began when Henry Sr., who is the grandfather of the Henry Somers who lives out on Geist Road (and great-grandfather to the young man you described who was involved in that awful incident at school) was blackmailed by someone Bridie called Old Man Skalecki from Polish Hill. This Old Man Skalecki had something on Henry Sr., apparently something very serious, Bridie wasn't sure exactly what, and Skalecki made some kind of a deal with Henry Sr. that essentially forced Henry Sr.'s son Henry Jr. to marry his daughter Alice.

Now, Jim, this is the most disturbing part of this whole story: Alice was expecting a child when she was forced by her father to marry Henry Jr. and the father of the child she was carrying was none other than her own father — Old Man Skalecki!

I know this must be shocking to you — just as it was to me — and when the baby was born, poor thing, he had several problems as you can well imagine. He was blind in one eye, and had a terrible cleft lip. Nigel was his name, and Bridie couldn't tell me whether he was still living.

Nigel...Nigel...cleft lip, blind in one eye. Nigel...Niney Vol...Ninety Vol...Ninety Volt...Nigel. Jim even replicated the man's speech impediment and repeated "Ninety Volt." Nigel. That poor son-of-a-bitch was trying to say 'Nigel'. Well I'll be dipped in shit. So, Nigel was half-brother to Henry Somers, young Henry's father. Jim continued reading.

Well, it seems as if Nigel was kept indoors most of the time and there were all kinds of rumors in the neighborhood about him. The poor boy was blamed for every dead dog on the block and every skinned cat, too. Henry Jr. and Alice eventually had more children together — a daughter named Mildred and then, several years later, Henry III, our Geist Road farmer. But that fuss Bridie witnessed in the store between Henry Sr. and Mr. Kowalski — the one Mother went on about-- was related, apparently, to Mr. Kowalski's knowledge of the reason for the blackmail — it must have been because Henry Sr. believed that Mr. Kowalski was about to betray some confidence that would have revealed whatever horrible crime or circumstance compelled him to offer up his own son as a husband to a woman who had relations with her own father. It's all so scandalous! Now, you know how I feel about gossip, but if this knowledge can help that poor young man at your school or help to understand those other issues that we discussed, well, I pray that the Lord forgives me for passing this on. Dear me, who would have ever thought that such salacious goings-on were happening in our little neighborhood in Brookline?

Who indeed? So, there was some evil connected with this family, but Millicent's detailed recounting of Bridie Hannigan's memory still didn't explain why Shirl Snyder was molesting boys.

XXI

Cathy sat directly behind Damon Ettinger in Monsieur Schmidt's class, breathing in the scent of Safeguard and another heavenly aroma that she couldn't quite place but reveled in nonetheless.

She could stare at the back of his head all day. He was simply beautiful, and even though she knew that boys weren't supposed to be thought of as beautiful, Damon was. He was like a Greek god, every muscle in his body defined, his moves graceful and elegant. At that moment, she wanted to reach forward, lay her cool, white hands with her 'Perfectly Pink' manicured nails on either side of his neck and smooth down the fabric of his sweater just so she could feel those sinewy muscles beneath her fingers.

Cathy closed her eyes and imagined the two of them, alone, standing together in a dark hallway where no one could see them, a place where she could walk toward him, seductively, placing her hands first on his chest then sliding down, her hands turning, then sliding even farther down, to the point at which she knew (based on her teasingly brief petting sessions with Biff Lord) that Damon, unable to help himself, would wrap his muscular

279

arms around her slender but curving body, pull her closer, his breath quickening, heavy, lowering his face into her freshly washed hair, and with the long fingers of one hand, he'd stroke her smooth pink cheek, then continue stroking her lightly, down, down, his hand coming to rest on one perfectly formed breast, finally burying his face between her cheek and her collarbone, his lips finding that place where her pulse foretold of future treasures to be found, pulling her tighter, the gentle warming of his body willing her to slide her hands farther and farther down until...

"Mademoiselle? Le dialogue, s'il vous plaît!" Monsieur Schmidt was standing over her, his eyes lit up like a Christmas tree, smiling as if he knew of her secret, beads of sweat beginning to appear on his vast forehead. Cathy's eyes flew open. She shook herself out of her fantasy and was shocked to find that her breasts were swelling, tingling, and heaving up and down, that her heart was racing, and that she felt an unaccustomed dampness between her legs.

What is happening to me? Cathy thought to herself, alarmed at the loss of control over her thoughts and her body's reaction to those thoughts. She could feel her face turning hot and imagined that her bright red cheeks told everyone in the class that she had been thinking about Damon, about how she wanted to touch him and how *he* would touch *her*. She fumbled through "le dialogue" clumsily, unused to being put on the spot, and thoroughly embarrassed by her impure thoughts.

This is no way for a future May Queen to be carrying on, she reminded herself, sounding much like her own mother would if she had any inkling that Cathy was thinking these thoughts about *any* boy. If she had any idea that Cathy had thoughts about Damon Ettinger, she would simply cast her withers and die.

Cathy calmed herself finally and turned her attention to the next speaker. She certainly wasn't the academic genius of a Debbie Vukavich or a Mary Dietrich, but she did work hard to stay on top of her studies and maintain at least a B+ average. After all, her guidance counselor Mr. Bixby assured her that her flight attendant training would not require her to have a stellar academic record, just a winning smile, a trim figure, and perky attitude. Well she had that, in spades.

Jim was shocked when he read the agenda for the January school board meeting that contained no old business addressing the most appalling issue that Jim had ever faced as a teacher or principal, so he anxiously awaited Boots Malloy's call for new business. Jim asked to be recognized.

"Ladies, gentlemen, at our last meeting, I disclosed to

you the details of an incident that occurred between two of
our students at Mercyville, and I asked for guidance in the
matter. Has the board made a decision as to how to
proceed with the handling of this delicate situation?"

The board members looked at each other, eyes raised,
as if Jim should have already known of their decision.
Boots, as was his custom when dealing with an
uncomfortable issue, Jim noted, cleared the gob of phlegm
from his throat and began, "Mr. Adamson — Jim — I believe
that we deliberated over this at the December meeting.
The matter is closed and not up for examination or
discussion. We're all in agreement." Boots, for effect,
looked at each of the other board members for affirmation
of this position, and heads nodded in understanding. It
was evident that the board, in his absence, had chosen to
ignore the matter, and whether it was because Henry was
still AWOL or that no one else had come forward with any
complaints, they evidently believed that no crime had
been committed and that there was no reason for any
further investigation or consideration of the matter.

"Gentlemen, ladies, if I may," Jim said, feeling his
blood pressure rising and his heart thumping in his chest,
"with all due respect, I think that," he paused, knowing
that he was about to step into a huge pile of shit but
unable to stop himself, "it is wholly and completely
irresponsible on our part, as educators, as adults, as
282

parents, to ignore what I have come to realize was not just a random act between two hormone-driven teenagers, but was an actual rape. A crime has been committed, and for the life of me, I can't understand the board's insistence upon sweeping this under the rug."

"Now just a…" Boots began.

Jim put up his hand. "No. Let me finish, please. I've held up my end of the bargain. I've not spoken to anyone about this, per your directive." At this point, he certainly didn't give a shit if they ever found out that he had shared this with Ruthie or Millicent, neither would they *ever* find out. Millicent was a veritable vault when it came to secrets—he knew he could trust her; their bond was far greater and stronger than that of most siblings, and he trusted Ruthie with the same amount of confidence. Feeling his face beginning to get hot, he knew his anger was making itself evident. He stood up; his one last chance at proving to the board that he was committed to his position. "Ladies, gentlemen, a child has been hurt…"

"Hurt under your care, Mr. Adamson," Olive Orly pointed at him accusingly, the wart on her face quivering rage. "Under your care. What were those boys doing on the stage in the first place, may I ask? Why weren't they properly supervised? How did they get access to that part of the building? You can't answer those questions, can you? Can you?"

283

Jim at once understood where this was heading and he sat back down, defeated.

No one spoke for an uncomfortably long time. Jim avoided looking at anyone else in the room, lost in the sick realization that his "sweeping it under the rug" comment may have just rendered him unemployed. Moreover, the psychological damage that Tommy Jankovic had suffered would never be addressed, and the boy would live the rest of his life thinking that he had some strange condition that attracted animals like Henry Somers.

Boots Malloy stood up and moved to adjourn. Meeting over.

XXII

Januarys in Mercyville were notorious for snowstorms, blizzards, school delays, school closings; a hibernation of sorts seemed to occur every January when families who had put up canned goods in the late summer and stocked up on meat, wrapped tightly in white waxed paper and stored in basement and garage freezers, sat back and enjoyed the satisfaction of having prepared for the winter. Mercyville's kids, on the other hand, just enjoyed the satisfaction of a snow day.

Once the weather reports confirmed that a considerable snow was on the way, the students at Mercyville were electric with excitement at the prospect of a day off. The drama that preceded the announcement of the snow day was nearly as exciting as the announcement itself. Will they or won't they? Who actually makes the call?

Unbeknownst to the 500 or so pupils at Mercyville, it was their own principal Jim Adamson's job to "make the call." Jim and Carol threatened the Adamson children with the rolled up newspaper if they were to ever breathe a word that Jim was the man with the power to deliver the edict regarding their schools' closing. For Jim, the

285

reliability of the forecast and the possibility of a snow day meant that at around three in the morning the home phone would start ringing—parents who didn't actually know that it was Jim who "made the call" still knew that he would be the first one to know if school would be closed, so they just figured they'd get a jump on their day by calling him at home. After all, his number was in the book. "Mr. A.? Are yinz callin' off school today? I need to know if I should hitch up the plow so's I can get them young'uns to the end of the driveway..." or "Mr. A.? Clyde wants to know if he should start milking now, 'cause he's guessing with all a this snow, them cows is going to be slow gettin' into the barn, and he don't want to miss the bus again, but if yinz aint havin' school, then he can sleep a extra hour..." Jim would suit up in coveralls and a heavy jacket, walk down to the end of their long driveway with a flashlight, check the road, then traipse back up and "make the call." Making the call involved calling WICU TV in Erie to tell them that the Mercyville schools would be closed that day. Jim then gave them the "secret password"—at least that's what Julie, who was often awake at that hour just so she could be the first child in the family to discover the serendipity of a snow day, guessed it was. Jim then gave the station their home phone number so that they could call back to confirm that he really was James Adamson, principal of Mercyville

High School — the man charged with making the call.

January 26 was such a day, and it just happened to be Julie's sixth birthday. The snow continued falling throughout the day, and even though her father usually braved the roads and made his way into school on snow days — he was able to accomplish an amazing amount of work in a short time without the usual interruptions — on this day, he wasn't even able to get the car down the driveway. Whereas Julie's birthday was usually celebrated with a special dinner at Ricci's, presents, and a cake, it was just the presents this year that made the day special; well, that and the fact that she didn't have to go to school and she could snuggle with her mummy on the couch and watch game shows and her mummy's "stories" all afternoon.

The snow continued to fall throughout the day, that night, and into the next morning, and what had started as a snowstorm had now become a snow emergency with upwards of ten inches predicted for the following day. Boredom started to set in on the second day of the snowstorm, and the Adamsons had run out of ingredients for cookies (and had grown bored not only with the variety of cookies they had produced but tired of actually eating the cookies). Jim, after a marathon shoveling session, was somehow able to get the Falcon down the driveway and decided to risk the roads and go into

Mercyville to the grocery store.

Not much was happening in town, and though the grocery store was open for business, few people were inside. Jim picked up a half pound of chip-chop ham, two loaves of bread, a gallon of milk, a pound of butter, a box of Cheerios, a dozen eggs, and a carton of cigarettes. With one arm wrapped around the bag of groceries and the other hand clutching the milk, he made his way out of the store and back to his car when he saw what appeared to be a man walking toward his car carrying a long parcel wrapped in a bed sheet.

Jim put the bag of groceries and the milk down on the snow-covered curb, trudged through the not-yet shoveled sidewalk, and, addressing this man who was the only other person on the sidewalk, said rather abruptly, "Hey, fella, whatcha got there?"

The man raised his weathered face at Jim with tears streaming down the rivers of folds, his beard caked with ice. He spoke to Jim in heavily accented English. "Wife...she sick...you take, please?" The man tripped forward just in time for Jim to receive the wrapped parcel in his outstretched arms—the parcel that he would soon discover was the dead body of Radmila Jankovic, Tommy's mother.

Wilson's was the only funeral home in town, and so

after Jim had bundled Mr. Jankovic inside of the Falcon and the remains of his wife in the back seat, he wrangled the Falcon out of its parking space and down a block, turned right, and slid to a stop in the funeral home's freshly shoveled asphalt drive. He carefully led Mr. Jankovic, who was crying in earnest now and reluctant to leave his wife, into the reception area of Wilson's and called for Hank Wilson.

Funeral directors must possess an innate ability to digest the most bizarre circumstances and calmly address the matter at hand and take care of business. Hank led Mr. Jankovic to a chair while Mrs. Wilson appeared out of nowhere with a cup of tea, placed it gently into Mr. Jankovic's hand, and muttered some soothing words that, if he couldn't understand, he would at least, by the tone, recognize them as comforting. Jim's thoughts, though, were entirely with Tommy. Why hadn't he accompanied his father into town? Was he sick? Hurt?

Once he explained to Hank that Mr. Jankovic would need his son to interpret the details of his wife's demise, he again made his way to the Falcon, and, groceries long forgotten, drove in the direction of Tommy's house — trying to remember exactly how to get there from town. Remembering his trek out to Mel Banks' place two summers ago, and his more recent jaunt with Tommy in tow, Jim drove as carefully as he could, but in some places, the roads had yet to be touched by a plow. This made him wonder if Mr. Jankovic had walked all the way into town with his wife in his arms — he could see no evidence that any vehicle had been on the roads since before the snowstorm hit. The blowing snow could be to blame, but Jim thought that at the very least he would see some sign of tire tracks.

After turning down a once familiar road, Jim realized that any landmarks that he could have counted on to help him navigate to the Jankovic's place were buried under nearly two feet of snow. Why hadn't Tommy's dad walked to a neighbor's to use the phone? Surely, an ambulance would have been able to make its way out here. Then he remembered that Mr. Jankovic, with his limited mastery of English, might possibly have felt that his best chance for help would be to simply carry his wife into town. But why not send Tommy? The feeling that something was horribly wrong, even more devastating than the death of Tommy's mother, began to creep into Jim's consciousness.

Unable to ask the Falcon to take him any further, Jim got out of the car and plodded through the snow for at least a half a mile, recognized the small house with the shed in back, and lumbered the rest of the way to the front stoop. He banged on the door, and when no one responded, he tried the knob — unlocked — and walked

290

inside.

Calling out for Tommy proved fruitless, so Jim inspected every room of the small, two-story house. Much of the house was in disarray, dishes with congealed food stacked in the sink, and it was cold, very cold inside. No fire had been lit in the fireplace for a while, it appeared, and the stove in the old kitchen was cold. Tommy was nowhere to be found.

Jim left the house through the kitchen's frosted over back door and trudged out to the shed. Inside, he saw Mr. Jankovic's workshop—cabinetry and furniture scattered the area. His tools, materials, and finished work, though, was organized much the same way that Jim would have organized a woodworking shop, though, and for a moment he forgot why he was there and looked about admiring the man's handiwork.

Further, toward the back of the shed, though, behind a small child's table and chairs carefully hewn out of oak, he saw Tommy, curled into a ball, shivering and rocking, making small child-like panting sounds. He did not respond to Jim at all.

Jim reached down and picked the boy up in his arms — a seventeen-year old boy who weighed probably the same as his ten-year-old son—and returned to the cold, empty house.

The Gym Show

XXIII

Life in Mercyville returned to normal for most everyone in the town after the previous week's snowstorm. School resumed the following Monday, and the majority of Mercyville High School's student body had been ready to be back at school well before their confinement was over. After an entire week at home, the prospect of having to make up the week's worth of school come June combined with the boredom of finding things to do at home made their regular routine of classes, practices, and games rather attractive.

For Jim, though, life was anything but normal. Last week he had been fraught with worry, anxiety, and the knowledge that Tommy Jankovic would, in all likelihood, need some kind of psychiatric care after the trauma of being raped back in November, then losing his mother (and nearly his father) and almost freezing to death in that cold shed.

Tommy's mother, he had learned, had been sick for some time. Darko Jankovic had tried ministering to his wife using homemade concoctions, remedies that had apparently worked for people in his family generations ago but were of no use to poor Mrs. Jankovic who,

293

according to Hank Wilson, had probably succumbed to some type of cancer. Though she had been seen by Dr. DeKreif for what might have been mistaken for a cold, Hank confided in Jim that the state of the woman's lungs suggested a disease that appeared to have been around for quite a while.

On that awful day when Mr. Jankovic had fallen into Jim's arms with his wife's stiff, cold body, Jim had first thought of taking Tommy to Wilson's funeral home where Tommy could, Jim was hoping, talk to his father, and then explain to Hank just how his mother's illness had progressed. Ten minutes into the car ride back into town, though, and Jim knew he needed to get Tommy into Erie and to a hospital.

The drive to Erie seemed to take forever, and Jim had kept one eye on the still-treacherous roads and another on the rearview mirror and the image of Tommy shivering underneath the pink blanket that Carol had always kept in the car for emergencies. Once at St. Vincent's, Jim briefly explained who he was and the strange and surreal events of the past couple of hours that led him to the emergency room of an Erie hospital with a pale, frighteningly cold, and close to non-responsive seventeen year-old boy. He did not think to tell them how Tommy had been brutalized two months previous and that his anxiety about the event may somehow surface. Later, he would find himself relieved that he had, if even in his unconscious mind, left out this most important detail.

He had called Carol from the hospital in Erie and assured her that he was all right. After that brief conversation, he left his name and home and school telephone number with one of the nurses and left. On the drive home, he contemplated telling Carol all about Tommy. The burden of sharing this with only Millicent and those idiots on the school board was beginning to take a toll on his spirit.

Now, where could a guy find a State Store in Erie?

Carol ran Gym Show practice for an extra hour the week after the snowstorm in order to try to make up some of the time lost. January was always a tough month to keep kids motivated, and February was proving to be just as challenging. So far, she had five girls each with solid floor exercises, and two who looked promising. That was better than last year, and she could only attribute it to, grudgingly, of course, the girls' desire to impress the seven boys from the junior and senior class who were now part of the Show and who just happened to have some talent and skill for gymnastics. They were proving themselves rather adept at each of the men's apparatus—parallel bars, horizontal bar, rings, and horse—and they weren't bad tumblers, either.

295

Dreama had planted herself into the fabric of each day's practice, and though Carol did her best to avoid her, Dreama seemed constantly to be at her side. She would mimic what she said and did to direct the girls as if she was a cheerleader who felt that it was only her continual rah-rah-ing that inspired some of the girls to push themselves toward executing their next trick, to push through their fears of falling, of grinding bone against wood, of missing the bar or the beam. To Carol, Dreama's interference was distracting, but somehow, the girls responded to Dreama and tried new stunts they would not otherwise have tried under Carol's direction. Dreama was their muse; Carol could tell the girls were eager to be appear talented, graceful, and worthy of Dreama's attention.

"If that's what it takes, oh well," Carol would smile and sigh to herself, but inside she was a pressure cooker about to explode into a million wretched and frustrated fragments. Oh, and the way that woman dressed was positively obscene! Dreama's attire at practice consisted of a long-sleeved black leotard, sans bra, and an ankle-length, black and gold skirt, and ballet flats. Pink. Sometimes, though, she would forego the skirt and instead wear footless tights over her long legs and bare feet, glimmering gold rings surrounding each startling pink toe. Her movements were practiced, precise, and meant to draw attention—contortionist-like bending, folding herself and her legs into impossibly grotesque balletic positions, the stretching, her body breaking apart like ripe fruit. She once managed, to the collective amazement of the girls and the not-so-easily hidden arousal of most of the boys, to place each of her legs over the top of her head, resting her feet on her shoulders. It was on those days that she fought to keep Dreama on the girls' side of the gym—no vinyl curtain this time, but Carol had insisted upon some kind of division—if for no other reason than to guard her girls against having to witness the boys' reactions to the Dreama Show and their subsequent burgeoning erections.

Almost like a proud father, Vinnie liked to lean back against the stage, light up a cigarette, and watch Dreama in action. Carol wondered, nauseatingly, if he derived some perverse sexual thrill from watching the boys' reactions to his wife's overt sexuality, but then everything about Vinnie disgusted her.

Despite her initial reluctance to accept Vinnie's boys into her sanctum of the Gym Show, she was actually proud of the boys, all of whom she generally liked. These were the boys who did not play basketball and who, during the winter season, were happy to have something to occupy their time aside from ice fishing and hunting. And besides, who could argue against spending every afternoon after school with a bunch of good-looking girls dressed in nearly skin-tight leotards?

One afternoon in early February, a flushed and nervous Barry Cubby appeared in one of the gym's doorways, a clipboard clutched in one chubby hand, leaning into the gym looking as if he was expecting a formal invitation that would officially welcome him into Carol's domain. Spying him out of the corner of one eye, Carol finally walked over to him and spoke. "Barry, you can come in and watch. Our practices are open until the end of March. Did...did you need something?"

Practically gushing, Barry moved forward, "Well, Mrs. Adamson, I was wondering if you'd given any thought to our earlier conversation? About the music? Piano? And a jazz ensemble?"

"Oh...yeah. That. Well, yes...um, I mean, no, but—well, tell me what you had in mind, and we'll go from there." Shit, Carol thought. She was happy with the old record player and the music that the girls usually picked out, but, hell, she let Vinnie in, she might as well give this little pink-faced boy a chance.

Given the green light, Barry Cubby excitedly, and with only a dribble of spittle emitting from his tiny rosebud of a mouth, described for Carol the veritable panoply of musical numbers that would accompany the gymnasts and dancers during the show. With little background in musical genres, Carol half-listened to Barry go on and on while she kept one eye on Dreama whom, it appeared, was attempting to spot Christy Bundy on the balance beam. Christy had just recently overcome her fear of the unknown and had performed a back walkover on the small beam, only four inches from the ground, and it looked as if she was about to try a back walkover on the regular beam, more than four feet from the ground. Holy shit.

"Barry — Barry, hey, I hate to cut you off, but I'm needed." She gave Barry a quick backhand slap on his flabby bicep — a habit she had developed back at Slippery Rock when she was playing field hockey. Carol scooted quickly over to the beam and yelled for Christy to stop just as she was about to execute her move — she bobbled and jumped off the beam. Barry Cubby, meanwhile, rubbed his upper arm and lowered his clipboard to just below his pudgy belly in order to hide the unfamiliar evidence of his excitement at Carol's touching him.

"Christy, this is something I want you to practice at least 100 times before you even attempt it — even with a spotter — on the regular beam," an exasperated Carol implored. Turning, she addressed Dreama. "Ms. Tag, may I talk with you, please?" She motioned Dreama away from Christy and the balance beam.

Dreama followed Carol over to the stage and away from the eavesdropping ears of most of the girls; however, some were clever enough to look as if they were busy doing anything else but straining to listen to this parley. A confrontation between the implacable Mrs. A. and her obvious rival Ms. Tag would be a battle for the ages, and no one wanted to miss this.

Carol drew in a deep breath and began. "Dreama, you are not, under any circumstances, permitted to spot one of my gymnasts on the beam—on any apparatus for that matter, unless you have permission from me, do you understand?"

Dreama said nothing, just stared at Carol, those green eyes flashing contempt. Vinnie cautiously approached the women, and an audible hush among the gymnasts was evident. Most of the kids within earshot had given up trying to look as if they were not paying attention to what was sure to become an all-out catfight.

"Carol, uh, is there a problem?" Vinnie asked, casually grinding out the last of his cigarette on the wooden stage and flicking the butt under the velvet curtain, but it was evident that even he was afraid of Carol.

"Yes, Vinnie, there is a problem. These gymnasts are my responsibility. I am their coach. I am responsible for their safety. Dreama is neither qualified nor knowledgeable enough about gymnastics to spot a girl who is about to execute a back walkover on the balance beam when that girl has never attempted it before." Turning to Dreama, she continued, "Dreama, I appreciate your help, but I think it would be best if you would stick to the dance portion of the show — I'll talk with JoAnn and the two of you can work together. But remember, I chose JoAnn because of her extensive background in dance. Please try not to undermine her efforts, please."

Dreama, who still hadn't uttered a sound, released a loud sigh, turned and dramatically marched out of the gym, which suited Carol just fine. Vinnie blew out a breath, flared his nostrils, and went after her. Good. I can do this without either of you.

"And I was just beginning to get used to the idea of their intrusion into my show," Carol said to herself. "Jesus, Mary, and Joseph."

The Gym Show

XXIV

Without thinking too much about it, Jim had taken it upon himself to shepherd Tommy Jankovic through his brief stay in the hospital. He had contacted the priest of an Eastern Orthodox Church in Erie who could talk with Mr. Jankovic about Tommy, whose condition the doctor had attributed to the shock over his mother's death, the storm, the lack of heat in the home, and the inability of both Tommy and his father to find help for Mrs. Jankovic until it was too late. Add all that to a freakish molestation of the worst possible kind, and it's not much wonder the boy hasn't permanently checked out, Jim thought.

Jim had, through the priest acting as interpreter, managed to let Mr. Jankovic know that he, Jim, would retrieve Tommy from the hospital and bring him home. Meanwhile, he had called Mel Banks and asked him to take a look at the home's furnace, get it up and running, and send the bill to him. A discretionary fund existed at Mercyville High School that only Ruthie and Jim knew about, and he would pay the bill out of that.

During the ride back to Mercyville, Jim tried again to get Tommy to accept some kind of help. Tommy, though, blamed himself for his mother's death; he felt that God

303

was punishing him for allowing Henry Somers to violate him.

Jim quietly explained, "That's not the way it works, son. Your mother was probably sick long before all of that happened, and besides, that's not how God operates. You did nothing wrong, Tommy. Henry was the aggressor, and though I'm not excusing him, something set Henry off that day. He's a victim, too. I know that may be hard for you to understand, but I've thought a lot about it, and I've done some digging..."

"Mr. A. you promised! You promised you wouldn't say anything," Tommy cried.

"And I haven't Tommy. I've kept my promise," Jim certainly didn't think the boy needed to know that he had confided in the school board, and since the board didn't want the information out there anyway, none of them would tell, and, of course, he trusted Millicent and Ruthie implicitly. She had only the best interest of Tommy and to a lesser extent Henry at heart.

"Tommy, listen to me. I've been around the block a few times. I've seen a lot in my days on this earth, and this kind of thing—this thing that happened to you—it was not in any way your fault. You didn't invite it, you didn't ask for it, you certainly didn't deserve it, and I wish there was something that I could do that would heal your wounds. What if I arranged for you to talk to...?"

"No, Mr. A.! No!" Tommy was adamant, "You can't tell anyone else!"

"But Tommy, I won't tell. A professional person, someone who's a lot better at this stuff than I, can help you. Hell, son, you don't even have to tell him about the thing with Henry—you could just talk about losing your mum. That in itself is enough to warrant a session or two with a psychiatrist."

"Mr. A., I told you I wanted to forget about that thing. I can handle everything else. No one can know about the thing...the thing that happened. I told you, and I'm very serious about this, Mr. A., I will kill myself, and I'm not just saying that to be difficult or anything, but I've thought a lot about this, and life just won't be worth living if anyone ever found...ever found..."

"Okay, okay, Tommy. But let's agree on one thing, okay? You and me, son, we're in this together. I want you to come to me if you need someone to talk to. I may not be a shrink, a counselor, a priest, or anything, but like I told you, I've seen a lot. And I have kids, too, Tommy. In my line of work, every kid in school is like one of my own kids."

Jim suddenly realized while saying this that it was, indeed true. Jimmy was ten, Jenny nine, and Julie now six. As sickening as it was to think about it, what would he want if the situation involved one of his own precious children—children who he would die for, who he would kill for?

Something had to be done about Shirl Snyder.

"Goddamn, woman," Damon muttered to himself. There she was again, walking toward him, her hips swaying, that come-hither look in those green eyes. Dreama Tagliaburro was making a habit of meeting Damon at his locker after third period. Kids in the halls would watch her in fascination as she did all those little flirty things in front of Damon that women do when they're trying to stake a claim on a man—tilting her head to one side, reaching out and smoothing down the collar of his shirt and then touching her own neck, brushing her hand down between her breasts, laughing at stuff that wasn't really funny. Damon would get so embarrassed, but he didn't know how to handle these advances. It was getting to the point that now the guys on the basketball team were starting to rag on him during practice—making snide remarks about him screwing around with Ms. Tag, and Bill Shepherd, the one guy on the team who had actually read a book, started calling him 'Mandingo'.

"So, Damon, we meet again. Practice tonight?" What a retarded-ass question, Damon thought. The basketball team practiced every night after school. She knew that because she was usually sniffing around out in the hallway waiting to get inside the gym for Gym Show practice — she had "run" into Damon a couple of times, but he soon got wise and started leaving out of the locker room from a little used side door that led straight out into the parking lot. Then he'd have to double back and wait for his dad to pick him up in front of the main entrance. Just another pain in the ass thing he had to do to avoid her, but he knew better than to give her more opportunities to corner him, especially with Coach and Mr. Tag lurking around. Damon didn't need his ass kicked by some greasy dago, and he sure as hell didn't need Coach thinking he was putting the moves on Ms. Tag.

"Uh, yeah. Gotta get ready for Hannover Heights. Um, I actually gotta' go...I need to talk to Mr. Harvey about my homework. So..."

"Mr. Harvey? Doesn't he teach some kind of really hard science course? Wow. I guess I didn't know you were that smart that you were in such an advanced class. It's okay — I can write you a pass. I may be just the Home Ec. teacher, Damon, but I *am* a teacher."

Jesus Christ, lady, just get the fuck out of my *way*! It had gotten to the point that, while he still fantasized about Ms. Tag in the sanctuary of his bedroom — who doesn't picture a hootchie-momma when he's trying to spank it — in reality, he was no fool. He fully understood the danger of any interaction with a white lady, white girl, white anything. Life was all fine and dandy when he was averaging twenty-five points a game and making the honor roll, but start talking to a white chick and the game's over. His dad had warned him over again about shit like this.

"Damon, you're a fine looking kid, and that's all well and good, but you need to understand how some women, well, they have a thing for colored men. It's almost like something taboo, you know, exciting. But let me tell you, son, no man is going to abide your having any kind of friendship with his daughter or his sister. Next thing you know, you're hanging from a tree, even up here in Pennsylvania. Trust me on this, son."

Yeah, Daddy, what do I do about this crazy bitch, huh? "Nah, that's okay, Ms. Tag. Gotta' go."

Dreama followed him down the crowded hallway with her eyes gleaming seductively, knowing that, at some point, he'd come around. They all do.

XXV

The February school board meeting came and went, again, without a word from any of the board members about the incident with Tommy Jankovic. Jim had Ruthie take Henry Somers' name off the school records—he didn't necessarily want or need to follow up to see where Henry was; it was probably for the best that he just stayed away for now. Jim kept a close eye on Tommy, though, and met with him as much as he could without drawing any suspicion. Without asking why, Ruthie had arranged for Tommy to help in the office during his lunch period, and when Tommy wasn't running passes or fetching supplies for Ruthie, Jim would call him into his own office on the pretext of assigning him some low level task when in reality, he took the opportunity to try and get a read on how Tommy was doing. If anyone had ever questioned Jim's sudden interest in Tommy Jankovic, a teacher's dream and a boy who was known for being responsible, Jim would simply say that the death of Tommy's mother had been hard on him—who could argue with that—and that Jim felt it was his responsibility to make sure that he was available if Tommy needed someone to talk to.

No one questioned him, though.

It wasn't until Tommy had asked Jim if he could drop Honors Art and work as a student assistant for Ruthie during that class period that Jim became concerned. "Why do you want to drop Honors Art in the middle of February? Are you not doing well? I can hardly believe that, but if that's the reason..."

"No, Mr. A. I just don't like it anymore. Can we just leave it at that?" Tommy hung his head, and Jim did not pry further, but went across the hall to the guidance office and had Janie Fox change his schedule.

Though Jim had a desk full of work to attend to, he closed his office door and started going through the yearbooks from 1965 through 1969 looking for some clue that might tell him something more about Tommy and why he was so adamant about dropping Honors Art. After all, most kids would have done just about anything to get into Honors Art—Jim was forever hearing Bob Bixby, the guidance counselor, complain about the numbers of junior and seniors who wanted to drop whatever class they had and sign up for Honors Art, but Shirl Snyder was famous for carefully hand-picking his Honors students based on a portfolio that the more serious art students would begin to compile throughout their junior high, freshman, and sophomore years in the hope of being asked to join the Honors Art cohort.

There was no Art Club per se, but the Honors Art

students formed a de facto group that represented the best of Mercyville's visually creative minds and so apparently had earned an entry in the yearbook. Jim could see nothing unusual in the past four years' worth of Honors Art yearbook group pictures—it was an equal mixture of boys and girls, unlike the photography club, of which there were no yearbook pictures and no boys.

He read through captions listing the kids' names, and he saw the name George Jankovic. Must be Tommy's brother, although this boy looked to be a bit sturdier than Tommy. He wondered if George had been in the photography club, too. Couldn't check, because there weren't any damn pictures of the photography club in the yearbook.

On the way back from the Hannover Heights game, Cathy Snow made sure that she was seated in the exact same spot that Damon Ettinger had occupied on the way to the game, and even though the trip would only take about twenty minutes at the most, she planned on maneuvering herself so that she and Damon would somehow be forced to sit together. She was good at these things, apparently, because after casually changing seats a half dozen times while the players had ambled onto the bus, their bodies still emanating the heat from the game and their subsequent showers, Cathy had managed to find herself seated right next to Damon.

"Good game, Damon. Were you surprised we won?" Cathy worked her best Sandra Dee expression and fluttered her heavily mascaraed eyelids.

"Not really, no. Why?" Why was this girl talking to him? She'd never said 'boo' to him before tonight and now she was being all goofy and shit.

"Oh, I don't know. Probably for you, winning is second nature, you're so good. I love watching you play," Knowing that the bus ride would be rather short, Cathy seized this opportunity to utilize every ounce of her coquettish charms in order to engage Damon in some kind of playful conversation. She had been dreaming about this for some time. The problem was that she wasn't so sure of what she would do if he were to actually bite back. When she had imagined this moment earlier in the evening, she was straddling his lap, grinding against him to ease the inexplicable pulsating ache between her legs. Even now, she could feel her face becoming warm as she willed herself to remain seated, her slim ankles politely crossed.

"Uh, yeah, well, thanks." Damon had no idea where this girl's shit was coming from. Just like with Ms. Tag, his radar detected danger ahead. Let's get this ride over with, man.

"So, do you know where you're going to school next fall? I mean, you are going to college, aren't you? You're
312

smart enough, you know."

Yeah, bitch, I know I'm smart enough — I'm also black enough, in case you hadn't noticed.

"Uh, well, the coach at Clarion's been talking to my dad. And Kent. Kent State. It's in Ohio..."

"I know where that is!" Cathy cried. Her eyes, even in the darkness of the bus, were shimmering with silver light.

"Yeah, so, yeah. It's between those two." He knew he should probably ask about her plans after graduation, but he really didn't care, nor did he want to encourage this conversation from going any further.

She obviously didn't get the hint, because she said, breathily, "I'm going to be a flight attendant — that's why I'm taking le français, you know." She giggled like a little girl then continued, "I plan on flying on international flights, and I might just live in Paris. Hey, if you ever get to Paris, you could visit me!"

Like that would ever happen. "Yeah, sure." Damon turned away and pretended to look for his gym bag on the floor. Thank God, the bus was pulling into Mercyville's parking lot, 'cause he sure as hell was ready to be out of this seat, off this bus, and away from this crazy blond bitch.

"See ya'," Damon mumbled then pushed ahead of Danny Teague to be the first one off the bus. Cathy sighed heavily but knew that her brief conversation with Damon Ettinger would carry her through the rest of the night as she lay among the fluffy folds in her pink-canopied bed and dreamed about those hands, those creamy coffee colored hands running up and down her white, white body. That damp, tingling feeling between her legs returned, but this time she welcomed it.

XXVI

Jim decided this Saturday morning to drive out to the Somers' place and see if he could talk to Ninety Volt, whose name Millicent had confirmed was indeed Nigel, but he wasn't sure that he should use the man's given name—he wanted to see how much information he could get out of him first.

He wasn't exactly sure what he was looking for in the way of information, but anything that Ninety Volt knew about Shirl Snyder might shed some light on whether Jim's suspicions about the man had any validity. While Jim's "bullshit detector" was usually accurate, without any tangible proof or solid accusations made by students, he really had no reason to take any action.

Maybe it was just the fact that Jim's "bullshit detector" — along with the sick feeling in his gut he got every time he thought about Snyder — was telling him that he had to do something. He couldn't fire him; he had no just cause. He couldn't take his suspicions to the school board—they were about as helpful as tits on a boar. He certainly couldn't involve the law—he wasn't a lawyer, but even his Thursday night hero Ironside wouldn't touch this case with a ten-foot pole.

315

He pulled into the rutted, muddy drive just as he had back before Christmas, only this time the house looked as if it was sleeping, boarded up, old sheets of faded, warped plywood nailed over each of the first story windows. Shit. He got out of the Falcon and slopped through the mud-covered path toward the barn. Jim poked his head inside the open doorway and yelled out, "Hello?" No one answered.

A fat yellow tabby, red-eyed and feral-looking, ran at him from out of nowhere, damn near scaring the shit out of him. That the cat was looking well fed wasn't necessarily a clue that someone had been feeding him — barn cats existed on rats and mice. He did, however, hear the distinctive noise of a dog barking somewhere in the distance, and he followed the sound.

On the north side of the graying barn, someone had tied up a mangy Bluetick hound to a slapped together doghouse. The dog, though rather rough looking, his coat caked in mud, appeared to have been taken care of — a full bucket of water was chained next to the doghouse along with an empty food dish. This was promising. It must mean that Ninety Volt was at least still around to take care of the sorry looking animal.

Jim had seen no cows in the barn, but it was close to noon on a Saturday; they'd have already been milked and turned out to pasture. Jim went back inside of the barn

316

and, once his eyes had adjusted to the dimness and the sharp ammonia smell of cow urine, he surveyed his surroundings. Fresh manure, some still steaming, littered the row behind where the cows were milked, although it appeared that some of it was in the process of being mucked up. He could hear the low hum of the refrigeration system in the milk room. The hired man must be around somewhere.

At once, Jim felt a sharp jab in his back down near his kidneys. He moved to turn around, but a thick, knobby hand, its nails thick with grime grabbed his shoulder from behind.

"Where you hink you goin'?"

Ah, shit. The son-of-a-bitch had a double- barreled shotgun thrust in the small of his broad back. Without turning his head, Jim carefully responded while slowly raising his hands up to his sides, "Ninety Volt, remember me? I'm Jim Adamson from the high school."

No response.

"Come on, fella, I just came out to have a talk with you, that's all. Can you put the gun down?"

"Wha you wan?"

"Like I said, I just want to talk to you — it's about your--about Henry's landlord, Shirl Snyder."

Ninety Volt had apparently lowered the gun because Jim could no longer feel the grubby hand on his shoulder nor the disquieting feel of a double barreled anything on his lower back, and his heart rate had begun slowing down. He turned around carefully, still holding up both hands so that Ninety Volt could see that he was unarmed.

"Nyder? Why you akin' abou him? I don know nothin'."

Jim took another deep breath, this time confident that Ninety Volt wasn't going to shoot him, and began.

"Okay, I'm just going to come out and tell you something — it's actually a feeling that I have, and if there's any truth to it, I need to know. Snyder's a teacher at Mercyville High School."

" I know," Ninety Volt said.

"Well, then you must realize that he comes in contact with a lot of kids." He paused. "A lot of boys."

Ninety Volt stared at Jim with his one good eye, and in that stare, Jim could recognize a glimpse of pure, unadulterated hatred. Jim's statement had apparently struck a chord with the hired man.

"Ninety Volt, do you know something about Shirl Snyder? Is there a reason that he shouldn't be around students? I have to know — I *need* to know. It's my job to protect these kids."

"Boys," Ninety Volt said, and turned to walk away.

"Wait, wait! What? What about boys? Come on, man, this is serious."

The Gym Show

Jim followed the hired man out of the barn and around the back of the house. For a man of his age, Ninety Volt moved like someone much younger, nimble, almost gracefully. Attached to the house was a small, lean-to shed, and this was, apparently, where Ninety Volt stayed. Why he didn't stay in the house wasn't quite clear, but at this point, Jim was more worried about how he was going to keep Ninety Volt talking. Inside of the dwelling, two old chrome and vinyl kitchen chairs, their seats torn, yellow foam peeking forth from their innards, were among the meager furnishings in the plywood-floored lean-to. Ninety Volt sat down on one and Jim helped himself to the other.

"What can you tell me about Shirl Snyder?"

"He ricked Henry."

"He 'tricked' Henry? How? How did he trick Henry?"

"Said to ge ri of the yipsies."

"I don't, did you say something about…gypsies?"

Ninety Volt nodded.

"So Shirl told Henry to do something with gypsies."

He nodded again.

"Were there gypsies here at the farm?" Jesus, Jim thought, I feel like I'm on a goddamn game show.

Ninety Volt nodded again.

"How many?"

319

Ninety Volt held up the five fingers of his left hand.

"Okay, five gypsies—all adults? Any children?"

Ninety Volt held up two fingers then folded them back into his blackened hand. He raised his other hand, equally filthy, and held up three fingers. Then his leathery face crumpled into a mournful grimace, and he placed both hands over his face and sobbed.

Jim drove around the familiar countryside for at least two hours after leaving Ninety Volt back at the Somers' farm. There were still traces of snow on the ground on this late February day, but there was definitely something in the air—the sharp, cold, clear promise that spring was just around the corner. Buds on leaf-stripped trees were now visible, and he thought he saw some emerging crocuses popping out in one of the wintered flowerbeds at the Dvorjak's house.

The older Jim got, he realized, the quicker the time flew by. When he was a child, he remembered that the cold grayness of winter seemed to go on forever, but now, all four seasons in western Pennsylvania roller-coastered by him in the blink of an eye. Maybe that was God's way of preparing His followers for death and life everlasting. Jim may not have been a church-going man, but his belief in God and the promise of salvation were as real to him as the small hills of snow that still dotted the fields near his

320

beloved home.

There was no doubt in his mind now that Shirl Snyder was manipulating those around him into not only keeping his evil proclivities a secret, but was using Henry Somers and quite possibly others to feed his sick obsession with young boys. The story that Ninety Volt had relayed to Jim as they both sat in that cold, damp, lean-to shed was a story that no one could have ever possibly fabricated, and when Ninety Volt took him down into the remote and isolated portion of the eastern most pasture of Shirl Snyder's property and had shown him the grave where five gypsies—a mother and father and their three small children, two little girls and an older boy, lay buried, Jim had retched into the soft ground until his throat was raw and his belly was empty.

At the end of every summer, the residents of Lake County would often find themselves with some uninvited guests, a collection of gypsies, traveling folks who followed the county fair and its caravans and trailers from town to town. Every land owner in the area had reported, at one time or another, that these folks were squatting on their land—Josef Danof had even hired a man to chase them out of the creek bed near his property at the end of every summer. They were generally harmless, non-violent, but they did have a penchant for grifting, stealing, and entering homes and barns and generally helping

321

themselves to whatever they thought they needed. They were a nuisance, to be sure, but a nuisance like a raccoon in one's shed or a mouse under the sink.

The gypsies could often be found camping deep into the woods near some kind of running water, either a small stream or a larger creek. They would use their camp as their base, then send their children, some as young as five or six, into town to steal what they could from the Five & Ten, or from Collins' Cut Rate. Calvin, the town's only police officer, would usually be called, and he'd doggedly track them down, shoo them back into their campsite, and everyone would go about their business and know that they could tell their grandchildren the folksy stories of "when the gypsies came to town."

Two summers ago, a family of gypsies had made camp near the creek on Shirl Snyder's property. Ninety Volt had discovered them when he had gone in search of a heifer that was missing from the herd. Clear down in the east pasture, Ninety Volt had found the heifer, tethered to the rusty bumper of a small camper; he also found a man and woman sitting around a campfire roasting a rabbit on a spit.

Ninety Volt had explained to Jim that, having been the target of ridicule and derision most of his life, he had preferred to leave the gypsies alone, but there was the matter of the heifer. When he had explained his dilemma

322

to his half-brother, Henry became impatient and angry with Ninety Volt, and told Ninety Volt to go back down there by the creek and get that heifer and to hell with the damn gypsies.

During Henry's tirade, Shirl Snyder had snaked his way into the barn and heard the entire heated exchange between the hired man and his half-brother Henry Somers.

"Gypsies, huh? I say we go down there and educate those gypsies on the vagrancy laws here in Lake County. They're trespassing on *my* property."

Surprised, both men turned to see Shirl Snyder, standing in the open doorway of the barn, carefully putting on a pair of leather gloves while his .22 was tucked in the crook of his right arm.

"Goddamn vermin, gypsies. Come on, Henry, Nigel, let us teach them a lesson they'll not soon forget. Henry, why don't you go inside and get your deer rifle; make sure you're fully loaded. We're going to get rid of these gypsies once and for all."

Henry and his brother looked at each other, half amused, half horrified. Shirl Snyder had always been a strange specter of a man, but this conversation was beyond the pale. "What do you mean, Mr. Snyder? What do you mean by 'gettin' rid' of 'em'?"

"Why Henry, you know exactly what I mean. You,
323

Nigel, and I are going to go down by that creek bed of mine and first retrieve our property, well, my property. We had better prepare for the worst, don't you think? After all, these traveling gypsies have been known to be rather unpredictable. And I want my heifer back."

"You really think we need two guns?" Henry had asked, a strange underlying tone of something akin to fear in his voice.

"Absolutely! These carnival people can be dangerous. Why, just last week, Opal Crosby up on Reed Road had her home broken into by these thieving bastards, and one of them had stolen her dead husband's Saturday Night Special. Why, how do we that know your gypsies down by the creek aren't the same ones who now have Ned Crosby's gun most likely tucked under their filthy vestments? So while you stand their questioning my sanity, Somers, that heifer of mine might just be roasting over an open fire, so believe me we'd better make haste, don't you think? I want my heifer back." He turned and walked out the barn's doorway. Henry and Nigel caught up with him.

Knowing that he had their full attention, Snyder continued, "Now, Henry, while I was looking for you earlier, because, oh, I had a couple of things to talk over with you regarding young Henry, I checked the inside the house, you see, and Mildred, your lovely wife, is taking a nap upstairs in her sewing room snoring away, young Henry is at my place doing some little odd jobs, so we — that is you, me, and Nigel here — are going to go into the house, retrieve your deer rifle, make sure that it is loaded, and we — you, me and Nigel — are going to walk calmly down to that creek bed and take care of our business. And if we happen to enter into some kind of confrontation with those damn dirty gypsies, we'll be prepared."

Shirl had marched both Nigel and Henry to the home's back door. Henry, still not trusting Shirl and his insistence upon obtaining more firepower just to scare a couple of gypsies, had reluctantly walked up the four cement steps into the back porch, reached for the deer rifle that was leaning against the wall behind the door, and checked to see that it was loaded, while Shirl, his .22 still resting benignly in his arm, watched intently, his eyes following both Henry's and Nigel's every move. The three of them had then made their way out of the yard, through the shabbily constructed gate that led to the east pasture, and walked without a sound to the gypsies' campsite.

What happened next was difficult for Jim to understand through Nigel's nasally speech impediment coupled with his increasingly pitiful, wracking sobs, but he managed to understand the gist of it. Once the campsite was well within sight, Shirl had dropped the .22, and had retrieved from his person a pistol that he had

325

secreted in the inside of his hunting vest, trained it on Henry's temple and quietly demanded that Henry take aim and fire the rifle at each of the two seemingly harmless gypsies, a man and a woman, sitting by the fire talking quietly, their heads bent toward each other, a gentle and tender ease between them. Henry, the threat of his own demise imminent, his body now convulsing as if he was experiencing some kind of seizure, shakily aimed the rifle first at the man, and fired, hitting him in the shoulder, then aimed at the woman and fired, hitting her between her astonished eyes. Then, out of nowhere, three children appeared, and with Shirl's prodding, Henry aimed and fired at each of them.

As the frightened children, wounded but not yet dead, called for their mother, Nigel stood rooted in frozen and horrified silence. He had not seen any children around the campsite upon his first visit to the creek bed; they must have been inside the camper. The wounded man staggered toward his three children in a vain effort to protect them from the man with the gun, but despite his pitiful attempt to shield them from the slaughter, the children were the next to die. Shirl had cocked the pistol that rested against Henry's temple, thereby sealing the children's fate. Shirl forced Henry to pick off each of the three children. Shirl then ordered Henry to finish the job. Henry walked closer to the family and shot the children's father at point blank range.

After Henry had reduced the family to a bloody, shredded and heaping mass, their bodies still twitching in the deepening shadows of the afternoon sun, Shirl, without looking once at the carnage in front of him, picked up the .22, snatched Henry's rifle from his shaking hands, and had calmly walked over to the camper, untethered the heifer, and slapped it on the backside. Next, he directed Henry to dispose of the campsite and instructed Nigel to dig a grave to bury the bodies. He then walked back toward the house and barn, disappeared from their sight, and never once referred to that afternoon or his role in the massacre of five innocent human beings.

In shock, Henry and Nigel had set about to dismantle the campsite and began digging a deep grave, one large enough so that the family could be buried together and deep enough so that if anyone might happen to walk through that pasture in the future, they would never know that the ground upon which they stood contained the remains of five people. Five innocent travelers who were murdered in order to provide Shirl Snyder with the leverage he needed to continue his molestation of Henry Somers' teenage son.

Upon hearing Nigel's recounting of this horrific tale, Jim understood then that Shirl Snyder had set up the entire scenario in order to blackmail Henry — essentially forcing Henry to trade his son for Shirl's silence. Shirl secured his association with Henry, Jr., and Henry Sr. remained a free man. As for Henry's culpability, it was true that Henry had killed all five members of that gypsy family with a deer rifle registered in his own name, but who would ever believe that Henry had committed these executions under extreme duress and with Shirl Snyder's blessing—the Walther P38 that Shirl had pressed against Henry's right temple?

That's right. No one.

THE GYM SHOW

The Gym Show

XXVII

On his drive to school, Barry Cubby could hardly contain himself. His mother, all a-flutter about his newfound success, had gushingly said to him this morning, "Barry, you're about to bust your buttons!" to which he laughed hysterically. Bust his buttons, indeed! Barry's excitement was apparently written all over his face. He was writing the entire musical score for the Gym Show!

It had happened quite by accident, this project of his. After his initial meeting with Mrs. Adamson that evening in the gymnasium (when she had playfully touched him on the arm—oh, the joy of that touch!), he had decided to prepare for her a sampling of what his jazz ensemble could perform during the show. He had also prepared an original piano medley that he wrote himself and hoped to use as accompaniment for one of the gymnast's floor exercises. Though Mrs. Adamson had seemed a bit confused at first, Barry assured her that he had been researching the art of gymnastics and the musical accompaniment for the floor exercise portion, and this enthusiasm of his seemed to impress her. She had finally given him the go-ahead by saying, "Sure, Barry. Whatever

331

you come up with is fine."

Oh, what a day that had been! He relived it over and over again in his mind, the way she placed her trust in *him* to make these crucial musical decisions for such an impressive event as the Gym Show! He promised her that she would not be disappointed.

Next, he needed to bring Tommy on board. Poor Tommy, losing his mother during that awful snowstorm — Barry shuddered at the possibility of living even one day without his sainted mother — and so he had remained sensitive to Tommy's mourning period, refraining from getting him involved too soon, but it was now time, and Barry could think of no better therapy for a grieving son than to embrace his music and play that piano! And Tommy played so beautifully!

Tonight, his assembled jazz ensemble would play for Mrs. Adamson the sampling of intermediary music that they would perform during the transitional phases of the Gym Show. He would also have Tommy play the original piano piece so that Mrs. Adamson might envision one of her gymnasts (oh, Barry hoped it would be her *best* gymnast!) using that composition for her floor exercise.

A little birdy had told him that one of the gymnasts was planning to use the theme from *Exodus* as her selected accompaniment for her floor exercise. Perfect! Barry had ordered the music right away and had given Tommy the

332

piano score as soon as it had arrived so that he may prepare. This was an easy piece for Tommy to play — he nearly had it memorized.

He wondered if Tommy owned a tuxedo. Imagine Tommy in a tuxedo and tails! Oh, how marvelous he would look sitting at the piano, his tails flipped over the back of the piano's bench! Barry was planning to wear his tuxedo, a beautifully cut garment his mother had bought for him when he was in college. Barry frowned. He should probably start watching what he ate — Mother loved to bake but what she loved even more was seeing her Barry eat and eat and eat!

I'm going off on a bunny trail, Barry thought. I must stay focused. I've such an important task ahead of me today, and so many details to attend.

Never in his wildest dreams did Barry Cubby ever believe he could be so lucky as to be auditioning in front of Carol Adamson — he felt like bursting out in song! The only trouble was, there was never a song written that could capture his feelings for Carol Adamson.

Carol only remembered that the music teacher Barry something-or-other (she could never remember names) was coming to practice tonight when she saw some of the band kids wheeling the piano down the hallway toward the gym. Shit. I did tell him that he could play a little something, she thought to herself, but I'll be damned if I remember what that something was. In classic Carol fashion, she decided to think about it later. With too many details to remember, her Scarlett O'Hara-ness was beginning to take over now that the Gym Show was only a few short weeks away.

It was already March and there were exactly fifty-three days until the Gym Show, and she was planning to hold practice every one of those days except for Sundays. For the week before the Show, she had put together a "Traveling Gym Show" featuring her best gymnasts, and this group would travel during the school day to Iroquois Lake High School and Iroquois Valley High School to perform. The two schools were Mercyville's two most hated rivals, so by showcasing the unique talent of Mercyville's gymnasts — no other school in Lake County had anything even close to her Gym Show — this would serve as a sweet exclamation mark to a fantastic basketball season since the Mercyville Anglers had finished first in the Lake County League and were headed to the playoffs. Next to her Gym Show, she loved basketball, and she loved winning.

As she was heading toward the main office, she saw one of her favorite kids Damon Ettinger standing outside of Vinnie's office — probably waiting to get his ankle taped, she thought. He towered over her petite five-foot frame, but she managed to reach up slap him on the arm and congratulate him on making the playoffs.

"That game Friday was amazing, Damon. Way to go! I know you can't hear us during the game, but I was just as hoarse from yelling for you guys as the cheerleaders were! Your parents must be over the moon!"

"Yes, ma'am, they are. And thanks." Damon smiled shyly but continued standing awkwardly waiting for Vinnie,

"Go ahead and knock, honey," Carol prodded. "Mr. Tag's probably just in the john."

"Uh, it's okay, Mrs. A. I'll just wait."

Waiting was not one of Carol's strong suits; watching someone wait was almost as painful. "Oh, for crying out loud," Carol stepped in front of Damon and rapped on Vinnie's door. "Mr. Tag? Come outta' there! Damon's out here waiting for you."

At once, the door flew open and Dreama appeared looking like a mare that had been rode hard and put away wet. She stared wild-eyed at Carol, but her face softened when she saw Damon.

"Well, Damon, come on in. I've been waiting for you."

What the hell? Carol thought to herself. What is she doing down here anyway, and look at the way she's looking at Damon!

335

The Gym Show

And Jesus, Mary, and Joseph, she's not wearing a bra!

Disgusted with the overtly sexual manner in which Dreama was presenting herself, Carol, in a clipped voice, said, "Damon's here to get his ankle taped. Is Mr. Tag in his office?"

"No...but Damon knows that he can hang out here with me until Vin comes back, right Damon?"

"Uh, well...," poor Damon looked as if he was about to throw up all over the front of Dreama's freely swinging breasts.

After an awkward moment of silence, Carol said decisively, "Tell you what, Damon," I've got plenty of athletic tape in my office. I don't want you wasting any more of your lunch period, so why don't you and I just go on down to my office and I'll tape up that ankle. I taped up Cliff Dvorjak's foot for him all last year after he broke his toe during P.E., so I'm sure I'll do just as good a job as Mr. Tag would, okay?" She left out the part where Vinnie had been in his office looking for his cigarettes when Cliff had stubbed his toe on the ball cart that Vinnie had carelessly left outside of the locker room.

"Yeah, thanks, Mrs. A....Um..." Damon wasn't quite sure what to do next, but Carol, sensing his dilemma, simply locked her forearm into his and began walking at her usual breakneck pace down toward her office with Damon in tow.

Dreama, her eyes narrowed, watched Carol drag Damon down the hall with her. "So," Dreama whispered under her breath, "I see how it is with you, Mrs. A. Starting to get tired of Old Fatty, huh? Why *not* try something tall, dark, and handsome…"

XXVIII

Tommy nervously approached Mr. Snyder's doorway with the pass for Cindy Himmel that gave her license to get out of school early for a dentist appointment. Since dropping Honors Art, he had so far avoided any contact with Mr. Snyder, but when Miss Stone had handed him this pass to deliver, he didn't want to make a big deal about it and decided just to get it over with. He took a deep breath and knocked quietly on the door.

Snyder opened the door and looked down at Tommy. Tommy simply held out the hand-written pass for Cindy and mumbled something about his being sent from the main office, but before he could finish, Snyder stepped out of the room, closed the door, and folded his long, bony arms in front of his body.

"So, Tommy, I see you've dropped Honors Art and are now serving as an errand boy for Mr. Adamson, is that right?"

Tommy was not sure how to answer, but he managed to stammer, "Uh, well, you see, Mr. Cubby has me practicing all of the piano pieces for the Gym Show, and I knew that I wouldn't be able to..."

"Ah, Mr. Cubby—the nubile and young Mr. Cubby.
339

The 'Music Man'. I see. Well, Tommy, you have a rather eclectic appetite for, shall we say, certain 'partnerships', is that right?"

"Uh, I...I'm not sure what you mean..." Tommy had no idea what 'nubile' meant, but it sounded rather feminine. His head began to ache, and he felt as if he was going to wet his pants.

Snyder's eyes drilled into Tommy's throbbing skull. "I mean, Tommy, that Mr. Cubby exhibits that, oh, how shall I put it, that 'flair' for the creative arts, just as I do, and you've traded your loyalty to me and have given it to him, is that a bit more clear to you? Have you *given* it to him, Tommy?"

Given? Given what? "Well, no, not really, Mr. Snyder. I've always had a love for music, and, well, you'll probably agree that I was never really that much of an artist in the first place—I'm still not sure how I was scheduled into Honors Art, but anyway, music has always been very important to me." Tommy surprised himself with his ability to articulate this statement, becoming somewhat emboldened.

"Why yes, of course, Tommy, I quite understand. So, what was it that attracted you to your *other* friend...was it Henry? Ah, yes, Henry Somers. No longer a member of the student body here at Mercyville, I understand, but perhaps *you* would know the reason why. Do you know where Henry is, Old Sport?" Snyder glared at Tommy, his steely eyes searching Tommy's face for some kind of acknowledgement.

Emboldened no longer, the roar in Tommy's ears drowned out everything else that Snyder had said after he had invoked Henry's name, so nothing after that registered with Tommy. He stepped back, tripped, righted himself, and then bolted down the hallway as fast as he could toward the boys' restroom where, with heaving convulsions, he vomited what little breakfast he had eaten into the nearest sink. Thankfully, no one else was in the restroom at the time, so once his stomach was emptied, he splashed cold water on his pale, sweating face, rinsed out the bitter vile that remained in his mouth, and staggered out of the restroom, unsure of what to do next.

He ran right into Mr. A.

"Tommy, are you all right?" Mr. A. searched Tommy's face for some kind of sign that would tell him that Tommy was okay—that Tommy had not been harmed.

"You fucking *promised*!" Tommy cried.

"What? What are you talking about? Where have you been? I've been looking for you. Ru...Miss Stone told me she gave you a pass to take to Mr. Snyder. Have you been to his room?"

"You fucking *liar*! You *promised*!" Tommy began sobbing.

"Goddamn it, Tommy, what did that son-of-a-bitch say to you?" Jim hissed, dragging Tommy by the upper arm into an empty janitor's closet.

"He knows. He knows about...about...Henry. *You promised*!"

Jim took Tommy by the arms and shook him into submission. "Listen to me, son. I never, I *never*, said a word to that man, nor to *anyone* about what happened that night on the stage. Do you understand? Now," Jim took a deep breath, not sure how much he wanted to share with Tommy, "you have to trust me, Tommy, for Christ's sake, you have to believe that I only want what's best for you and that I will do whatever I have to do to protect you. Mr. Snyder," Jim began, taking a deep breath, willing himself not to tell Tommy everything he suspected about that twisted, old fuck, "Well, Tommy, I believe he might be a sick man, but just as I've kept your confidence, you must keep that information to yourself."

Tommy looked up at Jim, so pitiful, so vulnerable, that Jim just wanted to take the small boy in his arms and rock him back and forth, just as he did with his own son Jimmy whenever Jimmy would wake up in the middle of the night from a bad dream. The image of Jimmy brought tears to Jim's eyes, and at this point, he didn't give a shit if

Tommy saw that he was crying.

"Tommy. Please, son. I have children of my own, three of them, and one of them is not much younger than you are. I would kill someone who ever tried to hurt one of my children, and I feel the same way about you. Please, Tommy. Let's go back downstairs, let's get some lunch — hell, I'll send Ruthie out to the Dairy Isle and she'll get us some hoagies — but let's calm down and talk about what to do next, okay?"

Tommy, his face still revealing nothing, hung his head and followed Jim downstairs to the main office.

No amount of alcohol could keep the dreams at bay that night. He was high on an Italian ridge, alone, and a sniper lay somewhere in the distance taking aim at Jim and hitting him, blood spurting from various wounds all over his body, but he just kept turning around, looking for the gunman. There was no pain, just a loss of blood. Then the sniper found another target, and this time it was Tommy. Tommy was running toward him, the sniper's bullets riddling his body, but he kept running toward Jim, but never getting any closer. Then Tommy turned into his son Jimmy, and the wounds in his body doubled in size — Jim ran toward his son, but he couldn't reach him, and the sniper kept on shooting and shooting.

Jim woke in a cold sweat, Carol still asleep beside him,

343

so obviously he had not cried out. But the dream stayed with him every time he closed his eyes. He eventually gave up any hope of sleeping for the rest of the morning and went down to the kitchen to make some coffee.

Tommy's encounter with Shirl Snyder was all the proof that Jim needed that the man was responsible for this entire fucked-up mess with Tommy, Henry, and most likely a whole host of others. Thankfully, he was able to yesterday finally convinced Tommy that he had kept his confidence. To save the boy from hurting himself or even from killing himself, Jim had explained to him that the only reason Shirl Snyder could possibly have known about the incident on the stage with Henry and Tommy was that Shirl had, in all likelihood, been molesting Henry, and for some sick reason had convinced Henry to go after Tommy. Jim did not, however, share his discovery about the dead gypsies — that was a story he would never repeat.

Now I have crossed the Rubicon, Jim thought.

Tommy still insisted to Jim that he thought that death would be a far better than listening to the relentless voices in his head that told him again and again that everyone knew his disgusting secret. He couldn't move away; his father had no money, George was being sent to Vietnam, and he just wanted to curl up and die most days. The only thing he had to look forward to was the Gym Show.

The original piano piece that Mr. Cubby had written

and Tommy had played for Mrs. A. at Gym Show practice last week was a rather complicated piece, but once he sat at the piano, the voices in his head at once ceased their chatter, his mind became one with the notes on the page and the keys on the piano, and life felt normal again. If what Mr. Cubby said was true, there were at least seven girls who would need accompaniment during the Gym Show — seven beautiful pieces of music to learn and memorize and perform — seven opportunities each time he practiced to stop the voices from telling his secret.

But after the Gym Show, Tommy didn't know what he would do.

As for Jim, little did he know that he had not made his way through the Rubicon, but that his journey was just beginning.

The Gym Show

XXIX

Julie and Stanley were now regular collaborators in just about everything, and even some of their classmates were starting to sing, "Julie and Stanley, sittin' in a tree...," but Julie didn't care, and if Stanley minded his fellow kindergarteners thinking he had a girlfriend, he never said anything. Both of them loved drawing and coloring, and so during their free time, they sat together making up elaborate stories to illustrate. Someday, when they both could read, they would put some words to the stories, but for now, their artwork managed to tell all kinds of tales.

Aggie continued cleaning for the Adamsons, and now that her Stanley was essentially a member of the Royal Family for the Gym Show, the Adamson's house was extra sparkly every week. Aggie and Lube had already purchased for Stanley a brand new suit which he would wear next week for his First Holy Communion, after which, Aggie would brush it clean and hang it back in the plastic garment bag until the big night when he would wear it for the Show.

Stanley's stock was beginning to rise with his fellow

bus riders, too, except for that awful Billy Chapin who made everyone's life miserable. Since his mother was the bus driver, she never called him out for his obnoxious behavior, so while the rest of the kids on bus 163 had developed an easy, cooperative friendship, Billy remained a terror.

One afternoon in mid-April, Billy started in on Stanley. The weather was getting much warmer, no snow on the ground, mild winds, but Stanley's mother insisted that he wear a hat when he went outdoors. This hat wasn't the usual stocking cap that most kids wore – no, Stanley's affair looked like an old man's hat. It was a Tyrolean green with a red and black feather tucked into the ribbon above the brim, and it had grey earflaps, and, of course, no one in Lake County – no child, that is, ever wore a hat like that. The best thing that Stanley could say about the hat was that it kept his ears warm.

That particular afternoon, Billy decided that he needed to try on the hat just so he could illustrate to everyone else just how ridiculous Stanley looked in it. He grabbed the hat off Stanley's head and pulled it down over his greasy, unwashed, and badly needing to be cut hair then danced around the aisle of the bus, his hands flopping at his sides; his feet tapping like a leprechaun.

"I'm doing the fairy dance with my fairy hat! Look at me! I'm a fairy with a feather in my hat!" Billy's singsong

348

falsetto, his idiotic dance, and his repugnant behavior went completely unnoticed by the only person who might be able to control it, his mother, so the other bus riders did what they had learned to do over the past six months and that was to ignore Billy Chapin. Most of them were getting ready to get off the bus at Porter's Corners anyway.

Thus, Billy's bullying didn't last long. Once his audience had stopped paying attention, Billy took off the hat, threw it on the dirty floor of the bus aisle, and stomped on it for good measure. He then picked it up threw it Frisbee-like toward Stanley who didn't catch it but was forced to crawl under the seat in front of him in order to retrieve it. That set off another round of laughter from Billy and the crushing question, "How many Polacks does it take to catch a hat?" Billy laughed so hard at his own joke that he farted, thus ending the bullying session.

Stanley brushed off his hat as best he could, placed it back on his head, and then waited patiently for Mrs. Chapin to stop in front of his house.

The residual consequences of Billy Chapin's activities that afternoon were about to nearly derail Stanley's and Julie's participation in the Gym Show.

After the first couple of years of May Queen voting and selection, Jim and Carol had come to agree on a fail-safe and fair method for choosing the May Queen Court. The senior high students — those in grades nine through twelve — would, during their final class period of the day, choose five senior boys and five senior girls simply by checking off names on a roster of the senior girls and boys. Teachers, who were also permitted one ballot apiece, would collect the ballots and deliver them to Ruthie, and Jim and Ruthie would tally the results.

Jim's idea, after the first couple of years, was to streamline the process. In order to avoid having to do this all over again, Ruthie and Jim would rank each of the five girls and boys by the number of votes they received; therefore, Jim and Ruthie knew a month in advance who the May Queen and her escort would be, but they kept that information to themselves. Not even Carol knew.

The day after May Queen *Court* selection was always a Friday, and Jim would make the announcement of the court at the end of the day. The suspense was palpable, and in years past, Jim thoroughly enjoyed the electric excitement in the hallways and in the cafeteria on May Queen Court Friday, as it came to be known. This year, however, he almost wished he could have just walked away from the whole thing and let someone else handle it. But he didn't.

Jim would make the big announcement at a planned assembly that convened fifteen minutes before dismissal.

350

The entire student body came together in the gym, and a lone microphone on a stand took center stage in the middle of the gym floor. Jim would wait until everyone was seated and the students were completely silent before striding up to the microphone, a three-by-five index card secreted in the palm of his big hand. He did his best, as he had the past six years, to make his announcement suspenseful and full of excitement, feeling a little like Bert Parks, and if anyone noticed that this year his voice was less than enthusiastic, no one mentioned it.

"Ladies and gentlemen, I am pleased and proud to announce to you our 1970 May Queen Court!" The roar of the entire student body could be heard all the way up at the Dairy Isle, he was sure, but the minute he raised his hand for quiet, a hush fell on the gymnasium.

"I will read the names of the five gentlemen first—the gentlemen who have been chosen to escort the five most beautiful young ladies in all of Lake County. Gentlemen, if you would, please, join me on the gym floor once your name is called. The 1970 May Queen escorts are, in alphabetical order:

Donald Atherton
Ronnie Bashchevik
Tony Callebretti
John Church
and Damon Ettinger
351

The Gym Show

At the utterance of Damon's name, the student body first gasped then erupted into a foot-stomping, hand-clapping marathon that Jim, smiling big, allowed to go on for a minute or two then he held up his hand for quiet. The young men had lined up beside him, most trying to suppress their pleasure in having been chosen, but they certainly didn't want everyone to know how much of an honor they all felt it was to be chosen as an escort.

"And now, ladies and gentlemen, Mercyville High School's finest young ladies—ladies if you will, please come forward when your name is called and stand beside each of these young men as we introduce the 1970 May Queen candidates!"

Christy Bundy

JoAnn Donaldson

Lana Ferguson

Barbara Hollingsworth

and Cathy Snow

Each of the girls--after the requisite gasp of astonishment, hands to the face, and in some cases, tears of joy—took their respective places beside the boy who shared their proximity with the alphabet, but when Cathy Snow, whose selection was the least surprising of them all, walked up and stood beside Damon Ettinger, she actually reached down with her right hand and took his hand in hers, squeezed it, and then tucked her left arm into his.

352

Damon, clearly embarrassed, turned toward her, then quickly turned away, but made no move to remove his hand. Throughout the stomping and cheering, the student body remained oblivious to Cathy's bold move, or if they were shocked, they certainly didn't react. The faculty, though, were very much taken aback, and wondered just how Mayor Snow would feel about his lily-white daughter holding hands — no, wait, linking arms with a colored boy, even if that colored boy was Damon Ettinger.

That was only the beginning.

XXX

"Guess who's coming to dinner?" Jackie Pfeiffer chirped knowingly as she skipped into the locker room to change for P.E. class.

No one seemed interested in what Jackie Pfeiffer had to say, so she repeated herself, this time much louder. "I said, *'Guess who's coming to dinner?'*" She calculatingly folded her arms in front of her chubby middle, waiting for someone to bite.

"Don't know, don't care, Jackie — what the hell are you talking about anyway?" Taking the lead, Missy Pelley finally responded to her, more to get her to shut up than to hear what she had to say. Most of her peers knew that Jackie was generally a huge pain in the ass.

"Well, let me tell you what Ms. Tag told us in Home Ec. It seems as if our Mrs. A. has a little crush on escort number five — Damon Ettinger. Did you know that she wraps his ankle now? Every day? For basketball?"

"Basketball's been over for weeks, dumbass," Noreen Sanderson interjected, trying to avoid rolling her eyes.

"Well, when basketball *was* going on, it seems as if Mrs. A. had Damon *all to herself* right down here in her little office." Jackie's pointed at Carol's office, its frosted

355

windows giving Jackie license to gesticulate to her heart's content. Jackie's smugness was, at this point, the least annoying of her irritating habits.

"So?"

"What do you mean, 'So'? Ms. Tag said that Mrs. A. practically *dragged* Damon down here. She said that there was more to the story, but that she didn't think it was very professional of her to talk about it."

"Well why the hell did she tell you in the first place?" Missy cried. Missy liked Mrs. A. because she always let Missy use her office bathroom when she was having her period and never asked any questions. And, most importantly, Mrs. A. had a huge stash of Tampax on the shelf that Missy frequently helped herself to, unbeknownst to Missy's mother who feared the use of tampons would ruin Missy's virtue.

By this time, though, Jackie had lost her audience — no one liked her much anyway, but that didn't stop the rumor from snowballing out of proportion. By the end of the day, the seed that Dreama Tagliaburro had planted in her fourth period Home Ec. class was the talk of the school.

Whispers of, "Did you hear about Damon and Mrs. A.?" and "I heard Mrs. A. and Damon were *doing it* down in her office!" buzzed throughout the school the next day. Carol, caught up in preparations for the Show, was oblivious to the rumors, but the rest of the staff seemed to enjoy the talk, even if they knew it was simple high school innuendo. That is until the story grew legs when the whispers and overheard conversations in the grocery store and on telephone party lines fed Mercyville its first big scandal of 1970.

"Julie, quit scratching your head! What are you, one of the Itch Kids?" It was Wednesday night, two and a half weeks before the Gym Show. Carol had referenced her childhood nemeses, the Itch kids, whenever any Adamson child did something unseemly or impolite or wore something that was either dirty, smelly, or looked like it came out of a Salvation Army bin. Julie never learned if the Itch kids were real kids, but even as an adult, she would often find herself referring to her own three as 'Itch Kids' when circumstances called for it.

Despite her mother's scolding, Julie, was unable to keep her hands out of her long, brown hair, and just wanted to jump in the bathtub and put her head under the spigot and get rid of whatever was causing that itch. But her bath would have to wait. Tonight was the night that Pippa was returning from Florida, and Julie couldn't wait to see her. Pippa usually brought presents for the three of them, too—not anything funny or frivolous, but usually something practical but always perfectly suitable.

357

Spring was definitely on its way, and Julie had played outside during recess and again after school with kids from the neighborhood. They had been climbing trees, so most likely, that is where the scratching had originated, or so her father thought.

It was rare for Carol to cook dinner during the week — it was even more of a rarity during Gym Show season, but in honor of Pippa's and Uncle Bernard's homecoming (and Grammy's, too, but Julie wasn't sure she was looking forward to that), Carol had prepared homemade bleu cheese dressing for salad wedges, a potato casserole, and Jim was grilling steaks and garlic bread on the charcoal grill out in the driveway. Jim had even ordered a cake from the bakery in town for dessert, since asking Carol to bake something in the middle of the week was akin to asking her if she'd like to invite Vinnie and Dreama Tagliaburro over for cocktails — it was never going to happen. Somehow thinking that if she was outside with her daddy that Pippa would get there sooner, Julie thought about going out to where Jim was grilling and drinking Iron City, but it was a little chilly still, so Julie contented herself by watching him from the house, scratching her head, and looking for Pippa's car to come up the driveway.

Once Millicent and Bernard had arrived and all of the greetings, hug, kisses, and homecoming presents had been exchanged, the family sat down to dinner in the home's small dining room. Since it was unusually late for supper, Julie was getting sleepy already; Jimmy and Jenny were too busy stuffing themselves with garlic bread and cake — none of the adults seemed to care that the older two had helped themselves to dessert while they were still slicing away at their New York Strips.

"So, Jim, how's the school business going? Preparing all of those eager young scholars to take over the world, are you?" Bernard never ceased to give the impression that he felt that being a school administrator was a profession for those who couldn't do anything else — like he could — and his snide tone was never lost on Jim. Oh, Bernard, if only you knew.

"Well, you know, Bernard — well, maybe you don't know..." Jim sighed, "At any rate, we're gearing up, of course for the Gym Show, and Carol here has just about kid in the school involved in doing something. It's a great event for the school and for the whole community, really."

"Uncle Bernard, did you know that Damon Ettinger is on the May Queen Court?" Jenny couldn't wait to be the one to deliver this stunning news.

"Ettinger — isn't he that colored boy? They let a colored boy on the May Queen Court? Good God, whatever could be next? A colored May Queen?" Bernard laughed uproariously at his analogy; no one else

359

seemed to understand his humor.

"Yes, Damon Ettinger," Jim confirmed. "Nominated to the Court by his peers, all fair and square."

"I think that's wonderful! Bernard, isn't that wonderful? That just warms my heart," dear Millicent interjected, sensing where the conversation may be headed.

"Well, now, I don't know," Bernard said, pensive now, rubbing his chin with his thumb and forefinger. "What are you going to do, Jim, if he is elected to escort the May Queen?"

Jim looked first at Carol who gave a slight shrug and then at Bernard. Jim had drunk just enough beer to trigger his litany of sarcastic comebacks. Time to let 'er rip.

"Well, gee, Bernard, I don't quite know. Might have to call in the National Guard to help him out. You know, with all these redneck peckerwoods in town, ain't no tellin' what might happen. I'll just make sure he stays away from hotel balconies and...well, *you* aren't going to shoot him, are you?"

"Jim..." Carol began, but even she realized that once he got going there would be no stopping him.

"I'm just saying," Bernard continued, attempting to defend his position while chewing on a particularly tough piece of steak, "that I think it's admirable for the student body to think so highly of him, but come on. Mixing

360

white and colored like that? And he can't possibly serve as an escort for one of those young ladies—it just isn't done."

"Not my decision, Bernard. Damon's a great kid with a great future, and I see no reason why he can't escort any of our young ladies during the May Queen Crowning."

"Jim," Millicent, ever the tactful intermediary, changed the subject, "what do you know about corn futures?"

"Corn futures? What—you mean like the price of corn in September? You mean that?" Jim barely hid his disappointment at the change in conversation; he was about to regale Bernard with some snide references to his Jewishness, but, once again, his respect for his wife and sister won out. "Nothing. Why?"

"Well, we—Bernard and I—have been thinking about the trust." Way to step in another pile of shit, Pippa, Jim thought, but listened to what she had to say.

"If we—Bernard and I—invest the money I have set aside for the children's education in a diversified manner, I'd like to investigate the possibility of investing in futures. Bernard and I attended a neighborhood seminar earlier this spring about investing, and one of the experts presenting told us that grain futures—especially corn futures—are one of the safest avenues of investing because the factors that weigh into how high or low the price will

361

be have already been established. Things like drought or excessive rainfall."

Jim was no whiz when it came to finances, and it always seemed as if he and Carol were continually playing 'catch up', so he was not the person to ask when it came to financial advice. While he appreciated Millicent's deflection of the whole Damon argument, which could have become ugly, he had on the tip of his tongue a smartass remark on the less than ironic instance of a Florida neighborhood's Jewish members sponsoring an investing seminar.

Then he stopped. What *did* he know about the price of corn?

XXXI

Julie went to school that Thursday with an itchy head and a throbbing headache—she had tossed and turned in her little twin bed most of the night, and when she finally did fall asleep, Mummy was right there waking her up again for school! Oh, if she could only have stayed home!

Once at school, she tried to keep her hands out of her hair. Stanley, still seated next to her just as he had been on that very first day he had joined Miss Marpy's class, was also scratching his head, frowning under the heavy frames of his glasses. It didn't take long for Miss Marpy to notice the two of them scratching away, and when she finally walked over to them to ask why they were so itchy, she gasped in horror.

Luckily, Carol had remembered that the Erie Times was sending a reporter and a photographer to Mercyville High School today to interview her and Vinnie for a feature story slated to appear in this Sunday's paper. She spent extra time on her hair and makeup, and she wore a light blue sweater set, her pearls (a wedding gift from Jim), and a navy blue pencil skirt, completing her look by fastening her charm bracelet to her left wrist. Satisfied

363

with her appearance, she tossed an extra bag of makeup in her purse so she that could touch up right before the reporters were scheduled to arrive at 11 o'clock. Unfortunately, just as she was unlocking the door to her office, her phone started ringing. It was Ruthie.

"Mrs. A., Miss Marpy from the elementary school called."

Jim had been at work since six that morning, staring at the open folder on his desk, his door closed. There was not one single infraction or notation in Shirl Snyder's personnel file that could possibly warrant any kind of disciplinary action. In fact, there was little to his personnel file at all. The only thing remaining that interested Jim was an indication of Shirl Snyder's next of kin.

"What do you mean she has head lice? How in the hell...how on Earth did my daughter contract *head lice*?" Carol felt her heart begin to race, her face to burn, and she actually started shaking. Head lice? Head lice! For Christ's sake, *head lice*? "Yes, I know, I know, I'm a teacher, too. As soon as I find someone to cover my classes, I'll be right there."

Jesus!

Dreama Tagliaburro walked forward to meet up with

Damon at the usual time, but today, he was busy talking to that little snot Cathy Snow who was practically rubbing her tits up against his arm that she had just grabbed hold of. Who in the hell did she think she was? Dreama stopped, backed up, and tried to look inconspicuous, but she was visibly bothered by the fact that Damon was actually listening to that little bitch as she cooed and tittered and fawned all over him like she was in junior high.

Didn't she realize how pathetic she looked?

Jim's office phone buzzed. It was Ruthie. "I have Mrs. Orly on the phone for you," Ruthie said almost apologetically, knowing that whenever a school board member called and asked to speak with Jim, she needed to put that person through immediately.

"Hi, I'm Vinnie Tagliaburro, and this is my wife, Dreama," Vinnie enthusiastically pumped the reporter's hand; Dreama had trouble suppressing her delight in "standing in" for Carol Adamson. However, she would only elaborate if asked.

She winked at Christy Bundy and JoAnn Donaldson, two of the students who, it seemed, Carol had earlier arranged to be featured in the Erie Times piece along with Vinnie, and of course, herself. Well, Mrs. High and

365

The Gym Show

Mighty Adamson, if you can't seem to find the time to show up for work, I guess you don't get to be in the newspaper, Dreama said to herself smugly. The two girls, meanwhile, were adjusting each other's ponytails and making sure that bra straps were tucked in, giggling at the prospect of being photographed for the paper.

Dreama gave herself a private pat on the back that she had dressed so tastefully that morning in a short yellow skirt, white go-go boots, and a purple puffy-sleeved blouse unbuttoned just enough to show off her amazing décolletage. Her hair hung loose around her shoulders and cascaded to just above her full, voluptuous breasts. She smiled seductively at the photographer, secure in the knowledge that he, too, found her irresistible. Certainly, he would want a picture of Dreama with Vinnie—the two coordinators of the Gym Show!

"Mrs. Orly, I can assure you that whatever you heard amounted to nothing more than vicious gossip. If Mrs. Adamson had Damon Ettinger or any young man in her office, I'm sure that she had a very good reason." Jim clutched the phone in his right hand so powerfully that he almost broke the damn thing in two. How dare this cow, this holier-than-thou old bag of bones, this wart-faced dried up old bitch, how dare she suggest that Carol and Damon had done something inappropriate? Jim drew a

366

long, deep breath in order to calm his nerves and avoid saying something he knew he'd regret. "Furthermore," he calmly continued, "I think it's only fair that you let me know how you heard this story, Mrs. Orly." Just the facts, Ma'am.

"Well, it's all over town, Mr. Adamson, all over town! Why, I was in the beauty parlor yesterday, and it was the talk of the shop, it was."

"'But, I say unto you, that every idle word that men shall speak, they shall give account thereof in the day of judgment,'" Jim sighed, knowing that he was most likely really going to piss her off now, but not caring.

"Now, don't you go trying to school me on Scripture, Mr. Adamson! Pastor Orly himself is on his way over there to...to..."

"Is he going to come over here to kick my ass?"

It was at that precise moment that Ruthie appeared in his doorway, face ashen, and said, "Mrs. A. just called. Your mother's house is on fire."

The Gym Show

XXXII

Jim seldom drove fast, but he managed the four miles to his mother's house, which usually took him five minutes, in half that time. He parked in the neighbor's driveway across the road from the house and, without looking right or left, ran straight into the path of an ambulance, which, thankfully, had slowed enough so that the driver had time to come to a screeching, fishtailing stop before reducing Jim into a semi-permanent fixture plastered on the vehicle's hood. Carol had run, in her bare feet, no less, down the path through the woods between their house and his mother's in the same amount of time it had taken him to get there by car, and together they got as close as the firemen would allow.

Jim said a silent prayer of thanksgiving when he saw Millicent and his mother huddled together behind one of the fire trucks. It only occurred to him later that he wasn't particularly concerned with Bernard's safety at that point, but seeing his mother and sister seemingly unharmed flooded his soul with relief.

"Mother tried baking a cake—on top of the stove," Millicent said wearily, shaking her head. "I was upstairs, Bernard was in the shed, and it wasn't until I smelled

369

smoke that I knew something was amiss. Bernard's talking to the fire chief right now — the fire's out, there's minimal damage, but we need to talk, Jim," Millicent's eyes widened at the last part of her statement, and Jim knew exactly what she was thinking.

Evidently, the past few months in Florida were nothing short of exhausting for Millicent — their mother had made several unscheduled "field trips" throughout the neighborhood, there was an accident at the grocery store which necessitated Millicent's insistence on diapering Ida if they were to be out of the house for more than a half an hour, and Ida had managed to ruin two of Millicent's saucepans when she had burned the contents of whatever she was trying to cook on the stovetop.

In her prime, Ida had threatened to haunt her children like a savage specter if they ever even entertained the idea about putting her into an old folks' home, but at this point, Jim and Millicent were left with little choice. Carol had made a good point when she said that the risk to not only Ida's health but also to Millicent's was reason enough to look for an alternative living arrangement. Jim put his arms around his sister and thanked her for keeping everyone safe — yet again. Tomorrow they would talk about the necessary arrangements.

After Ida was tucked safely in her room and the firemen had left, with Jim's forgotten car still in the neighbor's driveway, Carol and Jim walked back to their house holding hands. Halfway there, Carol looked up to Jim and said, "Oh, and by the way, Julie has head lice."

Jim couldn't think of anything else to do but laugh.

Finally making his way back to school, a visibly upset Ruthie met Jim at the school's front door. Oh, shit, this can't be good, he thought.

"He's been waiting here for over an hour, and I told him that your mother's house was on fire, but he said he didn't care! I can't believe it! I'm sorry, Mr. A. I tried to get him to leave a message with me, but he insisted on waiting to talk to you," Ruthie was as close to tears as he had ever seen her.

"That's okay, dear, it's not your problem. I stepped into another pile of shit this morning — I'll handle it, don't worry," Jim sighed again for about the tenth time that day. Norm Snow was waiting, hat in hand, overcoat draped over one arm, squeezed into a chair that was much too small for his large six-foot frame.

"Jim? A word, please?" Snow rose and motioned Jim into his own office. Jim followed, preparing himself for the worst.

"Is Pastor Orly not with you?" Jim began, not dead certain how much he wanted to share with Norm Snow about what he had said to that old wart-faced she-goat

371

Olive.

"Pastor Orly? I don't know anything about that. I'm here to talk to you about my daughter."

"Cathy? Oh," Jim, at first surprised then relieved that he didn't have to rehash the entire episode with Olive Orly just yet, sat down behind his desk. "What can I do for you?"

"Well, Jim, as you know, Cathy is the most precious thing in the world to Mrs. Snow and I," Norm began, and Jim couldn't help but smile at the irony of a school board member who had no idea of what an object pronoun was.

"And, as you know, Jim, she's a beautiful young lady — and one that I'd bet my life savings is going to be elected as this year's May Queen."

Jim lifted the corners of his mouth in a semblance of a smile, but didn't say anything. What the hell did Snow want?

"And, well, I just want to make sure...um...that is, I want a guarantee from you that..." Norm Snow's mood shifted into righteous indignation. "Well, I'm just gonna' come out and say this, Jim, man to man. I won't have no nigger escorting my daughter down that gym floor in there next Friday night when she's crowned May Queen."

Jim damn near fell off his chair. "Whoa — oh, well, hang on, there, Mr. Snow," Jim cried incredulously, "I hope you're not referring to Damon Ettinger. Our

Damon? Why would you care..."

"Dammit, Jim! I don't give a good goddamn who he is, or how good he throws a baseball or shoots a basketball! My princess is not going to be walking arm in arm in front of the whole goddamn town with some colored fella! Now, I don't mean to be difficult, but I'm sure that, as a father, you understand how I feel." Norm Snow leaned back in his chair, confident that he had made his point.

Jim sat for a moment, not looking at Norm Snow, but just thinking about Damon and how he, Jim, would honestly feel if one of his own daughters walked arm in arm with Damon. I guess I've just never thought of Damon being anything other than, well, Damon, Jim concluded to himself.

"All right, Mr. Snow. I understand. I will certainly take care of it. You have my word."

Norm Snow rose, held out his hand to Jim, a rather faint imitation of a smile passing his lips, and said, "I knew I could count on you. After all, we're men who love our little girls, aren't we?"

Jim shook his hand and escorted him out into the main office. "Sure," Jim said, but privately thought, I wouldn't put it that way, Mr. Snow, but whatever. I'll take care of it.

The Gym Show

374

XXXIII

"You'll look just like Mia Farrow in *Rosemary's Baby!*" Gina cried, not truly understanding that a six year old would never have the foggiest notion of who Mia Farrow was and had certainly never seen *Rosemary's Baby*.

It was difficult to tell who was more heartbroken – Julie or her mother. As her beautician clipped off the long locks of mousy-brown hair, Carol watched, stricken. She couldn't bear to see all of that beautiful, wavy hair fall to the floor in a lice-infested heap. Julie watched herself in the mirror, fat tears rolling down her face, as Gina proceeded to give her what she promised was the latest style – a pixie cut.

It was determined that in order for Julie to return to school, her head had to be lice free – in order to render her head lice free, it was necessary to remove all of the nits. To remove all of the nits from hair that hung down to the middle of Julie's back, she had to resign herself to having her hair cut short. If she had been a boy, Gina warned, Gina would be shaving her head about now.

That Gina, as a favor to her most well-heeled client, had agreed to come to the house to cut Julie's hair was less of an endorsement of her fondness for Carol and more

375

because she certainly couldn't risk having a licey-headed little girl running around her shop. Either way, Gina had spared Carol further embarrassment once Gina had agreed to come to the house, and Carol was grateful for that, at least.

In the meantime, all of the sheets, blankets, pillowcases — every comforter, bedspread — all curtains and even the draperies in the house were in the process of being washed or dry-cleaned. Carol had even gone so far as to recommend to Jim that they hire a professional cleaning company and an exterminator to come in and fumigate the house and clean every nook and cranny, but he stopped her. Aggie could take care of the cleaning — that's what he paid her for.

Waiting until Carol was busy talking to Gina about what she could do with for Carol's hair for the Gym Show, Julie quietly pulled on Jim's big hand and led him out of the kitchen into the living room. "But Daddy, Mrs. Aggie might have lice, too," Julie said rather sheepishly, preferring to break the news to her father and not her mother that Stanley Czerniawski had just as much head lice as she had.

"Why would Aggie have head lice...unless...Julie, does Stanley have lice?" It was all coming together now.

Julie started crying again, this time because she didn't want to lose Stanley as her partner-crown-bearer-escort boy. She was fond of Stanley, and she didn't want to do anything to hurt his feelings. Jim didn't think this disaster could get much worse, so he resigned himself to keep Stanley's infestation problem to himself.

"Julie, let's just keep this to ourselves, okay, little bunny? Mummy doesn't need any more stuff to worry about."

Relieved, Julie wrapped her arms around her father as much as she could—his girth making it impossible to reach all the way around. She breathed in one of her most comforting scents—English Leather aftershave, cigarette smoke, and whiskey—and laid her head against his wide middle.

House on fire, Mother in a nursing home, lice infested kid. Could it get any worse?

The home phone rang.

"I understand, Boots, but I can assure you that there is absolutely no veracity in this rumor," Jim couldn't believe the naiveté of the school board president. Didn't he recognize   gossip   when   he   heard   it?

"Jim, any suggestion of impropriety looks bad for you and it looks bad for your wife. Now, all I can tell you is that you had better get to the bottom of this before I hear from any more 'concerned parents'. My phone's been ringing off the hook all night!"

"Tell them to call me. I'm in the book. I welcome the opportunity to set the record straight," Jim declared emphatically. "But first, I'm going to talk with both Damon and my wife. I'm sure they can shed some light on who started this bullshit."

"Jim, now, don't you go...," Boots began.

"I know, I know, Boots. I won't say anything inappropriate." Realizing that he had probably pissed off Boots more than he meant to, he managed to calm himself. "It's just that this whole thing is a slap in the face to Damon, he's probably too embarrassed to come to school, and that's not fair to him. That's my first priority — Damon. Carol's a big girl; I'm not worried about her."

In fact, the only reason he worried about Carol was that when she found out that a vicious rumor was spreading around town like a forest fire, she would probably hunt down and murder whoever started this whole story. He sure as hell didn't need his wife going to jail and leaving him to raise three kids.

The irony of the whole situation, though, was not lost on him. If he ever had any idea of taking care of the Shirl Snyder problem, he had better be damn sure he was right about his suspicions.

"I sure am sorry to bother you folks at home, and right around dinner time, too," Jim truly did regret having to interrupt the Ettinger's dinner, but he wanted to get this over with. He had more important things to attend to.

"It's no problem, Mr. A., we haven't sat down to supper just yet," Freda said warmly, welcoming him into the house. "Can I get you some coffee?"

"That would be lovely, Mrs. Ettinger, and please, call me Jim."

"Only if you call me 'Freda'," she said. "Cream or sugar?"

"Black, if you don't mind," God, I hope that was all right to say, Jim thought. As much as he tried to feel at home at the Ettinger's, he was unaccustomed to actually being among a colored family. He looked around at the living room, which wasn't too much different from his own—maybe a little homier; definitely more cozy. "If you don't mind, may I have a word with Damon? He's not in any kind of trouble or anything—I just want to ask him a couple of questions," Jim considered lying to Damon's parents and just telling them that he was here to talk baseball business since Damon had recently pitched his second no-hitter Tuesday night, but he thought better of it.

"Why sure...Pat?" Freda called for her husband. "Pat—oh, there you are, Pat, Mr. A. —Jim—wants to talk to Damon."

"The boy's not in trouble is he?" Pat Ettinger looked suspiciously at Jim who shook his head.

379

"No, just a couple of questions about—about something that happened with another student at school."

Damon came downstairs, surprised to see Jim standing with his father, but not necessarily afraid that he was in trouble. After all, if there *was* a problem, Mr. A. would have called him into his office and talked with him first.

Freda brought out Jim's coffee then she and Pat left the two of them in the living room and stepped inside the kitchen. Jim sat in a chair across from Damon who sat on the couch.

"Damon, I have a question to ask about a rumor that's been going around school and now around town. I don't believe a word of it, but I'm hoping that you might know how it started or who it was who started it. It's about you and Mrs. A." Jim sat back and waited.

Damon's eyes reflected the shock he felt. "Mrs. A.? What the he...what about me and Mrs. A.?"

"Did Mrs. A. ask you to come to her office recently? Or within the past couple months?"

"Yeah—she taped up my ankle that last week of basketball. When we were in the playoffs. Why?"

"Well, the rumor is that she dragged you down there, and then she...and you..."

"Oh God no! Oh, man! I mean, no offense, Mr. A., but...oh! Man! No. No, no, definitely not. She's old

380

enough…"

"I know…to be your mother," Jim smiled. "I know it's ridiculous. Do you have any idea who may have started the rumor?"

Damon took a deep breath and blew it out. He shook his head then looked Jim straight in the eye.

"I know exactly who started it, Mr. A., and I'd really like it if she'd stop messin' with me, too."

XXXIV

Dreama Tagliaburro would have to go. Jim had listened to Damon pour out his bottled up frustration with Ms. Tag and her daily overtures, the comments, the suggestiveness, and her over-the-top behavior in Vinnie's office the very first day he had asked to have his ankle taped. Jim had then asked that Freda and Pat join them, and together Jim and Damon told the Ettingers about the rumor so that if they heard something, they wouldn't be alarmed or, worse yet, unfairly assume that there was any truth to it.

It didn't take much convincing. Jim could well imagine Dreama concocting some ridiculous story that involved Carol doing *something* inappropriate; it was always clear that Dreama was envious of Carol. To have manufactured such a vicious lie that eventually ran like a polluted river all throughout school and town, though, well, that was beyond unforgivable.

That night, he told Carol about the rumor--how it had spread throughout school and then town. Then he braced himself and told her that, in all likelihood, it was Dreama Tagliaburro who had conjured up the whole mess. Then he patiently listened to Carol scream, shout, and rant for a good hour until she calmed down and settled for merely fuming. Once he felt she had most of her anger of her system (and that she wasn't about to hunt down Dreama and strangle her), Jim warned her that under no circumstances was she to say anything to anyone — he'd take care of getting rid of Dreama, and to hell with what Vinnie thought. And he not only had to fire her from her substitute teaching position — such as it was — he had to get her out of town for the Gym Show.

Goddammit, Jim thought. He liked Vinnie, but if Vinnie wasn't man enough to control that trollop of a wife of his then Jim had no choice but to find another more suitable replacement for Doris Pennycroft. He'd think about that later. Little did he know that he had to get through Sunday and his wife's discovery that Dreama and Vinnie had inserted themselves and their images into the Erie Times as Mercyville High School's co-sponsors of the Gym Show.

In his dream that night, as every night, he was being stalked by a sniper, but this time, he could see the sniper's face. It was Shirl Snyder, and, once again, Jim had found himself unarmed and unable to run from him.

Tommy had all seven pieces of piano music memorized for the girls' floor exercises, as well as "A Time for Us," the theme from *Romeo and Juliet*, which he would play as the May Queen Court introductions were taking place, but he knew once the Gym Show arrived that he would opt for the safety net of the sheet music in front of him. His friend Ramona had agreed to act as his page-turner during the Gym Show. Mr. Cubby had actually bought him a jacket and tie for the occasion, since Tommy's father was inexperienced in the matter of purchasing ready-made clothes for his son. He felt like he was prepared.

The past few months had been difficult for the two of them, Tommy and his father, to say the least, and the news from Washington that Nixon was planning to send troops into Cambodia was even more disquieting. He had just lost his mother, his father had just lost his wife, and the two of them simply couldn't bear to think of what might happen to George if he was sent to Southeast Asia. But Tommy had his music, and his near obsession with the piano — somewhat to the detriment of his French horn — was the only thing keeping him from jumping off a bridge. Only the music quieted the voices inside of his head.

The shootings at Kent State, a mere hour and a half drive from Mercyville, dominated the national and local news Monday, May 4, the week of the Gym Show. Jim could foresee the passionate reactions of Mercyville's students to the event even before most college campuses around the nation had shored up their own procedures for dealing with student demonstrations. While one part of him — the rule-following military part of him--agreed that when told to stand down you did just that and got your ass back to class, another part of him agreed that the continuation of the conflict in Vietnam was an exercise in futility. Goddamn LBJ for getting us into this mess, even though Jim knew it was far more complicated than that. He knew one thing: he'd break his own son's legs in order to prevent him from being drafted to fight in a war — any war.

Cathy's gown for the May Queen crowning ceremony was, of course, white, sleeveless, with a bateau neckline. The sash that encircled her small waist was of pink satin, her signature hue, and the long, opera-length gloves finished off what she believed was her haute couture look. In reality, fashion had taken on a more bohemian flavor in that spring of 1970, but Cathy and her mother would never have deigned to the level of a hippie, and besides, Ruth Snow thought this dress, with a few minor alterations, might serve well as Cathy's wedding dress someday in the near future. Yes, Cathy agreed with her mother, it was a gown fit for a queen.

Damon's white dinner jacket, black slacks, and black

bow tie set off the color of his skin beautifully, Freda Ettinger thought. How handsome her oldest son had grown to be, and how proud she was of him. He would be going to Kent State University in the fall on a baseball scholarship, and her joy at seeing him so enthusiastic about going to college was diminished somewhat only by the notion that she knew how trapped and alone he had felt here in Mercyville. While she and Pat had tried to do what was best for their boys, did they take away from them their opportunities to be among people who looked like, talked like, and thought as they did?

"Dreama, I've asked you down here for a couple of reasons. Ruthie is going to sit in on our meeting and take notes," Jim gave Ruthie a knowing glance before she bowed over her steno pad and began taking shorthand. Ruthie could be writing a shopping list for all he cared — he just wanted to make sure that Dreama Tagliaburro didn't have the opportunity to manufacture some story implicating him in any kind of inappropriate behavior during this meeting. And he needed to figure out a way to get her out of town. He sure as hell wasn't going to take a chance that this lacquered-up tramp, who probably spent more time counting ceiling tiles than she ever did attending a class at Slippery Rock, would be around to cause some kind of dramatic scene during the Gym Show.

"It's about a story that has been circulating around school and town—"

"I swear, Mr. A., I never, ever did anything with Damon, I swear!" Dreama's eyes were about to bug out of her overly made up face.

For Dreama, Jim feigned a look of puzzlement, but inwardly he was serendipitously rewarded with enough information to justify getting rid of her. But not until after the Gym Show. "Well, Dreama, I'm not sure I understand what you're talking about. What I was going to say is that some of the girls in the Future Homemakers of America have been telling tales on you, I'm afraid. Seems you're not really much cut out for homemaking, so I asked you down here to let you know that I've decided to, ah, have you represent Mercyville High School at the annual Future Homemakers of America convention in State College this weekend. You see, ah, Mrs. Pennycroft was going to go, but, well…"

Relieved that she wasn't about to be canned for flirting with Damon but dumbfounded at this out-of-the-blue request, Dreama stared idiotically at Jim, her dropped jaw telling more stories than it had intended to. "You want me to go to all the way to State College? For a Home Ec. convention? Really?" He could sense that Dreama, in her stupidity, had thought she had dodged a bullet, and it took all of Jim's powers of concentration to maintain the

388

serious look on his face. Especially with Ruthie in the background.

"Yes, you see, the trip is already paid for," Jim was truly making this up as he went along and behind Dreama he could see Ruthie's shoulders heaving up and down, but like a good girl, she kept scribbling away on her steno pad. "You'll get to—ah—stay at the Nittany Lion Inn for two nights—Friday and Saturday. All of your expenses paid, including your mileage and meals. Then you can come back Monday morning and report back to me everything you've—ah—learned. I'm sure it will be a tremendous educational opportunity for you. How does that sound?"

Dreama looked more than a little confused, shook her head and said, "You said, uh, there were a couple of things..."

"Ah, yes, well the other thing was that, um, Ruthie here is going to, uh, well, there's a contest at the convention. A pie-baking contest. The teacher with the best tasting pie from—uh—her region of the—uh—state wins. Here it is," Jim, pulling this subterfuge out of his ass faster than he could get the words out, shuffled some of the papers on top of his desk and pretended to read, "and apparently you have to design and wear a uniquely crafted apron that reflects your school and community. Yes, that's it. And the good news is that Ruthie here said she'd help you make it." Jim watched Ruthie's head snap up, her eyes cutting evil right through his skull. "So it looks like this week after school, the two of you will hole up in the Home Ec. room, Ruthie will teach you not only how to bake a helluva pie, but the two of you will make an apron you can wear during the contest. Let's see, this is Monday, so it'll probably take you at least three or four days after school. Now isn't this exciting?"

"What about the Gym Show? I've been, well, I've been an important part of getting our kids ready, and if I have to be baking pies and sewing aprons all week, and then, to be gone Friday and Saturday..."

"Yes, well, Dreama, it is unfortunate, but when you agreed to replace Mrs. Pennycroft, well, you kind of signed up for this. I'm sorry."

After a bewildered Dreama left the office, Jim told Ruthie, "When she gets back from State College, I'll fire her, I promise. And look, if it makes you feel any better, there is no Future Homemakers of America convention in State College this weekend. Call the Nittany Lion Inn, make a reservation for Friday and Saturday nights for Dreama Tagliaburro, and have them send the invoice to me, here at school—Jesus, not at home."

"So, Dreama's going to show up in State College on Friday afternoon, no convention, and then what?"

"Ruthie, have you ever been inside of the Nittany Lion Inn? It's gorgeous and very, very upscale—well, upscale for Dreama Tagliaburro. Trust me, I'm sure she'll find something or someone to 'do'. I just hope they don't mistake her for a hooker and throw her ass out. Once she gets back, I'll tell her that I had the dates mixed up, and then I'll fire her. How's that grab you?"

"You're forgetting that I have to help her sew up a gol-darned apron and bake a pie. Thanks a lot for that, Mr. A." It was one of the rare times he had ever seen Ruthie pout.

"Ah, Ruthie, you're my girl!" Jim patted the girl's large shoulder. "It's up to you to manage my expectations."

He only hoped he wouldn't have to look for a new secretary, too.

Following his early Tuesday morning practice session with Mr. Cubby, Tommy opened the door to the hallway from the music room and was shaken by the sight of Mr. Snyder waiting for him. He had clutched in his hand a newspaper and Tommy's Honors Art portfolio.

"So, you meet with the music man every morning?" Mr. Snyder asked, staring down at Tommy like a vulture ready to prey, "Here," he shoved the portfolio at Tommy, "your life's work in the visual arts. I can't have it cluttering up my room." He turned noticeably and began walking down the hallway past Mr. A. who was leaving the cafeteria.

Tommy had taken the portfolio, relieved that Mr. Snyder was gone, but shaking nonetheless. Mr. A. saw Tommy, then, instead of approaching him, he turned and followed Snyder. Tommy hung his head and wondered how he was going to get through another day.

"Shirl, may I have a word with you, please? In my office?" Jim had caught up with Snyder outside of the main office. The man stopped, sized up the situation, and followed Jim into his office where he took a seat.

"May I ask what you were talking with Tommy about?" Jim said, not caring at this point how Shirl Snyder might perceive this line of questioning.

"And may I ask why it is any of your business?" Snyder retorted, dropping the newspaper on Jim's desk, fishing a cigarette out of his shirt pocket and lighting it, undeterred by Jim's position and obviously comfortable with his own impertinence.

"It's my business because Tommy is a student here at Mercyville, a student who, very recently, lost his mother. It's my business because every kid in this school is my business."

"Well, if you must know, I was returning your Tommy's art portfolio. Anything else I can help you with, Mr. Adamson?"

Jim ignored the "your Tommy" reference, for now. "I don't know, Shirl, it just appeared as if you had upset the boy. What is your connection—your relationship with Tommy?"

Snyder's eyes turned dark, his face revealing his visceral hatred of Jim, "Let me ask you something, Mr. Adamson. Why are you so interested in my relationships with my students? You single-handedly dismantled my photography club, you obviously had a hand in removing Tommy from my 214 class and making him your office lackey, and for a man who can't even keep his own wife under control, you certainly do make a lot of assumptions."

It took every ounce of self-control that Jim possessed for him not to leap over his desk and choke the living shit out of Shirl Snyder, but the portion of his brain that controlled logic and reason had fortunately taken over. "What assumptions, Shirl? What assumptions have I made about you, or is there something about your character that you're keeping a secret from everybody?"

There it was again, that flash of *something*—was it fear? Whatever it was, it was indicative of the sewage that was running through the man's veins. Snyder pushed back his chair, and with his eyes still fixed on Jim, he retreated from the office. He left his newspaper behind.

393

The Gym Show

394

XXXV

Jim had decided that morning to take a proactive measure and address the Kent State shooting situation up front. The Gym Show was Friday, and he needed no distractions, interruptions, or demonstrations that would make this week any longer or more difficult than it had to be.

During homeroom time, and after the Pledge of Allegiance, Jim called for students in grades nine through twelve into the gym. He figured that the junior high kids would follow the leadership of the kids in the older grades, and the senior high students would be more receptive to his message if he spoke exclusively to them as the young adults that they were. He didn't ask anyone's advice, seek anyone's approval, or ask for anyone's opinion; he simply felt that taking this approach would be the best course of action and would alleviate any plans that the students might have, individually or collectively, of demonstrating their outrage about the actions of the Ohio National Guard.

Once in front of his student body, Jim began an impromptu speech. "Yesterday, on a college campus not too far from Mercyville, four students were killed when they were fired upon by the Ohio National Guard. The students were protesting the actions by government that will expand the war in Southeast Asia into Cambodia." The audible murmurs among the students were a mixture of anger, resentment, and in some cases, shock.

"The reason I've called all of you down here this morning is to acknowledge the feelings that many of you may be experiencing. I want you to know that I understand your frustration, the anger, the hurt, and the belief that no one over thirty should be trusted." He listened for a minute to gauge the mood among the students then continued.

"But trust *me*. War is an awful terrible business, and this war is especially terrible. It has gone on long enough."

"While we may not agree with our nation's reason for fighting it, in the words of Stephen Decatur, it's 'my country, right or wrong'." Jim thought it best to leave out Decatur's reference to 'intercourse with other countries'. "Though we're free to disagree, we can do so without violence or without sacrificing any of our goals."

"Seniors, in a few short weeks you'll be graduating. Let's look toward that goal and to all that awaits you after graduation. As for how we can honor those who died yesterday, I propose that during Friday night's Gym Show, we pay our respects by wearing black armbands. I will provide armbands to any student participating in or attending the Gym Show. This is, of course, optional."

That said, he dismissed the student body, and any plans of a student demonstration would have been regarded as reactionary and intransigent since the issue had already been addressed and a way out for those who wanted to recognize the tragedy had been given. Jim, though he never came right out and said it, saw both sides of the situation. For him, it wasn't his job to agree or disagree—it was his job to make sure that nothing interfered with school and to a greater degree, the Gym Show. He had his wife to answer to, after all.

Back in his office, he told Ruthie he was going to make a few phone calls. He shut the door, took his phone off the hook, and laid the receiver on the desk. After lighting a cigarette, he slid Snyder's personnel file out from under his blotter and opened it once more, studying it to try to find something in it that would help him get rid of the son-of-a-bitch. Then he picked up the newspaper that Snyder had left on his desk. It had been folded back to the stock section. On it, someone, presumably Snyder, had circled and underlined various charts and graphs, mostly having to do with the price of corn and corn futures. On the margin of the newspaper, he had written the words "Sell Now!!!" and "To Market!!!" and had underlined these several times.

Jim stared at the newspaper for nearly a half an hour, not necessarily reading its contents but allowing the words Snyder had written on the page to motivate him toward his next move. Never in a million lifetimes did he ever think that he had the capability of doing what he was about to do, but he knew that it was the only way to protect the kids at Mercyville. To depend upon those students who Snyder had molested to testify against him was ridiculous, if Tommy's reaction to his situation with Henry was any indication. To wait until he was able to catch Snyder "in the act" was to wait until Snyder damaged another boy, and that was unacceptable to him.

And then, of course, there were the gypsies.

He slid the personnel file back under the blotter and took the newspaper, intending to throw it in the trash on his way out of the building. He would leave through the kitchen and deposit the newspaper in the bottom of one of the garbage bins, just in time for the cafeteria ladies to fill up the rest of the bin with the detritus left over from their lunch preparations. Jim left his office and told Ruthie that he would be back in a couple of hours and to call Mr. Harvey if there was an emergency.

"Oh, Mr. A., just so you know," Ruthie then lowered her voice to a whisper, "she got the last room at the Nittany Lion Inn. There's a big Westinghouse convention there this weekend."

At first, Jim had no idea what she was talking about until he remembered his meeting with Dreama the day before. Poor Westinghouse guys — one of them was bound to go home this Sunday with a healthy dose of the clap.

Jim left school, stopped at the beer distributor and picked up a case of Iron City, stopped by the grocery store and bought a carton of cigarettes then headed out to see Nigel at the Somers' farm.

The dreams that night were the worst he could remember. This time, the sniper was in full view and every one of the senior high kids were with him on that rocky ridge in Italy. Then his own family joined him, and he watched as the sniper took shots at each of them — blood poured out of their mouths, but the sniper kept on shooting. The scene became more grisly, more macabre as more people he knew joined him on the ridge. No one but the sniper was armed; no one knew what to do — they kept asking Jim to help them, help them. He ran from one person to the next, and once he had stopped one person from bleeding, another would start to bleed, then another. Soon, a river of slick blood had mixed in with the mud and rocks and everyone with him on that ridge started slipping down over the side, over sharp rocks, and into a ravine with more and more bleeding and wounded, and

399

soon there was a heaping pile of bloody bodies buried one on top of the other. He woke up screaming his wife's name, covered in a cold sweat, and shaking.

Earlier, that afternoon, Jim and Nigel had talked for about an hour and a half. During that time, they had calculated a plan that would eliminate Shirl Snyder. It would provide the Somers' family with the opportunity to return to their home without the threat of Snyder's revealing Henry's culpability for the deaths of the gypsies. More importantly, the plan would ensure that Shirl Snyder would never again harm a child in Mercyville. It would be a fitting end for a man who had caused so much pain and so much grief for so many people in the town that Jim loved so much.

Removing corn from a silo was a two-man job. It was a dangerous job. After a morning spent calculating the risks and the consequences of what he was about to propose, Jim had a long talk with Nigel. The hired man showed little emotion, but was able to, with his broken diction, agree to the plan that Jim had laid out for him. Jim was convinced that Nigel was nimble enough and confident enough to make Shirl's demise look like an accident.

For Jim's part, he had studied Snyder's personnel file and had discovered that his next of kin was a great aunt living in Corvallis, Oregon. Someone, probably Ruthie, had updated this information a good eight years ago after Snyder's wife had left him, so chances were good that the old woman in Oregon was not even alive now.

That he knew he could form this plan with Nigel and trust Nigel to carry it through, to keep Jim's confidence, and to agree to it was never at issue. That day in late February when Nigel had poured out his ravaged soul to Jim, a symbiosis had forged between the two men. The fact that Nigel never wavered at all in his retelling of the story about the gypsies proved to Jim that Nigel trusted him; in turn, the pain that Snyder had caused Nigel's family and would continue to cause was reason enough for Nigel to want Snyder eliminated.

And so the two of them had devised a plan that involved Nigel and Snyder and the process of emptying a silo full of corn that Snyder was set to take to market. Only the two of them would know that Shirl Snyder would meet his fate at the bottom of a corn silo while trying greedily to extricate the last of the season's corn from the sides of the silo. It was a common accident, especially for those who tried to work the silo alone. If anyone came snooping around the farm, Nigel would know how to become scarce; furthermore, his perceived diminished intellect and rather frightening countenance would only serve to help him remain anonymous.

The plan was simple. When Snyder approached Nigel

401

to empty the silo, Nigel would insist that he would not be able to get all of the corn out without some help. He could hire out someone, but knowing Snyder as Nigel did, he knew that Snyder would never agree to putting out any more cash for something that the two of them could do easily. Nigel would direct Snyder as to what his role would be in the process and would make sure, one way or another, that it was Snyder who would end up being sucked into the bottom of the silo, buried under several tons of corn. Afterwards, Nigel would quietly enter Snyder's farmhouse and render the home as if Snyder had left of his own accord, and for good. He would make sure that the house told no tales that might suggest that Snyder's absence was anything but planned—by Snyder himself. Nigel would then empty half the silo and store the corn various places around the farm, using it for feed. Snyder's body would rot away at the bottom of the silo. Let the barn cats take care of the rats.

"How will you get word to me that he's...gone?" Jim had asked.

"Ou'll know when e doen come oo wor," Nigel replied. Fair enough.

That was Tuesday afternoon. Shirl Snyder missed his very first day of work on Friday, May 8, 1970. The day of the Gym Show.

THE GYM SHOW

The line had formed outside of the high school lobby's ticket window at four o'clock. Though most students had purchased pre-sale tickets, those in line were from other schools and other towns who had heard about the Gym Show from kids who had seen the Traveling Show at Iroquois Lake or Iroquois Valley. Before Jim left for home to shower and change for the big night, he hoped they wouldn't sell out before they reached the end of the line.

Carol was at her calmest in the hours before the show. Her nervousness had reached a fever pitch the two days prior during the two dress rehearsals, which, according to her, were simply awful. Even with months of practice, once the Show's participants tried putting it all together, the kids had no idea knew where they were supposed to be. The poor boy playing the music had to play parts over again, and then a second time, then a third, and even though he never complained, Carol felt sorry for him. Barry Cubby almost broke down in tears because his ensemble was missing its bassist during Thursday's rehearsal. It was always like this, though, Jim thought. Somehow, by some miracle, it all seemed to come together the opening night of the Show — tomorrow night would be even more relaxed since the whole May Queen crowning business would be history.

Bert Schmidt, the French teacher, was the show's emcee. He had a good voice and was poised enough to pull it off. He was enthusiastic, and best of all, he did it for free because he genuinely liked to do it, refusing the usual $20 stipend that the rest of the staff were paid to take tickets, help out behind the scenes, and control the crowd before and after the Show.

Jim and Carol arrived back at the school at five thirty. Carol was looking sassy. Gina had styled Carol's hair in a complicated up-do, and she was dressed in a white and silver haltered jumpsuit, her right arm decked out in silver bangles, punctuated only by the black armband she wore, while her treasured charm bracelet encircled her left wrist, her favorite piece of jewelry that she rarely wore except on special occasions.

Tonight, though, she felt as if she wore the bracelet as a talisman against any disaster that might occur even though she felt as if she had already wrapped up all of the loose ends and couldn't imagine that anything could go wrong. She had planned well. Looking at Jim, though, she sensed he was preoccupied. Maybe he should wear the bracelet, she thought.

Jim marveled at Carol as she calmly gave last-minute instructions to those she had chosen to pass out programs.

Bert, dressed in a natty looking tuxedo, was in the outer office practicing his diction into the school's one ancient microphone, while the girls in the Court began arriving and were ushered into a nearby classroom that had been converted into a dressing room for them. Cathy Snow, her gown held high above the ground by her mother, smiled regally and walked as if the crown were already perched upon her blonde hair, arranged in a complicated bouffant up-do even more sumptuous and extravagant than Carol's with several wiglets and hair attachments involved. She, or more likely her mother, had somehow found a hairdresser within a day's drive of Mercyville to copy Audrey' Hepburn's *My Fair Lady* complicated coiffure. Curiously enough, a distinctly empty spot was vacant in her elaborate Audrey 'do at the exact place where a tiara might sit.

No one could deny, however, how breathtakingly beautiful she looked.

Millicent arrived with the children in tow, and despite her new pixie haircut, Julie looked adorable. Millicent had fashioned for Julie a wreath of daisies that she wore around her head like a halo, and her white dress with its baby blue, pink, yellow, and light green ruffles was delightfully guileless yet sweet in its own simple way. She wore gloves adorned with tiny embroidered flowers colored to match the dress' pastel ruffles, and her socks and white patent Mary Janes perfected her look.

Stanley and his parents took their place in the outer office, Aggie and Lube nearly bursting with pride. Though his head had been shaved and he was missing his two front teeth, having lost the second one earlier in the week, he looked snappy and dapper in his First Communion suit—a light blue jacket, navy blue slacks, and a red bow tie. Aggie and Lube had even purchased an instamatic camera, four rolls of film, and a box of flashcubes and had begun taking pictures of nearly everything even before the Show began.

At last, it was time, and with the gymnasts seated in a double line on the gym floor in order to make an aisle for the May Queen Court, Bert Schmidt took the microphone.

"Ladies and Gentlemen, it is my distinct privilege to welcome you to Mercyville High School's annual Gym Show!" With that, the 1970 Gym Show began.

Tommy's rendition of "A Time for Us" from Romeo and Juliet was perhaps the loveliest melody Julie had ever heard in her life. She and Stanley, who were both taking very seriously their tasks as flower girl and crown bearer, performed perfectly their step-together, step-together walk that they had been practicing during every recess for the last month. To the collective "Awe's" of the crowd, they completed their journey down the aisle between the gymnasts in their green leotards with the black armbands—the boys in all white; they too wearing black armbands. Julie and Stanley didn't wear black armbands, had no idea why anyone else wore them, but they felt important and grown up nonetheless.

Looking back, for Jim, the highlight of the evening wasn't the obvious pride he took in his wife's accomplishment yet again this year. It wasn't the amazing performance by Mary Dietrich on the balance beam where she performed the first ever seen front walkover and nailed it, to the collective gasps and cheers from the standing-room only crowd. It wasn't even the boys' awe-inspiring Giants on the horizontal bar or complicated routines on the horse, an apparatus that, several months previously had merely served as a convenient place to sit if you were unlucky enough to have been eliminated from a P.E. class dodgeball game. It wasn't the beautifully choreographed dance by JoAnn Donaldson that surprised even Carol in its complexity and spirit nor was it tiny but mighty seventh grader Diane Michaelson's show stopping twelve back handsprings in a row—no, none of these performances came close to the look on Cathy Snow's face when she was not crowned this year's May Queen.

Of course, Cathy had gathered more votes than the other girls on the court did, but her slight victory, such as it was, was not a landslide by any means. Thus, Jim felt justified in making a rather bold decision—further

407

encouraged by Ruthie's wide-eyed affirmation. Jim had taken seriously Norm Snow's directive that "no nigger is gonna walk my daughter down that aisle," and so it was Christy Bundy, good old Christy who was crowned the 1970 May Queen. Christy, with her mischievous sense of humor, her funny-looking rectangular glasses, and her good natured and easygoing personality along with her unparalleled gymnastics skills came in a squeakingly close second in the running for the May Queen. At that point, Jim had decided that it would be Christy, not Cathy, who would walk on the arm of one of his all-time favorite kids Damon Ettinger.

For Damon's part, he had won by a landslide, easily gathering the most votes among his peers.

Weeks later, Jim would discover that the photographer that he had hired—in the absence of one Shirl Snyder—was able to capture perfectly the look on Cathy's face as Bert Schmidt unsteadily named Christy as the May Queen. Oh, that picture! Evidently, either the photographer was so enamored of Cathy that he paid little attention to anyone else, or someone had clued him in that Cathy, in all likelihood, would be named May Queen, and so prior to the big announcement, he had trained his lens solely on her. He then clicked away, one picture after another, seizing the exact moment before the announcement when Cathy had actually blushed, looked down demurely, then prepared to stand up, then to that horrifying moment when Bert Schmidt, with an uncharacteristic hitch in his diction that suggested surprise, had *not* announced *her* name but had instead said Christy Bundy's name.

Then came the tears — the pouting, the fuming, Cathy's crumpled face awash with anger, hurt, and disappointment while on the other hand, Christy Bundy appeared genuinely surprised then rather modestly pleased. Once the two of them were together, Damon and Christy had found themselves laughing at each other either about the absurdity of their situation or the appropriateness of two good friends winning over the popularity of the student body. With Damon waiting patiently, last year's May Queen Vicky Miholic took the crown proffered by a very serious Stanley Czerniawski and placed it on Christy's simply straight hair, then Christy bent down and kissed little Julie on the cheek as she accepted the dozen long-stemmed roses that Julie handed to her. It was at that moment that Julie fell in love with everything to do with the Gym Show, even though the best part had yet to be experienced.

With Damon offering Christy an arm, the two of them smiled at each other then laughed once again as they walked together down the "runway" in the gym. The flashing bulbs and ear-shattering cheers from the stands reaffirmed what Jim had always known in his heart — the residents of Mercyville were well accustomed at recognizing excellence when it walked in front of them.

He smiled. The town's collective "bullshit detectors" were in good working order, it seemed.

Christy then scooted off to the locker room and got down to the business of changing from her simple white cotton dress that she had bought just last night at Trask's, pulled on a green leotard, a black armband, and had fastened her light brown hair into a low ponytail. Her performance in the Gym Show was her absolute best, she executed stunningly on beam, bars, and floor, and Jim was as proud of her as if she had been his own daughter.

Tommy's piano accompaniment combined with the music from the jazz ensemble made this year's Gym Show unique and extraordinary, giving it a polished and professional feel. Though Carol had been skeptical of Barry Cubby's confidence, especially as his plans grew grander by the day, he really did know how to score a performance. After the Show, Carol and Jim had made a special effort to find Tommy and Barry Cubby and congratulate the both of them not only on their musical talents, but for adding something very distinct that Jim told them he was sure would carry on for years to come. Barry, with his Wagnerian mother on his arm, nearly burst into tears he was so happy, and Tommy smiled — it was the first time he had felt worthy of anyone's praise for a long time.

Dreama Tagliaburro was noticeably absent, and was, at that very moment, quite possibly charming some poor drunken son-of-a-bitch from Westinghouse into buying her another daiquiri at the bar in the Nittany Lion Inn.

At eleven o'clock, Jim and Carol left the school, happy, relieved, and in need of some libations. Millicent, dear, dear Millicent (whom Jim had already appointed as Doris Pennycroft's replacement) had graciously taken the kids home with Bernard promising to make them ice cream sundaes—proof, Jim guessed, that he was good for something. Jim and Carol headed to Iroquois Lake to their favorite little hole in the wall restaurant that overlooked the water, a table waiting for them with a view the moonlit lake and the twinkling lights of the boats still anchored out in the darkness.

"Congratulations Carol. You've done it," Jim said, taking his wife's tiny hand in both of his and placing a platinum silver charm of a gymnast in the palm of her hand.

"It's long overdue, my dear. You've made the Gym Show not only a part of our lives, but you've touched so many others at Mercyville with all of your hard work and your creativity. There's no one who could have done this but you. I love you. You never fail to amaze me."

The Gym Show

Carol dropped her head so that Jim wouldn't see the tears forming. She was never much good at accepting praise from her husband—from others, yes, she ate it up, but when it came from Jim, he had such a way with words. She felt deeply his sincerity. She also sensed that he had had something on his mind these past few months, and she felt guilty that she had been too busy to pay much attention to him to find out what it was. "Yep," she swallowed, "and I get to do it all over again tomorrow."

Carol shook her head, looked up at Jim and smiled, then examined the tiny silver gymnast charm. She felt a sense of relief wash over her like warm rainwater knowing that tomorrow's show would be far less stressful, far more relaxing, and her gymnasts would be primed to give it their all, especially the seniors.

Jim looked at his wife, this beautiful woman, this dynamo, the reason he lived and breathed. Many times, he had considered unburdening himself to her, telling her everything that he had been through with Snyder, with Tommy, and the whole sordid story about Henry Somers, Nigel, and those poor gypsies. That was what a partner was for, wasn't it?

He had once considered it, but no. It simply was not fair to her.

Jim knew that what he had done—or rather, what he had arranged to have done to Shirl Snyder—was akin to

412

playing God. Was it his place to destroy a man on supposition? What about the gut wrenching details of the deaths of the gypsies retold to him by the hired man? It wasn't the involvement in Shirl Snyder's demise that had Jim bothered—he had killed before, and justifiably. But this wasn't war, and so he had to ask himself once more, did he have the right to play God? Perhaps, Jim reasoned, if Tommy Jankovic—a boy who had not a care in the world seven months ago until Henry Somers had irrevocably changed his life— if Tommy was determined to keep his shame to himself, then Jim was firm in his belief that none of the boys Shirl Snyder had violated would ever be willing to come forward either.

But had he assumed too much?

What he had done had been his decision and involving Nigel was the only way that he knew of to rid the world—his world—of a man who had hurt so many people. If, for some strange reason, he chose to tell someone about his particular brand of justice, perhaps that person might think it was cowardly of him to have involved Nigel.

That didn't matter, though, because he had no plans to reveal to anyone what had taken place at the Somers farm this past week. He had taken care of business—his way. He was the one running this show at Mercyville High School.

413

The Gym Show

And he would spend the rest of his life asking God to have mercy on his soul.

The Gym Show

The Gym Show

Acknowledgements

Many thanks to my dear friends Anita Walls, Ron Crowl, and Debbie Ray who read my early drafts and gave me sound advice, heartfelt support, and valuable suggestions. Dina Silver, your advice was invaluable and I thank you. Mike Nickels, my friend, you're next, and I can't wait to read what you have to say. To my father-in-law, your sage knowledge about farming and what not to do when you're all by yourself on the farm was oh-so helpful. See, I told you he deserved it. Randy Panko, thank you for educating me on the finer nuances of gun ownership—knowledge that will be long remembered. And many, many thanks to my fellow cheerleader, biggest fan, and best sister ever Becky Panko.

To my children Caroline, Julianne, and Christian, I guess I should thank you for not making fun of me during my numerous attempts at trying to get you to read some part of this—any part of this. Will you read me now?

And Tim, thank you for giving me the time and the opportunity to write this. ILYBB!

417

32378516R00251

Made in the USA
Lexington, KY
17 May 2014